MW00899539

THE
FORGOTTEN
HOUSE

-- A NOVEL --

Written by: J. Marie

This book is a work of fiction. Any references to historical events, real people, or real places are used fictitiously. Other names, characters, places, and events are products of the author's imagination, and any resemblance to actual events or places or persons, living or dead, is entirely coincidental.

THE FORGOTTEN HOUSE by J. Marie
Copyright 2018, J. Marie

www.jmariebooks.com

All rights reserved. No portion of this book may be reproduced in any form without permission from the publisher, except as permitted by U.S. copyright law. For permissions, contact: jmariebooks.com

Cover art by Kelley Nemitz & Katie Eney 2018

He just couldn't finish it. His best yet, and he couldn't finish it. The words that had faithfully shown up like tulip sprouts in April soil, the words he counted on these past fifty years, they had never failed him.

Now, they suddenly hid from him, almost like they were haunting him, taunting him with their incessant cadence, "Those fifty years, they were a dream, old man, and surprise. This is reality."

He closed his eyes against his pain – and it was a physical pain, he shook his head stubbornly – no matter how often they told him it was all in his head. But, he knew better. When you miss someone like he missed her, it was more than emotional, it was physical too. It impacted everything in your life. And because of that, it impacted *everyone* in your life too. Especially those you loved the most.

Pulling the soft wool plaid blanket tighter over his knees to ward against the chill in the evening air, he closed the laptop and pushed it aside. Try as he might, the fog was too thick, he just couldn't envision the end, the words would not come. If he could only be happy once again...after all, *happiness* is really such a simple thing.

◆ ◆ ◆

CHAPTER 1

*... Sometimes life throws you a curve ball, and
you forgot your glove in the garage ...*

"I'm sorry, Mallory. We just aren't seeing the results we were hoping for. You know how our business is, we survive on the very thin edge, our advertising can only reflect the very, very best."

Mallory's boss Jameson smoothed down his already slick blonde pompadour and slid his trendy, 50s-retro framed glasses back over his bright blue eyes as he sat forward in his chair, trying his best to be engaging.

"Now, before you lose it on me, I want you to know that I've secured something else for you here at Wishful Thinking Creative. Something more – suitable to your talents."

Did he just demote me? She could feel the heat rising in her cheeks, and her knee started to bounce uncontrollably in an embarrassing display of nerves. He's actually expecting me to ask what this other opportunity is, like I should be grateful that they "found something for me to do" here.

When she didn't respond, Jameson folded his hands together primly, crossed his legs and continued.

"I could really use an assistant, someone to pick up the loose ends around here. And, since I think we work really well together, I was hoping you would see this as an opportunity to shine! Copywriting isn't for everyone, you know."

He smiled stiffly and tilted his head to the side. And as she stared at the irksome look on his face, Mallory had an overwhelming urge to grab one of the antiseptic hand-wipes she had sitting at her desk and wipe that fake smile clean off his perfectly tanned face. Oh, I'm sorry, did I just ruin your $200 spray tan? My bad.

"Well, Jameson, forgive me for being underwhelmed by your offer."

She had to admit though, he was right, she did want to lose it on him, and considered it a significant victory that she didn't "accidentally" spill his almond milk, low fat, sugar free caramel latte all over his perfectly organized, perpetually empty desk. He needs help picking up the loose ends all right. Half the time, Mallory wondered what he did all day.

"Now, Mallory, let's be reasonable. You know we are very supportive of our employees here. We like to think that we have a very nurturing, very cohesive work environment where everyone is encouraged to reach their full potential-" His reckless overuse of the word *very* was very, very annoying.

"Jameson, please. You can save me the sales pitch. And, if you want to encourage people to reach their full potential, you could start by paying them what they're worth." She forced her mouth to shut down just then, cautioning herself, now would probably be a good time to just button it.

She thought over her work here, and the friends that toiled along beside her, always trying to find a tiny bit of joy in their day. They often joked that sometimes you took the small moments and made them grand, just to make yourself feel better.

Like writing some scintillating advertising copy for an electric utility company that would run on Pandora or creating an imaginative campaign for a chain of dental clinics in the area. Contemplate that one for a moment – no one, absolutely no one, enjoys going to the dentist – you try writing copy for that.

They all, Mallory included, really tried to find value in the writing they did here. Now, he was taking even that away from her.

Wow, the realization sunk heavily inside her, that thought just sealed the deal.

"You know, Jameson, let's just consider this my exit interview. I'm done. I'm so *very, very* done."

As she stood to leave his office, she noticed her knee had stopped nervously shaking. That was a good sign, she congratulated herself, it seemed her body had decided to act in concert with her mind. She must face it. And, she *refused* to be nervous about quitting. It was time to go, something new had to happen.

A few minutes later, after signing the HR forms like a dutiful ex-employee, she packed her few personal items and three potted succulents into a box and caught the sad sight of herself as she passed the mirrored door of the conference room.

Her brunette hair curled out from under her indigo-colored, Boho-style hat and fell in full waves along her shoulders and back, looking rather stylish, she had to admit; but then she noticed her light blue eyes with the hint of past-3PM smudged eyeliner. Those eyes looked vacant and scared, not Instagram-worthy at all.

As she hugged her few friends on her way out the door, she wondered, we all say it now, but will we really keep in touch? With that thought, she made a mental note to text as many as she could to make weekend plans right away.

Vaguely she realized, if she didn't keep these friend connections, she could quickly find herself slipping into cat-lady-recluse status, and even though she didn't currently own a cat, she might be tempted.

In fact, maybe she should channel these feelings into something positive by writing a series of posts about all this on her blog "The Twenty-Something Dreamer." You know, when you quit your job and question your sanity - she could title it "I'm So Very, Very Done."

While she waited for the 6th floor lobby elevator doors to open, Mallory turned her back to the office suite behind her and gazed sadly out the window at the Baltimore business district across from the building, catching a slim glimpse of the Patapsco River to the north. It had started to rain, and the big drops left rivulets trailing through the dust on the outside of the windows.

Great. Rain in the city, so close to rush hour. What a day.

"I'm sure you will find another job, you're an amazing writer, hon." Jasper called out loudly from across the table at the tavern later that day, as he casually tossed some peanuts into his mouth. "You just have to get out there and search for your next opportunity."

He sat back on his chair, loosened his tie and smoothed down the front of his cashmere, merlot-colored sweater vest which peeked out from under his tailored suit jacket. And, even though the tavern was obviously packed with thirsty-after-work office dwellers, he still was the best dressed guy in the place. He had driven into the city straight from work to meet her, not that it made that much of a difference in how he dressed; Jasper always looked his best, truly believing that the clothes made the man.

"Yes, Jasper, but unfortunately my career path is less secure than yours. Working for Daddy has its upside, he can't fire you and demoting you wouldn't sit too well with Mommy."

Mallory laughed ruefully as she took in his charming smile; long ago she had given up finding fault with him about his privileged upbringing and rather lavish lifestyle. And, without a hint of guilt, he freely admitted that he rather enjoyed the silver spoon his father's chain of east coast Mercedes dealerships bestowed on him. Frequently she would have to remind him he had become so accustomed to this silver spoon, that he sometimes forgot that the rest of the world ate with a regular fork and knife.

"Hey, I've been a productive employee for over a year now, give me some credit. Just today, I sold another GLS class to Guinevere Albott. This one will go to her house in the Hamptons. That's the second one I've sold her in less than a year!" He smiled proudly before raising his glass of imported ale in a mock salute to himself.

"Of course, you are productive. I was kidding, Jasper." She paused, looking into her glass of untouched beer, not enjoying their usual banter tonight. "I'm sorry. I'm just kind of... off balance now, I guess. I don't know what to do, where to go."

She looked back up at her on-again-off-again boyfriend of two years, hoping for some consolation. But his smoky gray eyes were gazing over her right shoulder, and she knew before she turned what she would find. As she followed the trajectory of his eyes, there she was of course. Another pretty girl.

This one had lush silvery blonde hair extensions that reached to her waist and her wide, glamorous eyes were adorned with feathery, false eyelashes.

Pursing her lips in annoyance, Mallory realized, one thing was certain in this epically chaotic world - Jasper's appreciation for women. He was hopelessly drawn to them, like a bee to honey.

A distant memory prodded her - strikingly out of place while sitting here in the noisy, city tavern. She recalled the lively hum of bees in a grassy meadow with mountains rising in the near distance, the memory so strong and sweet, it tugged at her to stay. Back there, in that meadow. But, she couldn't stay, listening to the grass move in the breeze, feeling it whisper past her fingers as she walked in it, that place was too far away, too long ago. This is now.

She forced herself to smile at Jasper, pretending that he was still with her at the table, when it was clear he wasn't. "Hello, Jasper. I'm still here, hon." She used his pet name for her intentionally, would he even notice?

"Yes, of course you are, hon. Sorry, what were you saying?" He reached across the top of the table to take her fingers in his hand, as if that would keep his wandering eyes focused in one direction.

"Nothing. I wasn't saying anything." Mallory sighed, and suddenly losing the energy to continue the discussion of her disastrous day, she took a long swallow of the cold beer. As she regarded him sitting across the table from her, she noticed that he was fidgeting in his chair, crossing and uncrossing his legs under the table, like he couldn't wait for her to vacate the room. Like she was in the way somehow.

Ok, she thought with a challenge, let's see what he does. She pulled her fingers from his, picked up her small clutch purse and shifted out of her seat, "Excuse me, Jas, I'm going to the restroom. If he comes to take our order, just get me the usual fish and chips."

He nodded, smiled an airy acknowledgement and glanced around the room looking for their waiter. Mallory continued across the crowded restaurant, turning back to look at him as she reached the hallway that led to the restrooms.

It didn't surprise her at all to see Jasper's chair was now empty. She scanned the patrons until she saw him leaning in oh-so-cool-and-casual next to the blonde who now sat poised, with her legs on full display, at the bar. That sure didn't take long.

He'll never change, a small voice whispered inside her, he's like a bee to honey...

Knowing there was a side exit in the hallway near the restrooms, she continued towards the door and made her escape into the chilly late autumn evening, saving them both the hassle and embarrassment of a confrontation.

Of course, she was hurt and of course she was mad. But, in the end, she was just tired of it, the constant stream of other women, the feeling like she was never good enough to keep him interested. She was tired of him and she was tired of this pretense they called a relationship.

As she walked east towards her apartment, she felt heavy and aimless, like a slug, making his way slowly back under a rock. And, as she dodged the dirty puddles pooling in the worn patches of sidewalk, she thought, there had to be more to life than this. There just had to be.

CHAPTER 2
... I'm sorry, but I must go now ...

Another job prospect, down the drain, Mallory swiped the button on her cell phone to close out the conversation. Well, that's the last advertising agency in town...and in D.C. Now what? Philly? New York? How much rejection was one person expected to take? And, how could she afford the cost to move, and deposits, and the rents in New York? She turned her coffee cup in circles on her desk, and propped her knees up tighter against her chest, turning nervously on her office chair.

Had it already been three weeks since she quit her job and broke off the relationship with Jasper? She opened the calendar app on her phone. Yes, it had been three weeks. Wow, time flies when you're having fun, she thought derisively. For his part, Jasper had called and stopped by a few times, trying to mend things. Of course, she told him No.

But, as she watched him walking back to his car the last time, his head and shoulders bent low, she found herself wavering. Maybe this was her future? Maybe Jasper *was* her future? No one was perfect after all. Didn't all guys have issues with fidelity? It seemed to be a common thread in the relationships of her friends and co-workers.

But, here it was three weeks later, and still, she just couldn't force herself to call Jasper and open herself up to more of the same. She attributed it to pride, but a small, though stridently willful, part of her just wanted to be special to him. Special enough to keep his undivided affections.

And, adding to her stress level was the job hunt – three weeks into it, and no prospects. The finances were going to get really tight here if something didn't break soon. True, the extra time was allowing her to work on her blog more, but that certainly didn't pay the bills. Her eyes moved over her email screen to the folder marked JOBS, YO. Clicking it open, she remembered the day she made the folder, secure in her abilities, and in her future. Now, not so much.

Scrolling through the few emails in the folder, she clicked on the email from Bradford, her friend who worked in the fashion industry, regarding freelance copywriting for his online catalogue clients. At least it's some money, and I could keep looking for something more stable, she thought as she started typing him an email.

A few minutes later, her thoughts were interrupted by her cell phone buzzing, and, just as she was swiping it open, she noticed the caller ID signaling it was Grandpa J. Funny, she thought, her brows frowning in slight confusion, she didn't even remember having his number saved in her new phone and the last time she heard from him was a voicemail saying he would call around Thanksgiving, and it was only the first week of November.

"H–hello?" Mallory spoke hesitantly, never quite prepared to talk to him and certainly not now after such a long time.

"Hello, Mallory? Is that you?" Further confused, she held the phone out from her ear to look a second time at the screen, checking the caller ID again. This didn't sound like Grandpa J at all.

"Yes, this is Mallory. Who's this?"

"Hello, Mallory, this is your Uncle Canton in New York." Her mind froze, what in the world?

"I'm calling from your grandfather's phone because we didn't have any other way to reach you. I'm glad he at least had your number in here." It dawned on her then, like a slow fog rolling off the bay, if they needed to talk to her so bad, why didn't Grandpa J just call her?

"He's very sick, Mallory. He's had a massive heart attack. The doctors say he might not make it through the night. We just wanted you to know, in case you wanted to come. Maybe to see him for the last time."

That was Monday and already it was Thursday evening, and she was on the train headed for the city. As the train neared New York's Penn Station, the cabin lights blinked in short succession and the train rocked as it changed its momentum, reminding her that she wouldn't be able to stay cocooned in here forever. She would eventually have to get out and face the world again.

She wiped at the window where her breath had created a faint haze, blurring the lights of the city. He was gone. He was really gone. She repeated the thought, rolling it over and over in her mind, examining it from all angles.

Her Uncle Canton had texted her back later Monday evening, and typical to his usual terse style, he told her don't bother rushing to the city, it was too late to say any goodbyes. The public funeral would be this Friday, expect it to be a media affair. If she wanted to avoid all that, she could just come for the reading of the will on Saturday at 10:00 am at Windhurst & Bannon in their office on Park Ave, he will send a text with the address. As the only living survivor of the youngest son - his brother Parker - she really should be there, but if not, someone from the firm would contact her so they could get her signature for the legal documents.

Mallory read, and then re-read, his text at least twenty times. And even now, three days later, the day before her grandfather's funeral, she still felt numb. A sinking, all-encompassing blankness had taken over the moment he said, "maybe to see him for the last time" and the additional careless comment that she was the "only living survivor" of her parents Parker and Nicole, was just another reminder of her particularly pathetic place in life. She willed her mind not to dwell on the memories of her grandfather, and her parents, and the deep chasm that separated them until her parents' sudden death over ten years ago.

And, the bitter realization that she and her grandfather had done nothing to bridge that chasm - in some ways it had even grown - that realization just left her numb. She forced herself not to think about Grandpa J's recent voicemail about a month ago, the one where he said he was sorry, that he had finally "found his compass," and that he wanted to see her when he came back to the city for Thanksgiving.

She just couldn't let herself think about the "what could have beens," and "what should have beens." That would drive a person crazy.

Mallory sighed heavily as she glanced down once again at the newspaper folded next to her, tucked snugly against her leg as if by not seeing it, she could avoid reading it. Frowning in frustration, she finally shook it open, forcing herself to turn the paper over to read the other front-page article, the one below the fold, lower right-hand corner. Foolish to try to avoid it any longer.

JL McMICHAEL, A LITERARY AND FILM LEGEND
LAID TO REST TOMORROW

He looked distinguished in the photo, taken within the last few years, his bright, inquisitive eyes were smiling and his short, cropped at the sides and longer on top, white-blonde hair was perfectly groomed. His wardrobe for the photoshoot that day was his typical, personable, not-too-stuffy crew neck sweater and tie. And except for the clothing, since her dad was much more the outdoorsy-type, more comfortable in a ski jacket than a tie, he looked so much like how she remembered her father, sometimes it took her breath away.

Funny thing, DNA was. They shared the same gray-blue eyes, the three of them, and the same long straight nose, high cheekbones and, although hers was dark brunette like her mother's, where theirs was blonde and fair, they shared the same thick, wavy hair. But, beyond the physical similarities, they shared precious little else.

The brief article praised the life of the "legend" including his literary work and film credits and the other businesses and philanthropy that mushroomed from his stellar literary career. It mentioned the children of his first marriage to Rosalind, son Canton and daughter Jasmine, and their involvement running the "business enterprise" that JL McMichael crafted from his humble beginnings as an English professor some fifty years ago.

Mallory swallowed hard against the hurt and resentment when she noticed they didn't even mention his second wife Camille and his youngest son Parker, her father. Blinking hard, she reminded herself, this wasn't the obituary; this was just the surface persona, pretty much what everyone else knew of JL McMichael.

The article reflected the life that the "literary legend" allowed them all see, it was the extent of what he wanted them to see. And, the public was all too eager to believe it, the public facade that the legend and his family embodied. She did her best not to let the tears burn through her resolve, the world might call him a legend, but she called him Grandpa J - and a few other names that she wouldn't allow herself the gratification of saying out loud this week, the week he was laid to rest.

Mallory laid her forehead against the window, tired of thinking about it, but closing her eyes didn't help. It just opened the door to the memories, and when that happened, they rushed in unchecked.

it's a memory, forgive me if it's faint and a bit out of focus

"So, what do you think of your Grandma's little house, Mal? She always called this place her heaven on earth." Grandpa J shut the car door, leaned against the side panel of the Chevy convertible and crossed his arms over his chest, regarding the odd stone house with quiet appreciation, the same look he got when he scored a first edition rare book or one of those paintings that he loved so much at his place in Palm Beach.

Having ridden the past couple of hours in a convertible with him, Mallory's long dark curls were a mess of tangles and she pushed them out of her eyes and behind her ears again, as she walked around the car to stand next to him. She looked past the rustic, wrought iron fence with its little iron gate and across the patchy green grass, her eyes following the stone path leading up to the old, one and half story river stone house, with a simple shuttered window peeking out from under a dark gabled roof and a sturdy, antique wood double door between two old, paned windows. She took in the massive oak and cedar trees surrounding the little house and the rather steep hill with its tangled brush that rose behind it, which seemed to hover over and all around, as if protecting it from the bright sun. There was a sound of water, but the stream wasn't visible from where they stood on the street. Judging by the little bridge they had just crossed, it must cut through the backyard, meandering along the base of the hill.

Grandma's little house - purchased because it was close to her family in Minnesota. If this magical place was her "heaven on earth," Mallory cried again inside, her heart seizing up, she sure wished she could have met Grandma Camille.

But, somehow, when she spoke all she could say was, "It's cool, I guess. Is there air conditioning?"

She crossed her arms in front of her, mimicking his stance, trying to get a rise out of him. What did he expect her to say? Thanks for dragging me, your fourteen-year-old-recently-orphaned granddaughter, halfway across the country from New York City to this forgotten spot of soil in Minnesota - for God knows how long - where I will surely shrivel up and die of sheer boredom or severe depression?

"Ha! Yes, there is!" Grandpa J's light gray-blue eyes twinkled at her attempt to goad him. He was too smart to be drawn into her sour disposition, she hadn't quite broken his resolve yet. Give it time, it will happen eventually, she assured herself. He said they would be here all summer.

"But your grandma preferred to open the windows when she was here. She loved the sounds of the birds and the brook. Come on, Mal, let me show you the place."

With that, Grandpa J reached over the backseat of the car, grabbed his worn, leather laptop case and waved her along behind him up the walk.

◆ ◆ ◆

The day of the funeral dawned bright and sunny, but the crisp November air was portending some more nasty weather. A low-pressure system was stalled out in western Pennsylvania and was so far from the city that it seemed non-existent. Like all life west of New Jersey, to New Yorkers it didn't really matter until it had crossed the Hudson River.

As Mallory walked the three blocks from her hotel to the church where the funeral was being held, she noticed with dismay that her black suede boots were no match for the Manhattan sidewalks which were covered in a slick mess of heavy November slush after last night's nasty weather. She pulled her gray plaid wool coat tighter around her and lifted the faux fur collar up to protect her neck from the cold drafts that blew up and down the streets in a crazy dance between buildings.

Miserable day to be in the city, she thought as she spied the church a block away. The street was cordoned off to allow space for the media vans with their satellite dishes and their reporters standing outside, microphones in hand, attempting to score a big moment with the mayor or one of the Hollywood celebrities that were expected to attend today. She panicked inside at the mayhem, how would she get through that throng of people? As she drew nearer, she skirted along the fringes of the crowd, trying to spot a side door or a security desk.

"Mallory? Is that you?" She turned as someone briefly touched her shoulder. Guillory. Oh, thank God. He texted her yesterday that he and his wife Suzanne would be on the look-out for her today.

"Guillory! Am I glad to see you!" He took her into a light hug, smiling in his quiet way and patted her on her back.

"It's been far too long, Mallory. We've missed you." Tom Guillory was her grandfather's assistant and best friend. She noticed he had different glasses now, these were frameless, and he wore his gray hair a little longer, it curled down his neck and onto his collar. But otherwise, Guillory, as everyone called him, looked the same as he always had since he was hired over fifteen years ago. She didn't have to see under his wool overcoat to know he would be wearing a neat, fitted sweater over a button-down shirt with a tie and gray dress pants. She had teased him many times over the years, did he even own a pair of jeans? No, he'd replied. And, if he did, she would never see him wearing them.

"I've missed you too, Guillory. I was planning on coming here for Thanksgiving this year, but then – this." The tears pricked her eyes suddenly and she brushed her lashes quickly. This weather, the cold seemed to be biting right through her coat, it was so frigid it was making her eyes water.

"Why don't you come inside? Suzanne is on her way, caught in traffic. I told her I would find you and we would wait for her in the guest area." He politely took her elbow and walked with her to a side door where a security guard stood with a clipboard. They didn't need to check him off the list, they knew him well. As Grandpa J's assistant, he most likely had hired the security team for this event, and Mallory was sure he had managed most of the details. They checked off her name, and then they walked into the church and down a hall into an open area with a comfortable couch and two chairs. Guillory motioned for her to sit down and, taking off his wool overcoat, he laid it down neatly on the couch and sat across from her.

"I'm so sorry about your grandfather, Mallory. It was so unexpected." He looked at her with compassion, and she was reminded that somehow her grandfather had connected with this nice man for many years, certainly there must have been some common bonds they shared. But, compassion couldn't have been one of them.

"Yes, Uncle Canton called me Monday and then later he texted me don't bother coming because ... he was gone already." She found she had a hard time getting the words out, and she looked down at her black leather gloves, pulling them off slowly one finger at a time.

"Yes, we were so surprised. One moment he's happily writing - I think he said he was at the ranch - and the next moment, he's back here saying he's not feeling well." Guillory shook his head slightly, his eyes perplexed at the unexpected tragedy.

When he looked at her again, Mallory was sure that he had much more to say, "If he was still with us, I would never betray his confidence this way, but he shared things with me when he got back here. Meaningful, important things. He was re-evaluating his life, his journey, his faith. And, then suddenly, he's gone."

Guillory sighed softly and paused as if he wanted to say more but he was choosing his words very carefully, "He spoke most lovingly about you, Mallory. Before he left us." He reached over and patted her hand softly, holding it loosely, "I just think you should know that."

As they sat there for a moment, Guillory waited patiently for her reaction, but she realized she didn't have anything to say. It was a little late, wasn't it? She didn't really know how to feel at this moment, so many years had gone by without dealing with any of it.

If Grandpa J had suddenly found a faith in a higher power, good for him, but it didn't change the words that were said, all the pain. The years between then and now had gradually just piled up on each other, until the mountain between them was almost insurmountable.

"Guillory, honestly, I just don't know what to say to that. I'm sorry, and I don't want to be bitter, but I'm having a hard time with all of it. You've seen some of what's gone down, it hasn't been good."

Mallory's voice trailed off softly, she knew that he was well aware of how she felt. He had been a witness to how her grandfather had treated her, and how he treated her father before her.

"Yes, yes, Mallory, I know. He was an ...enigma." He gazed out the old, diamond pattern lead-glass window to his right, and then a soft smile crossed his mouth, "But, he was your Grandpa J, the only one you'll ever have. That's something, Mal. It's worth something."

Reminding her of his unique position as employee, personal friend and substitute family, he intentionally used the name she gave her grandfather and the name her grandfather had given her. She recognized it and couldn't help but smile weakly back at him.

"He was lucky to have you, Guillory. And, you're right, he was an enigma." She lightly patted his hand which still held hers and tried to put an end to a conversation that was going nowhere.

"Where are you staying while you're in the city? Please come to his house to stay." He looked at her with a crooked, sad smile on his mouth, "It's so very quiet there these days."

"Haven't you been going home this week?" She blinked in surprise at his comment. Guillory and Suzanne had lived in Brooklyn for forty years; Mallory knew their brownstone home well, having spent many holidays with them and their two children over her teenage years. "Certainly no one expects you to stay there to watch the place, Guillory."

"No, that's true. Your Uncle Canton stopped in Tuesday to go through your grandfather's study and papers and he made it clear that the decision to continue on for a while was up to me. But, I've just felt like someone should be there. It's hard...you know, Mallory. It's hard to let him go."

"Yes. Yes, it is." She looked out the paned window, wondering did she really feel that or was she just agreeing because she could feel his pain at the loss of his friend?

She shook her head slightly, trying to sort out her feelings. As always, when it came to her grandfather, her heart was open only just so far, just far enough for her to feel human, but not far enough to get hurt again.

A few minutes later, the family and close friends were ushered into a room for a brief private service and to view the deceased. Mallory waited towards the back of the room while the other family members, her aunt and uncle and her cousins and their wives walked past the casket, saying their goodbyes to JL McMichael.

She wondered, what were they saying to him as he laid there, defenseless, his cunning mind and quick wit silenced once and for all? Did they all have the history of hurt that she harbored deep in her heart? If so, how did they resolve it and forgive him, especially when he died before it could be aired out?

Finally, unable to avoid it any longer, Mallory took her turn walking past the open casket, knowing that the gazes of her family were ones of judgement, not compassion. After all, she was the black sheep of the family, a role magnified by her darker complexion and hair (a tribute to her mother) in comparison to their fair skin color and blue eyes. Bottom line, she didn't belong, she didn't look like them and she wasn't one of them.

She knew this was what her family thought - her Uncle Canton's family and her Aunt Jasmine's family - they were all cut from the same privileged, entitled cloth.

After her parents' death, when she came to live with Grandpa J in New York, her cousin Geoffrey had come right out and told her what they were all saying - she was the product of Grandfather slumming around, picking up his second wife along the way, "that woman from little house on the prairie."

And, he'd continued, no doubt that's why her father Parker was such a loser, drifting around the country and ending up in Colorado. It was clear he couldn't cut it working in the business. Lucky for them all, JL McMichael had two other children he could count on for that.

She tried to blink away her tears and leaned against the casket slightly, feeling a little off balance as she struggled to focus on him, lying there silently in his dark blue suit, so very unlike the Grandpa

J she knew. But, it was hard to keep her thoughts in order. He didn't even look like Grandpa J. She had the absurd urge to poke his chest, wanting him to open his eyes. I will never see his eyes again, she thought sadly, my only connection to Daddy is gone forever.

And, as that realization settled heavy onto her heart, Mallory turned from the casket and walked out of the family service and didn't stop walking until she was far away, down the hall, almost out the back door. She didn't really belong in the private, family service anyway.

Later, at the public funeral in the ornate church sanctuary, seated at the end of the second row, next to her cousin Michael, Mallory watched as various dignitaries and celebrities shared their soaring accolades for the icon JL McMichael and his many accomplishments. A man of many talents, they said, a man who touched the lives of so many, his influence in literature, film and philanthropy so great that we cannot know today the full impact, let the future generations be the judge, etc etc.

As the funeral continued, and her mind started to wander, Mallory noticed a woman sitting on the end of the row ahead of her, dressed in a stylish, perfectly tailored black and white suit with a beautiful red leather Prada bag peeking out from beside her on the church pew. She hadn't seen Grandpa J's first wife Rosalind for many years, and from the looks of her unnaturally tight face and highly arched eyebrows, Rosalind was trying to erase the years as fast as they crept up on the calendar.

Grandpa J met Rosalind while they were both attending college in Maryland and married her just before accepting his first job as a part time college professor at American University and part time public information officer at the Department of Defense.

While living in Arlington, they soon had their son Canton, and then Jasmine arrived the following year. But, a few years into the marriage, Rosalind, not content with life as a wife to a poor college professor, was swept off her feet when a doctor, with much stronger social standing and financial prospects, arrived in her life. Soon, she left the college professor – and closet story writer – taking her two children along with her.

Not long after, the college professor finished his first novel, and moved to New York City where the novel was published, and a literary legacy was born. The burgeoning novelist did his fatherly duty, trying to be involved in his children's lives as much as he could, given the distance between them, but the pattern was established. It became a habit of his to think his children were a distant responsibility, determining that they were more of their mother's concern.

He had more important business to take care of, he had stories to tell, stories that would transcend the ages, timeless stories of loves lost, and lessons learned, lives lived, and hearts broken. Mallory was always struck by the nature of her Grandpa J's novels – how someone so clueless on the essentials of humanity could write novels filled with such moving tributes to humanity. An enigma, as Guillory said. Boy, was that was an understatement.

But, the real gold mines, the rich, textural work that leapt from his mind and onto the page with feverish abandon, those happened after he met Camille that fateful day in 1970 at a northern Minnesota lake lodge writer's camp. JL McMichael was attending this event at the request of his publisher as part of their nationwide effort to promote their new "undiscovered talent" brand.

Camille, not a writer but always a supportive friend, was attending at the request of her neighbor Betty, a wishful romance novelist, who asked Camille to come along for moral support, and to split the hotel expenses.

Her Grandpa J and Grandma Camille met quite by chance, forced to share a table that busy Saturday morning, because the Whisper Pines breakfast buffet was a popular draw for the summer crowd and tables were scarce. JL was entranced beyond words and Camille fell head over heels in love. Soon, they were married and not long after, they had a son and named him Parker. And the words, the stories, they flowed with abandon.

CHAPTER 3

"Just do your best to get through it, Mallory. You will be fine." Guillory replied with a smile and patted her knee while she griped about having to spend the morning with her family at the reading of Grandpa J's will. As the cab pulled to a stop in front of Windhurst & Bannon offices, he handed the cab driver payment and turned to open the door, waiting for her on the curb.

I don't even know why I'm here, this is a total waste of time and a source of unnecessary torture, Mallory thought as they walked together into the skyscraper and took the lobby elevator to the 23rd floor where the law firm conference room was located. The doors opened to an upscale lobby, tastefully decorated with marble floors and textured gray and silver papered walls. Upon their arrival, they were greeted by a receptionist who ushered them down a dark wood-paneled corridor and into a conference room, with an impressive bank of floor to ceiling windows along one wall and outfitted with a massive dark-leather topped table and upholstered leather rolling chairs.

As she entered the room with Guillory, Mallory tried to smile back at the brief acknowledgements from her family members who stood in clusters around the room. Homing in on the table set up with a coffee pot and a spread of fresh fruit and baked goods, Mallory headed that direction, with Guillory following her lead. She had already had two cups of Guillory's coffee this morning at the house before they left, but somehow, she was dying for another one right now.

As she laid her coat on a chair, and smoothed down her hair, she tried not to focus on how her simple white silk blouse, navy blue velvet pants and floral-patterned boots contrasted with her family's attire, all of whom were dressed in expensive designer suits and shoes.

It just doesn't matter, she reminded herself. This is how I dress every day, I don't care what they think. Feeling more secure after her internal pep talk, she said good morning to her cousins Alton and Christopher who were standing near the coffee buffet and helped herself to a steaming cup.

"Good morning, welcome to you all," The taller of two men spoke as they entered the conference room, followed by a young woman who held a stack of folders in her arms. "I am William Bannon, JL's lead attorney and this is David Yardley a staff attorney who has worked on JL's estate for the past few years and this is Donna Kent, our legal assistant. Please help yourself to coffee and pastries and then, if you're ready, let's please sit down and we will begin."

Everyone found a seat and Mallory couldn't help but feel the eyes of her family focused on her, with Guillory seated next to her. It was obvious he was not family, at least by blood, and they were confused by his attendance at today's meeting. This morning at the house, he told her that the attorneys had unexpectedly called requesting that he attend the reading of the will today.

She wondered, would anyone explain that, or would he be forced to endure these uncomfortable looks for the duration of this event?

"Let me start by giving you my condolences on the passing of your father, and grandfather, JL." William Bannon pulled a pair of glasses out of a leather pouch and placed them carefully on the end of his nose as he reached for the stack of folders Donna Kent handed him, "I have known him for many years and consider him a dear friend. When he returned to the city this last time, he called me over to his home and we reviewed his estate. Of course, he must have had some inkling that his health was deteriorating in some fashion, but I can assure you, he did not mention anything to me about that. And, as was said many times yesterday with words much more eloquent than I have, he was a true artist and will be truly missed."

He looked around the table at each of the family, his eyes resting for appropriate moments on each person. Nice touch, Mallory thought, an attorney who seemed human.

"I know Canton and Jasmine personally, but some of you I have never met, so if you don't mind, could you please introduce yourselves by going around the table?"

After the introductions were made, William Bannon began reading the last will and testament with all its legal language and formalities. Most of which Mallory spaced off, wondering ... really, why was she here? Certainly, it was expected that her uncle and aunt would be the beneficiaries of the estate of her Grandpa J. And rightfully so, they had devoted their entire lives to his career and businesses.

William Bannon droned on about the literary proceeds, and future royalties, current and future relationship with the publisher to be willed to Uncle Canton, which he managed anyway so no surprise there. The film production studio and associated California operations to be willed to Aunt Jasmine, which she managed anyway, so no surprise there. The hotel franchises, which were operated out of the Florida office, were willed to them both with a stipulation for a trust to JL's selected charities, including a significant donation to the homeless in Miami and for hurricane disaster relief efforts in the state of Florida. The JL McMichael Foundation charitable organization focusing on literacy, already set up in trust, which was managed by Geoffrey, was beneficiary of another significant cash amount and significant holdings in Grandpa J's investment accounts.

After discussion of the businesses was complete and Mallory felt her eyes completely glaze over while she strategized a subtle way to leave for the restroom - dang, those three cups of coffee - William Bannon read through the section regarding the grandchildren trusts.

One by one, each name was read, each was granted a million dollars in trust to be granted upon their thirtieth birthday, to be used as they chose, with his request that they use it thoughtfully and with purpose to improve the life of not only themselves, but others around them.

What the heck, oh my gosh! Not expecting it, Mallory wasn't sure she heard it correctly at first and immediately felt guilty for the nasty thoughts that she had been having about Grandpa J.

Ever since she'd known him, Grandpa J had money. Lots of it. He used to say he had too much of it and it felt good to give it away sometimes. But, today's reading of the will was proof that, even though he had given a lot away during his lifetime, it seemed he still had some left when he died.

She glanced around the table at her cousins, they all seemed to take the gift in stride, some even grimacing slightly. I guess a million dollars to them is but a minor blip in their trust funds, too paltry to notice, possibly even an insult. But, for her, just the thought of it was tinged with the smoke of guilt because she couldn't believe she deserved it. Like, it can't possibly be that easy, can it? A million dollars ... oh, what she could do with a million dollars! She was already trying to figure out how many days it was until her thirtieth birthday.

"... and, as for residential properties owned by my estate, I bequeath the following residences, and all contents so contained, as of this day and all rights to the said contents, as follows: proceeds from the sale of my Palm Beach, FL residence to be held in trust for the JL McMichael Foundation, residence Beverly Hills, CA to daughter Jasmine, residence Jackson, WY to son Canton, residence New York City to Tom Guillory, my long-time friend and business associate..."

Mallory heard Guillory's sharp intake of breath as the words sunk in and she turned to him, a smile bubbling onto her lips while Guillory just sat there staring at the attorney like he had two heads.

In her excitement for Guillory, it didn't occur to her that this turn of events would be received less than enthusiastically by her family. Their blank stares and open mouths said enough, and inside, Mallory's heart was singing. *You owned everyone with this one, Grandpa J, thank you for doing what's right for once.*

"...and to the aforementioned residence keeper I bequeath $250,000 for his faithful service and, while I would be willing to bequeath more, I would not want to offend and he would likely not accept, so I give him my eternal gratitude that no amount of money can express..."

Lost in her thoughts about Guillory's new upper east side home, Mallory didn't hear what that was all about, but obviously someone had made a good impression on her Grandpa J. And, her heart was softening with each of these paragraphs as his generosity was displayed.

A few minutes later, after dispensing the instructions for stocks and investments, trusts and endowments, it seemed like they must finally be getting to the end–

"...and this completes the reading of the final will and testament."

William Bannon removed his glasses and put his hands palms down on the papers in front of him. "Are there any questions or sections you want read again or clarified?"

With his eyebrows raised, he turned to Uncle Canton, who had stood up towards the end of the reading and drifted over to the window behind Aunt Jasmine's chair. Mallory wasn't sure if it was intentional, but she noticed that the attorney avoided eye contact with Guillory, probably thinking he was in shock and would be unable to form a question in his current stupor. She couldn't help wondering if Guillory was even breathing yet and she worked hard not to high five him right there in the conference room.

"No, I have no questions." Aunt Jasmine spoke first, adjusted her dark rimmed glasses on her nose and gracefully smoothed her silky, straight blonde hair behind her ear, revealing a glittery pear-shaped diamond earring. Mallory wondered fleetingly, how much did it cost, and how much time did it take, to have such perfect hair, skin and nails?

Aunt Jasmine turned and looked to her brother slowly, as if waiting for his agreement, but Uncle Canton just continued to stare out the window, deep in thought. It was hard to tell what he was thinking from his expression.

Then, Aunt Jasmine turned her gaze across the table towards Mallory, a somber look shading her eyes, and suddenly she felt singled out and utterly defenseless in the quiet conference room. Except for Uncle Canton, all their eyes were now focused on her, and she felt like she was the only kid in the classroom - the one who came in late - that didn't know there was a test scheduled for that day.

When she spoke, her aunt's voice seemed abnormally strident in the hushed room, "I'm sorry, Mallory. I thought father would leave more to Park- I mean to you. I had hoped that ... after all these years and since he'd experienced these "changes" recently ... he would have moved past their differences and would have forgiven. I'd completely forgotten all about that little house ... I'm just so sorry..." She finished with a soft whisper, her eyes misting over, right there in front of them all.

Mallory's mind went blank as she tried to catch up to what she was saying. What about the little house? She'd forgotten about it too. Who did he will that to?

Wait.

Did Grandpa J leave Grandma Camille's little house to her? She didn't even hear that part, it must have come right after the part about Guillory, but, obviously, it had been in there.

A tangled mess of thoughts and emotions, Mallory tried to process the fact that Aunt Jasmine considered it an embarrassment, and hurtful - actually, spiteful - that he had left that little forgotten house to her.

When she couldn't think of how to respond, and the pause became unbearable, William Bannon cleared his throat and assertively pushed documents across the table towards her cousins while the legal assistant started handing out pens to everyone and pointed to the lines for them to sign. Each of her cousins and Guillory were signing, while on the other side of the room, her aunt and her husband Craig and her uncle and his wife Desiree, were talking to the other attorney going through their own thick set of documents.

Then, William Bannon, still sitting across the table, pushed a set of documents towards her, holding his hand on them until she looked up to meet his unswerving gaze.

"These contain the Deed for the property in Minnesota and other instructions from your grandfather regarding this property. He said that it's up to you if you'd like to sell it and, if you so choose, he recommends you talk to the residence keeper. He will likely be a potential buyer and his number is listed in the documents."

William Bannon smiled, his eyes crinkling up at the corners, obviously he missed the part about this house being an embarrassingly public display of Grandpa J's deep-seated repugnance towards her, and her father.

"It's a pleasure to meet you, Mallory, your grandfather spoke highly of you. He took special interest in this property and said that, while most might not recognize it, you would appreciate it's true worth."

CHAPTER 4
... Nice to meet you, neighbor ...

"Hey, Paul, can you upload those photos you took of those bar stools we did for that microbrewery in Duluth? When I get back from this meeting, I have to send the pictures to that new designer in Minneapolis."

As he walked out of his office into the upholstery room, Harris shrugged his arms into his black down-filled jacket, dropped his cell phone into his pocket, and slowed down by the back door to look at the UPS box that sat partially opened on the floor. This was not the box he hoped to see. Yesterday, they were supposed to get those leather swatches from that new supplier in Denver, and from the looks of it, he would have to wait until Monday to see them. With a frown, Harris turned to his younger brother Paul who was stretching over his broad table, laying out a rich caramel-toned microfiber suede for some custom pillows.

"I know, I know. They didn't come in yesterday." Paul addressed him without waiting for the question. "I've already sent them an email, but you know, some people actually take Saturdays off, so I don't expect to hear from them until Monday."

Laughing, Paul smoothed his impressively long blonde beard with his right hand and then bent over his work again, pulling his white headphones from around his neck up onto his ears. "And, yes, I will have the photos uploaded by the time you get back." He gestured towards his computer where the digital camera was connected, and Harris could see the photos were uploading.

"I don't feel sorry for you, you'll be out of here by noon." Harris said as he picked up the pair of sunglasses from the shelf near the door and put them on, turning to his brother, "You know, I could be really mad that you refuse to come with me today, but instead, I will go and do the deal that will help us continue to pay your exorbitant salary."

Harris knew he could hear him through the headphones when he saw the smile from under Paul's mustache, "But, thanks for the photos, you're the man. If I ever tell you any different, just ignore me."

Paul's laugh followed him out the door and, relishing the warmth of the bright Saturday morning sunshine on his face, Harris began to feel the load on his mind lighten just a little.

If today's meeting went well, Lake Country Customs would be one step closer to a full-service custom furniture and cabinetry shop. Will Benson's building, located just a few miles from here, had twice the equipment and space of their shop. And, having been in the business for over thirty years, his relationships with home builders in the Twin Cities and north lake country went deep.

They were a perfect fit, these two companies. Lake Country Customs was growing too large for their location here and Will, whose wife had been a furniture customer of theirs for years, wanted to retire. And, while Paul was averse to being involved in the detailed business aspects of the merger, the two brothers had been praying about this for months, and they both felt the momentum was in the right direction. It was all so tantalizing, Harris could see it laid out right in front of him.

The early morning sun had some power and already the snow from last night was starting to melt on the street in front of his shop. He turned his Chevy pickup truck out of the driveway and by force of habit, he glanced over his roughly ten acres of land and trees and towards his house and smiled, never growing tired of the sight of it sitting there in the distance, against the backdrop of evergreens, river birch and maple trees.

Distracted slightly, unless today's temps melted it, he realized that he needed to shovel snow off his front walk. Not that anyone used it - the postal service and UPS came to the shop - no one except his family came to visit him at the house, and if they did, they came to the side door by the garage. But, the snow-covered walk gave the impression that no one lived there and something about that bothered him. He really had to get a life.

Slowing at the stop sign at the end of his street, he felt his cell phone buzz with a text and he retrieved it from his pocket. Hoping it wasn't Will wanting to reschedule today's meeting, he blinked slightly and then smiled when he saw the text was from The Wandering Poet, the contact name in his phone for his next-door neighbor and friend.

It's about time, he thought as he glanced over at the small stone house behind the trees that shared the small clearing with his larger home. His neighbor lived in Florida, but he spent random vacation weeks in Minnesota as he worked his way towards retirement. Recently though, he was starting to wonder what happened to the guy, two voice messages and a few texts later and no reply, he was starting to think the guy had died.

He swiped open the text,

Sorry for the delayed response. This is JL's son Canton. I regret to inform you that my father died of a heart attack earlier this week. I gather from your texts that you knew my father well, so I want you to know he died suddenly and didn't suffer. Thank you for being his friend.

What? Harris's mouth dropped open and he had to re-read the text three times, trying to comprehend. Why was this guy on Mike's phone? Why did he call him JL? And, did he mean that Mike was dead?

Harris's phone buzzed again just then, with a call from Paul.

"Harris, you need to call Cindy Hallgren. She said you promised to stop by her house this week to get her a price on those built-ins. And, you need to come back here to get that leather framed mirror you said you'd give to Will Benson. He said if you showed up without it today, it could be a deal breaker."

And, with that, Harris knew he should focus on the business at hand, but inside, he felt a hole had formed, a part of him felt hollowed out suddenly. And, still sitting at the stop sign, he put his truck in park and stared at the small stone house in the distance. It was empty now. His friend Mike was gone. Just when he finally got to know him.

Later that afternoon, as she rode the train back to Baltimore, Mallory mulled over the day's events. To say that the family was shocked by Grandpa J's generosity towards Guillory would be a monumental understatement. Even though the upper east side townhouse was purchased over twenty years ago for a much more reasonable figure, today's market value was beyond anything Mallory's bank account could comprehend.

Guillory obviously was surprised - and beyond self-conscious - about such an extravagance. After the meeting was complete and her family members milled around the room, most of them surreptitiously glaring at Guillory, he pulled Mallory aside and said certainly there had been some mistake. He couldn't possibly have the house, it was the family's house.

As he nervously whispered his concerns, her mind flashed back to that first Christmas, less than a month after her parents' accident, before she had enrolled in the Connecticut boarding school where she would stay for a few years. Even though New York was his home, and by default it became her home too, Grandpa J didn't feel responsible to be in New York that Christmas, the first she would spend without her parents. He was busy with two movies in production in California, he couldn't make it back to New York, he said. She would get along just fine without him, Guillory was there.

That holiday was the first of many that she would spend with Guillory and his family at their Brooklyn brownstone. To Mallory, in many ways, Guillory was more family than her own relatives. Obviously, Grandpa J considered him family too.

Which made it even more hurtful that he couldn't be more generous towards his own youngest son, and by birthright, her. It wasn't about the money, even though that would have come in handy right now, she thought as she realized her rent would be due next week, and soon she would have to tap into the rainy-day fund from her parents' nominal life insurance policy.

No, it wasn't about money, it was about rejection. And bitterness. And control. It was another reminder that Grandpa J had always wanted to control her father, and after her father was gone, he wanted to control her. And, since he hadn't been able to master that while he was alive, he would control them after he died. This had been their life's struggle, and now, Grandpa J had settled the score.

Later that night, after texting a few friends and a phone call from her friend Bradford with whom she shared some of the news of the day, Mallory was brushing her teeth when she heard her phone pinging again. The photo of Jasper lit up the screen – three texts this week and now a phone call from him. How long would he continue this? Mallory rinsed and wiped her mouth on the hand towel next to her sink, debating whether she should just pick up and get it over with. Finally, unable to bear listening to the ring tone any longer, she plucked the phone off the counter and answered.

"Hey, Jasper. What's up?" And why are you being such a jerk, her voice came out flat and unemotional as she finished the thought in her mind.

"Oh, hi! I thought you wouldn't pick up." Mallory heard booming loud music and people in the background. Did he really think she was going to talk to him, especially when he was out drinking? "I've been thinking about you, Mallory... you know, with your grandpa's funeral and everything. Could I come over ... maybe we could talk?"

"No, Jas. You know that's not going to happen. Just let it go, ok?" Mallory wandered into her bedroom, shuffled her still-unpacked luggage off her bed, spilling out some of its contents, and plopped down, every inch of her body suddenly very tired.

"Uh, that's the thing, I know I should let it go. But, I just can't seem to do that. You know that you do this thing to me, I can't stop thinking about you." His voice had that balmy, low-pitched tone that she had heard many times before and she could picture the way his mouth curled up when he said it. His charm used to make her smile, but now she realized, it made her slightly sick to her stomach.

"Well, it sounds like you're out tonight, it shouldn't be too much trouble to find someone to help you move on." She didn't try to hide her sarcasm and she heard him laugh slightly. He must have stepped outside or into a hallway, somehow away from the crowd, because the background noise had dimmed considerably.

"Really, Mallory, I'm serious. I am sorry."

He sighed heavily, and she imagined how he would be standing, his dark hair neatly trimmed, with his imported oxfords highly polished. She wondered, was he dressed down tonight in jeans or was he in dress pants, his more typical nightly attire? Either way, she was sure he was wearing one of his expensive, Italian-made tailored shirts with the perfectly pressed collars.

"You know I love you. I want us to try again." He waited for her answer, and she heard a few people laughing and chattering as they passed by him, "Can you at least please consider it?"

"Honestly, this is the last thing I want to think about. I'm tired, it's been a long few days. I don't want to keep doing this-" She closed her eyes and lost her voice as her throat filled up – finally feeling the weight of the day, and the sting of her grandfather's rejection, starting to settle in.

"Mallory, I'm sorry. Can I come over? You should have someone there with you." Did she imagine it, was he actually using her grandfather's death as an excuse to come over? My gosh, the nerve of him!

"No, you can't come here." She fought for some way to put an end to this conversation, her eyes coming to rest on her opened luggage with the property deed peeking out from under her pajamas. Seizing on the thought, she said, "I'm leaving tomorrow for Minnesota anyway. I have some things to wrap up with Grandpa J's estate."

The beginning of a plan was starting to take shape in the back of her mind – Yes, she reasoned with herself, that's what she'd do. She would go to Minnesota to sell this house.

"Oh. Well, then, let's get together as soon as you're back? Promise me, Mallory, you will let me see you when you get back?" The urgency in his voice sounded real and she pondered his persistent calls these past few weeks. Surely there must be something behind the fact that he kept reaching out to her, maybe he really did feel something for her?

"Maybe." She conceded, her anger gradually dissipating, she was feeling herself weakening inside. For some reason, she still loved him. How pathetic was that? "I need to put a property up for sale, it could take a while."

"I'll wait. And, thanks Mallory." He hesitated briefly, as if he was looking for the appropriate words and through the phone she heard a siren in the distance and his quiet sigh, "I love you."

Mallory hung up the phone without saying goodbye, opened her Google Maps app and entered Minneapolis/St. Paul International airport as starting location, with Beck's Creek, MN as her final destination.

Maybe Beck's Creek wasn't technically located at the end of the earth, but the last hour of driving convinced her that the end of the earth had to be close to here. Mallory squirmed in her seat again to bring some sensation back to her right butt cheek and rotated her shoulders to try to alleviate the stiffness. Funny how this two-hour-plus drive across the flat lands of mid-Minnesota and up towards "lake country" seemed so much faster ten years ago.

That day ten years ago, even though she was doing her best to be mad at him, and they had gotten a late start - he was hungover from too much vodka at the hotel bar the night before - the drive had pretty much flown by.

It was an exquisite summer day and her grandpa, looking surprisingly refreshed in his golf shirt and Ray Ban sunglasses, was driving the convertible that he stored in a garage near the private airport next to the main terminal at the Minneapolis/St. Paul airport. He told her she could choose whatever music she wanted on the radio and he cranked it up really loud and tried to sing along to the songs he recognized.

When they had travelled many miles away from the Twin Cities, and the selections of radio stations became scarce, he introduced her to a game that he said he used to play with her dad. He would select an old, dilapidated house or a historic brick building they passed along the way, and then she was asked to come up with a story for it.

There were only three rules: One, the story had to originate out of that building; Two, the characters must be engaging and unique; and Three, there must be a twist, something unexpected, something "so compelling that you simply had to turn the next page."

Funny how she remembered those rules, she thought as she squinted into the last sliver of the setting sun in front of her. Funny how she remembered any of it after all these years, including the proud feeling she had when, after her third story ended and they were rounding the bend into Beck's Creek, he looked at her, propped his sunglasses up on his head and said with a smile, "You have it, kid. I knew you would!"

Beck's Creek is a typical sleepy, small town, like any other. You know the type - every state in the country had them - a few residential streets cobbled together, anchored solidly by four blocks of yawning, weathered brick buildings which housed the businesses on the main street.

In Beck's Creek, the residential neighborhoods embraced the main street on all sides with a mix of houses including some brightly painted grand old ladies, with welcoming sloped porches who graciously shared their stately, oak tree-lined streets with their neighbors' more modest, simple dwellings with their neat yards and single stall garages.

Mallory pulled up to the stop sign on main street, glanced to the north at the irregular skyline of red and gray brick buildings punctuated black against the setting sun, and tried to remember the landmarks. She looked at the street signs and remembered that, although this was the town's main street, it was called Beatrice Blvd and it intersected with Bjorn Street.

She always wondered about that, who were Beatrice and Bjorn? Were they married? Were they the Beck's - founders of Beck's Creek? She was sure Grandpa J could have come up with quite a tale about those two.

The streets looked about the same as she remembered, with a few new tenants in the storefronts. She knew for sure there hadn't been a coffee shop/bakery on the corner before, it had been a bank when she was last here, and a new boutique had opened two doors down already dressed up with clear twinkling lights and greenery in its window boxes, decorated for the holidays.

She continued a few blocks down the hill towards the bridge in the dip below. The sun was setting quickly, with brilliant fuchsia pink and neon orange colors slashed across the horizon, and the hills on either side left this street in deep shadows. The near darkness didn't bother her though, she didn't need to see clearly, she remembered the turn well, having ridden bike over these streets many times that summer.

Turning the corner, her car's headlights swept over the pretty snow-covered clearing on the left side of the street, it's cotton-smooth cover interrupted by jack pine evergreens and river birch where it met with the hill on the other side; no houses over there, just a smooth layer of downy snow, almost glowing eerily pink in the spots touched by the setting sun.

And, there on the right side of the street, behind the fence line trimmed with red twig dogwoods, and some overgrown oaks and maples, sat the little stone house off in the distance. It looked dark and forgotten. Her inheritance.

She pulled slowly into the driveway that curved lazily around to the left side of the house and noticed that the lights were on in the only other house on this street. The Big House, as her grandpa used to call it.

It was a beautiful old house, built in similar style to the little house, with muted colored stone work covering three quarters of the way up the two stories and finished with dark wood shakes and steep gables on the last quarter. Although the shades were drawn, Mallory could see light coming through some of the large, paned windows that were trimmed in deep amber-colored stained shutters and she could smell the applewood smoke of a fire burning in one of the two imposing stone chimneys. If they had a fire burning, the Andersons must be home, and she realized she might need to visit them if her grandpa had decided to change his hiding spot for the key.

When William Bannon gave her the envelope for the house, he said that there wasn't an extra key for this house and, while it might be on her grandpa's key chain, there was really no way to know for sure unless she tried every one of them. Mallory assured him, no worries, I think I know where he keeps his spare key.

Now, standing in the cold snow, with the light of day gone completely, she thought better of her bravado. A lot has happened in ten years, maybe she shouldn't have been so confident.

She glanced again at the Andersons home; they would likely have an extra key, but would they remember her after ten years? Had her grandpa even thought to mention her to them ever again after that summer?

She walked gingerly along the snowy walkway towards the broad stone steps and front double doors that were protectively inset into a small alcove by large, rough-faced rocks. And using the flashlight on her cell phone to light the way, she swung the light across the rugged, heavy wood doors, and the two timeworn, weathered black lanterns that hung on either side of them.

Mallory stood on her tiptoes and reached a finger into the gap between the lantern on her left and the stone wall behind it. Not feeling anything, her heart sank.

This is the lantern where he stored it. She was sure of it. She lifted the phone closer to the gap, rested her cheek against the cold rocks, and tried to see if somehow she had missed it. Nothing. Great.

She swung her phone's beam across the stone steps and towards the other lantern on the right side of the door. Maybe he switched up his hiding spot?

But, no. Nothing. Again. Where would he have left it? There wasn't anything else on these steps under which he could hide a key. No mat, no false rock, no little frog figurine. Nothing. Great.

She stopped moving, her nerves firing. What was that? Did something just move out there in the yard? She could have sworn she heard the snow crunching behind her.

"Hey, what's up? Can I help you?"

A resonant, throaty voice called from a slight distance away, hidden behind the bright beam of a flashlight. He looked very large, like a hulking dark shadow, in the dim light bouncing around him.

"Well, I ... I don't think so. Who are you?" Mallory found her voice after a moment, who did this guy think he was? Sneaking up on her and scaring her like that!

"I was going to ask you the same thing."

She was irked by his tone, she didn't owe him any explanation after all, it was her property. He walked a little closer and put the light down slightly as he reached the steps. She caught the smell of applewood on his plaid flannel jacket and she noted thick, dark hair and the hint of a white smile as he leaned one foot onto the first step, but then stopped.

"I'm Harris Lake, Mike's next-door neighbor." He said as he reached into the pocket of his jacket and then dangled a set of keys. "I look after the place when he's away."

He had a disarming way about him, all confident with his foot on her steps like that. Mallory bristled to herself, this guy acted like he expected everyone to trust him, just because he said so.

"Mike? He told you his name was Mike?"

"Well, yes, he did. And, by the way, you haven't told me who you are..." He let the question hang there, waiting for her response, obviously he felt protective over the place.

"I'm J - I mean Mike's - granddaughter Mallory. He used to keep a set of keys hidden here, but I guess he moved them." She gestured towards the lantern and peered through the light of the flashlight, trying to read his expression. She wondered, did he know about Grandpa J's death yet?

"Oh, ok, yes, he's mentioned you before. He gave those keys to me. Here let me open up for you."

Harris moved past her, unlocked the creaky, antique door and stepped aside to let her walk in. After she passed, he reached around the inside edge of the door and flipped on a light switch setting off two table lamps that perched on a rustic wooden side table guarding the wall in the front hall.

She glanced to her right at the austere, rock-walled living room which boasted an impressive set of bookshelves snuggled around an imposing brown-brick fireplace and to her left at the closed door that she knew led to a bedroom and bath.

Turning slightly, she noticed he stood waiting in the open doorway, patiently watching her as she surveyed the dimly lit rooms.

"Ah … if you don't mind," He spoke up as she glanced at him, "I have a few questions to ask you about your grandfather, Mallory." For some reason, it startled her slightly that he remembered her name.

Taking a second look at this guy - Harris Lake, is that what he said his name was? - Mallory clicked through her observations. He was handsome, no doubt, with high cheekbones and light skin shadowed with just-enough-to-be-sexy dark stubble on a strong chin and deep, dark eyes framed with dark lashes. As she appraised him standing there, not knowing him at all, she debated about how to tell him about her grandfather's death.

"Well, by now, you've probably heard, my Grandpa J died last Monday. It was sudden, a heart attack, they say he didn't suffer."

Her gaze swept downward at the snow dusting the tops of her black leather knee-high boots. Every time she recounted this, it hurt somewhere deep inside.

After a momentary silence, she glanced up, not sure if he heard her because he didn't immediately offer the typical platitudes, the same ones she'd heard countless times over the past few days.

Instead, Harris Lake looked at her with the deepest coffee-colored, brown eyes that she'd ever seen, a lost expression in them that seemed bottomless. He squinted slightly, and Mallory was almost certain that she noticed tears welling up in his eyes before he looked down quickly and dropped the flashlight into one of the large pockets on his jacket.

"Oh. Okay. So, it's true." Harris wiped his eyes with his long fingers and sighed deeply, as he gazed off towards the living room and out the back windows, deep in thought. Not really knowing how to react but sensing there was more to Harris than she originally thought, Mallory walked around him and closed the door.

"Do you want to sit down?" Mallory continued down the short hall and into the open kitchen, flipping on the light switch and gesturing towards the primitive wood stools that sat at the butcher block top center island. With the exception of some new furniture, thankfully, Grandpa J hadn't changed much around here. She had always loved the slightly cheeky charm of this simple little house.

Harris followed her, pulled out a stool and sat down, not uttering a single word. Finally, extremely aware that she was sitting next to a stranger and feeling one of them should say something to fill the silence, Mallory continued.

"Did you hear about it on the news? Or, read it online maybe?" She pulled off her gloves and set them on top of one another on the counter, gathering her long hair out from under her scarf to let it fall out around her shoulders.

"What do you mean?" He looked confused, his dark brows frowning and his eyes squinting again in confusion. "Yesterday I got this strange text from Mike's cell phone, but it was a guy named Canton, saying something about Mike - he called him JL - that Mike had died. I didn't really know what to think. I guess I hoped it was some mistake. I tried calling Mike's phone again, but the number just went to voicemail all day."

"That's my Uncle Canton. He must have Grandpa J's phone." Mallory regarded him, sorry that he seemed so shaken up about this. "Did you know my grandfather well?"

"Yeah, I did, I guess. We hung out a lot when he was here - you know, when he took breaks from his work in Florida. It's such a shock, he was just here a few weeks ago."

"Really? I didn't know that, I thought he was at the ranch in Wyoming." She thought over what he said. Grandpa J was here in Minnesota that recently? She was sure Guillory had told her that he was in Wyoming before he came back to the city because he wasn't feeling well. Did that mean that Grandpa J was hiding out here for some reason? Hiding, even from Guillory? Why would he do that? And there was something else Harris said, something...

"Wait, he told you he had some work in Florida?" Mallory inquired, confused.

"Yes, of course. You know, the two hotels he managed in Florida. He never mentioned that he had a vacation home in Wyoming too."

Suddenly, it was becoming a little clearer to her.

"Harris, do you live next door with the Andersons?"

"No, they moved out over six years ago and the place was empty for a couple of years. I bought it about four years ago now. Why?"

"And my grandfather – who you know as Mike – told you that he managed two hotels in Florida. Did he tell you anything else about what he did for a living?"

"No, why? What else did he do?"

"Have you ever read anything written by JL McMichael, or watched any of the movies?"

"Of course, I have. I think the "Stand Tall, Son" novels were two of the best books I've ever read –"

He blinked slowly, comprehension lighting his eyes and Mallory saw the bright white of his smile as he laughed slightly, shaking his head in disbelief.

"Are you telling me that I've been taking care of JL McMichael's house for four years – I've been his friend for four years – and I never knew?" He laughed out loud this time, his shoulders shaking with laughter. "And, all this time, he's told me, and others here in town, that his name is Mike Jones and he's got to watch his finances because he's retiring for real sometime soon. That old fart!"

He shook his head again, glanced into the living room and then back to her, uttering a final soft recognition with a bemused look, "Wow."

Mallory couldn't help but smile at his reaction, they must have been good friends because – even given the deception – this guy was appreciating the humor of it all.

Suddenly shivering in her wool coat, feeling the cool temperature of the house, Mallory looked around for the furnace thermostat.

"Well, don't feel slighted," She was warming up to this new neighbor, he wasn't so bad, "In some ways, you got more of the truth than most people. His real name *is* Michael Leland Jones, it's just everyone forgot that decades ago, he's gone by his pen name for so many years. I think most people have forgotten Mike Jones ever existed." She smiled slightly, thinking, I bet he loved the fact that, even after all these years, no one knew who he was when he was here in Minnesota.

When she stayed with him that summer ten years ago, she remembered they kept mostly to themselves. And, when she asked why the Andersons called him Mike, Grandpa J told her that he was working when he came to this house, and he didn't want the distractions of celebrity, so he never discussed his career and he chose to use his real name when he came here.

Outside of a few artistic-bubble communities across the country, including New York and LA, and serious literature or film nuts, it was actually quite common that authors and movie producers weren't well-known faces. And, if you wanted to go incognito and had the motivation to hide who you were, it wasn't completely impossible.

Shivering again, she said. "It's cold in here. I guess I didn't even think about calling before I came today. I suppose Grandpa J would always call you ahead of time and ask you to get things ready?"

"Yes, he would." Harris stood up, reminding Mallory how tall he was, and walked over to the back wall of the kitchen, turning up the thermostat. "I have a list of things, turn up the heat or the air conditioning, basic grocery list, freshen the bedding, you know. So, I guess it's not quite ready this time." He shrugged and opened the refrigerator, showing it was empty.

"Oh, no big deal, I'll just go to the store tomorrow."

"I'm sure you're hungry though. There's a sports bar uptown, Spike's. It's not fancy, but they make a good burger. I haven't eaten yet either, would you like to go?"

"Well..." Mallory shifted uncomfortably, suddenly not sure how she felt about all this. Was the guy married?

Mallory noticed he was wearing an interesting ring, it looked like it was made of wood and sterling silver, but it was on his middle finger next to his ring finger, so that left things a bit confusing. Sensing her hesitation, Harris spoke up quietly.

"You can drive separately, if you like." He reached into his jacket pocket again, retrieved the keys and set them on the butcher block island. "Here, these are yours. So...?"

He glanced at her, putting his hands in his jeans pockets and rocking slightly on the heels of his leather lace up boots, waiting for her reply. Obviously, he would bring her along if he had a wife, and if he had a girlfriend, he must not feel awkward about having a burger with a perfect stranger. He didn't seem threatening, and her grandfather must have trusted him if he watched the house these past four years. How bad could he be?

"Okay, sure, I will bring my things in and I will meet you up there."

"Okay! See you there." He walked towards the front door, turned slightly to look into the living room again before he left, and shook his head, smiling softly to himself, lost in a memory.

As he left, Mallory realized that she wanted to know more about his friendship with her Grandpa J and she realized it wouldn't hurt to get to know this guy Harris a little better too.

CHAPTER 5

"... so, this little house is my inheritance, and I've been checking a few realtor websites, thinking I will list it, but it's going to be difficult to sell it during the winter, I think."

As they shared the booth near the bar at Spike's, Harris watched as she moved her cheeseburger over further to the side of the heavy white ceramic plate and squirted ketchup across her French fries in a zigzag pattern. Under the sweep of her brunette bangs, he saw her raised eyebrows as she held the ketchup bottle out towards him. He waved his hand slightly and shook his head No while he tried to swallow a bite of his burger before he spoke.

As he listened to her plan, he thought, I don't want her to sell the place right away, hopefully I can convince her to stall on that idea for a while.

"Mmm, that's so good." He closed his eyes slightly and smiled contentedly, as he relaxed into the booth a little further, "I forgot I worked through lunch today, didn't realize that I was so hungry."

He was doing his best not to stare at Mike's granddaughter, but it was proving very difficult. She had a way about her - all confident and self-reliant - that was super attractive.

And, when she spoke, her voice had a low caliber, kind of raspy tone, with a hint of an accent he couldn't quite identify. It wasn't east coast, and it definitely wasn't midwestern. He enjoyed listening to her, and played the game in his mind, trying to identify where she came from.

"It's Sunday today. Where do you work?" She scanned the pile of fries, choosing one that had the most ketchup on it.

"My brother Paul and I have a wood and upholstery shop just down the hill from my house, we renovated an old barn on the property. We sell custom furniture, fix up antique furniture, do upholstery for classic cars, that sort of thing. So, except for church on Sunday morning, every day could be Monday to me."

"Oh yeah, I remember that barn! I always thought that was the coolest building with its stone basement and the big hayloft." She smiled then, the thought must have taken her back to a happier time.

When she smiled, Harris found himself wishing she did it more often, it lightened the shaded look in her gray-blue eyes.

Some of her features were so similar to Mike, her wide eyes with long, thick lashes and the shape of her face, the way she tilted her head sometimes when she spoke, and yet, many things were so different.

Once he had gotten to know Mike, he found him to be very open, generous with his conversation and his time. So far, Mallory seemed very guarded, almost jaded, which was surprising for someone who must only be in her mid-twenties.

"Oh, that's right, you spent some time here when you were younger." When she frowned at the comment, Harris felt like he'd said something inappropriate - borderline creepy judging from the look on her face - and he explained further, "Mike told me some things about his children and his grandchildren over the years. Of course, now I see that he conveniently left out some pertinent information, but I remember him telling me that you were his only granddaughter and that you had stayed here with him one summer years ago. I asked him why you never came around while he was in Minnesota, but he said you were busy living your life."

Harris watched her expression as he took another bite of his burger and as he chewed, took his time wiping his mouth with a napkin. Would she share anything personal about herself, he wondered, anything about her rocky relationship with her grandfather? Probably not.

"Yes, I spent the summer here with him when I was fourteen, before going to boarding school that fall." She glanced around the sports bar, suddenly very interested in her surroundings. "So, Harris, you mentioned a brother, do you have other family around here?"

That's a bummer, he thought to himself, he knew there was more to tell, but he could see she wasn't ready, so he responded to her change of subject with a smile.

"I do. My parents live in Alexandria, which you probably drove through on your way here. My brother Paul is married to a lady whose first husband left her alone to raise their son. The guy gave up his parental rights and now Carissa and Peyton are part of our family...and we have aunts, uncles and cousins in the area. So yeah, it's a big, happy crew most of the time."

"Cool. No wife or kids for you though?" He noticed her looking at the ring on his left hand and he felt the familiar twist inside when the question was asked. He self-consciously pulled his hand off the top of the table and rested it in his lap.

"No. Divorced two years ago now. No kids." He tried his best to let the words just flow out, like they didn't bother him in the least, but they always seemed to get stuck somewhere in the back of his throat. "What about you?"

He was pretty sure he knew the answer, thinking Mike would have told him if she was married, but he was desperate to keep her talking, so he wouldn't have to.

"Married? No. In a confused relationship state? Yes." She laughed a little derisively and rolled her eyes, pulling some of her long dark hair behind her ear, revealing a delicate die cut bronze flower earring dangling against her neck, just above the lace-edged neckline of her fitted, black sweater. This girl was strikingly pretty and smart, he thought, but she seemed so sad. Obviously, there was a guy somewhere not helping the situation.

"But," She continued, casting her eyes downward, avoiding his gaze, "It's whatever, you know. It will work out. In the meantime, I have a house to sell." She sat back a little on the bench, pushing her plate away slightly, and met his eyes with a serious look.

"Grandpa J left word that you might be interested in purchasing the house, if given the chance. I don't want to pressure you to do that, because I have no problem listing it with an agent, but it would be good to know if you are interested. Maybe we could come to an agreement and avoid using an agent?"

Wow, for someone so young, she sure had a way of getting right to the point, he thought as he paused with a French fry midway to his mouth.

"Well, that would be great – and I know you're probably not here for long – but let me think on that for a day if you could."

Harris chewed the fry and took a long drink of water, giving himself a moment to consider what he was feeling. He would like to purchase Mike's property, it sat directly next to his and, although he didn't have a use for the house, he couldn't really imagine anyone else living there. It was Mike's place, it would *always* be Mike's place to him.

"Honestly, Mallory, I am still struggling to come to grips with the idea that Mike is gone. I can't quite believe that he won't be coming around ever again." He looked at her across the table, her face betraying no emotion.

Man, she must have ice water in her veins, she seemed so cold. It kind of bugged him, if he was honest. Whatever her relationship had been with Mike, his relationship with him was completely different and it was worth something to him. It meant a lot to him, and regardless of what she thought, he wanted her to know that.

"I miss him already. We had some really good times."

"Great. That's great." She looked off again, across the room at the large mirrored wall with a screen-printed Minnesota Vikings logo and brightly colored mirror-chalk inscriptions from the local fans scribbled all over it.

Harris waited again, hoping she would broach the topic of her grandfather, so he could share more about his friendship with Mike. But something held him back, he had the strong sense that she needed to open the door, he didn't want to force it open.

Finally, she continued, totally ignoring his comment, "Ok, then. You take a day or two to think about it. I will do some looking around for agents in the meantime. I'm between jobs, doing some freelancing now, so no need for me to rush back home. I should check though, Grandpa J still has internet at the house, right? I assume since he was writing there, he must."

"Yeah, he does I think. I don't know his password though, hopefully it's written down somewhere at the house."

Her comment renewed his shock about who Mike really was - this crazy ruse - and how unsuspecting he was in it, "I can't believe that he was writing books the whole time he was here. When I asked what he was doing on his lap top so much, he always told me he was writing poetry, that it was his way of relaxing, you know a break from managing the hotels."

Harris laughed again, it was all so surreal to him. Mallory had a lifetime to know that Mike was a big-time writer and film producer, he had only heard about it a couple hours ago. As he mulled it over in his mind though, he decided he was glad - glad that Mike had kept the truth hidden from him - because it made his friendship more personal somehow. Their shared experience meant more because of it.

"Yes, well, he loved to write and always was most relaxed when he was doing that. It makes me wonder what he was working on, you know, the weeks before he died. I suppose Canton knows, he's his agent..." She left the statement unfinished and lowered her eyes slightly, a somber look passing over her face, "Harris, over the years my grandfather had issues with alcohol, serious issues. Was he drinking a lot when he was here?"

When she let her guard down like right now, Mallory had the look of a young girl, innocent and trusting, and it struck him that she must have been totally unguarded like that at one time in her life.

Harris knew some of Mike's demons and had heard some of the stories of his past mistakes with Mallory, but somehow it felt like a betrayal to freely discuss them with her now. He turned the thought over in his mind, was the messed-up history between her and Mike really any of his business?

"No," Harris answered diplomatically, "I didn't see him drinking at all this past year or so. He did tell me that he recognized he had a problem and from what I could see, he hadn't started drinking again."

Her thin shoulders lifted slightly as she took in a breath and let it out slowly, her body seeming to relax as she did so, "That's good, glad to hear. It's something, I guess." She nodded slowly and glanced down while straightening the arm of her sweater, lost in thought again.

They finished their dinner while talking about the weather and the differences between living in the backroads of Minnesota versus the city streets of Baltimore.

Harris found out she was born and raised near Telluride, Colorado (which explained the laid back, slight tang of a slow drawl that he heard sometimes) until, at age fourteen, after her parents were killed on an icy mountain road in a freak car accident, she was forced to migrate between Mike's multiple homes and boarding schools.

She stated, rather dispassionately, that her grandfather had no prior experience being a parent, and was in no condition to suddenly become one, and it was probably for the best that he shifted the responsibility of a teenager to boarding schools and his assistant, a guy named Tom Guillory, who still lived in New York.

As she recounted her childhood in such stark, emotionless terms, Harris's heart went out to her in a way so physical, it took willpower not to reach across the table and take her hand in his. He wondered, after the moment passed, should he have reached out to her? Of course, he didn't really know her, he hadn't built any type of rapport with her, but he couldn't help but wonder, was it ever a good idea to resist an impulse like that if it came from a place of pure compassion?

After they left the sports bar, Harris followed her back to Mike's house, telling her he would come over to double check that the furnace was working and help her light the fireplace after she complained that the Minnesota night was "mind numbingly cold."

He showed her where the linens were kept and made sure that the water heater was working. A few minutes later, with the fire crackling nicely and with a book and a cup of hot chocolate, she was buried in a blanket in the leather and crushed velvet chair that Mike had purchased from him last year.

As he walked back to his place, enjoying the bright stars in the cold early-winter night, Harris realized that he was already looking forward to surprising her tomorrow morning with some coffee and breakfast. She didn't have much of anything for food in the house and, of course, it was the neighborly thing to do.

CHAPTER 6

What *was* that sound? Mallory tried to burrow deeper into Grandpa J's comfortable king size bed with its soft, plaid-flannel sheets and white down comforter to avoid hearing it again.

All night she had been on edge, hyper-sensitive to the foreign creaking and cracking sounds of the house, and now she grudgingly acknowledged that the dim light of morning was shining from under the wooden blinds on the bedroom window.

She listened again, trying to pick out the sound that woke her up just now. It was so blasted quiet here - absolutely no traffic sounds - so every other sound seemed magnified, and she guessed the sound she heard again this morning was the same one she'd been hearing on and off all night - a haunting ooo, ooo, oooo

There. There it was again! She whipped the down-filled comforter off the bed and stuffed her arms into her fuzzy chenille robe that had been draped over the end of the wrought iron bed frame. Not waiting to put on her slippers, she moved to her window, flicked the wooden shades open slightly and peered out and over the snow-drenched shrubs towards the front yard.

It sounded like it was coming from right outside this window, but she didn't see anything. She searched the trees - it had to be an owl - but, where was he?

Still scanning the trees, suddenly she spied the blur of movement and found Harris, dressed in blue jeans, a black down-filled jacket and black stocking hat, striding alongside the house with an insulated bag hanging from his arm. On the other side of him, a silky-haired, copper-colored Irish setter dog bounced happily in the snow next to the sidewalk.

Oh my gosh, she panicked, I'm not dressed, what's he doing here?

She snatched her cell phone from the bedside table and saw that it was already 8:30. Normally an early riser, she numbly realized that she had overslept. But then, where did she have to go? Wasn't she allowed to sleep past eight o'clock, given the situation?

She glanced across the room at the mirror above the dresser, hurriedly tried to tame her bed head and yanked the belt of her robe tighter around her flannel pajamas in a vain attempt to hide the dancing-cats-in-party-hats pattern. Oh well, she thought, giving up the pretense ... Good morning, neighbor.

Stuffing her feet into her pink fluffy slippers - this wooden plank floor was incredibly drafty- she hurried out into the hall and opened the door before he had a chance to knock.

"Oh, hi!" Harris smiled in surprise while the dog sat next to him, his tail pounding the stone steps excitedly, "I probably should have called, but I realized that I didn't have your number. I brought you some breakfast and coffee since I know you don't have any groceries."

Really? Was this included in the management contract? Mallory fought the urge to be cranky about the intrusion. He was just trying to be nice.

"That's nice of you. Come in." She opened the door wider and they both came in, Harris and his dog. When he didn't say anything to stop him, and the dog immediately ambled over to the fireplace and perched on the braided rug like he'd done it a million times, Mallory just shook her head, "Looks like he's been here before."

"Oh, yeah, *she* acts like she owns the place. Mike loved Penny, she spent many days over here, sitting right there for hours." Harris walked to the kitchen, began taking containers out of the insulated bag and glanced up with a question in his eyes, "Course if you'd rather her go outside..."

The dog Penny looked up at her then, panting softly and thumping her tail on the floor. And how was she supposed to say "Out!" to a creature with that adorable face and those dreamy brown eyes?

She smiled at the dog and walked into the kitchen, "No, that's fine. Wow, this looks great, but you didn't have to bring me breakfast."

She washed her hands in the kitchen sink, having to walk around him and noticed how close it suddenly felt in the small kitchen. His clothes still had the cold Minnesota morning air on them and she was standing here, no make-up, and in her kitties in party hats pajamas, with a perfect stranger. Ok, this felt weird.

"I know, but it gives me a good excuse to delay the inevitable with the guys at work today. I'm still trying to figure out if I should tell them about Will's shop yet. But I know I need to tell them soon, otherwise the rumors will start to fly and rumors rarely reflect reality in small towns."

Mallory reached into the cupboard for plates and coffee cups, thinking he must plan to eat here with me given the amount of scrambled eggs and sausage he was setting out on the kitchen island.

And, him discussing this business merger again after sharing the basics with her last night, had her feeling a bit unsettled, especially since he told her that very few people knew about it. I don't even know this guy, why is he so comfortable sharing this stuff with me? Almost like he wants my opinion, but what do I know?

"I bet. Probably best to get ahead of the rumors then. I'm sure you will do what's right."

She handed him a napkin and silverware from the drawer next to the dishwasher, realizing that Grandpa J hadn't rearranged anything in the cupboards or drawers in all these years. She knew right where to find the salt and pepper, the napkins, and the aspirin...he had her retrieve a lot of that for him that summer ten years ago.

On a whim, she reached up to open the small cabinet door next to refrigerator, the cabinet to the right of the glasses - his liquor cabinet. Empty. Nothing there except an old coffee pot and a small, forgotten Crock Pot. She must have stood looking at it for a moment too long.

"Are you looking for something?" Harris held out a plate towards her, steam rising off a heap of scrambled eggs and sausage.

"Ah, no, nothing. Just thinking that's all." She took the plate from him with a smile of thanks, noticing that he had shirked off his coat and he was smoothing down his hair after taking off his stocking hat. Mallory sat down on a stool and pulled the insulated coffee carafe towards her.

"You seem to have all the tools for a picnic here. Do you do this often?" She poured him a cup and, even though she didn't have her usual shot of cream, she took a swallow of the deep rich coffee herself, immediately warming up inside.

"No, not really." He regarded the insulated bag and coffee carafe with a wry expression, "These are some old wedding gifts actually, they're from one of my college friends. My ex wasn't much into picnics, I guess. We never used them." He busied himself with unwrapping the buttered English muffins he had wrapped in tin foil and set them on a plate for her.

"Oh. Well, that's a shame. You're very good at them." She smiled, feeling herself drawn deeper into his brown eyes when he looked at her, his brows furrowed in confusion, "Picnics, I mean. You seem to be an expert, I wouldn't have guessed you were a novice."

He flashed a smile then, laughing a little and she noticed his shoulders seemed to relax as he started eating his eggs.

Really, this guy was very unusual. He didn't seem to have a game at all - no cat and mouse banter - nothing. I don't know what to make of him, but I know I'm starting to trust him for some reason and for someone with diagnosed trust issues like I have, this whole thing is making me nervous, she battled her misgivings in her mind as she ate alongside him.

Suddenly, she remembered something that occurred to her last night when she was exploring around the rooms of the house.

"Harris, I found the internet password written in a notebook in Grandpa J's desk, but I was wondering, did he ever mention what he might have in that small safe in the living room? I don't remember him having that when I lived here."

"No, I don't know specifically. And, sorry, I don't know what the combination would be, or where he would have written it down."

"Oh, that's ok. I will probably find it somewhere. I have to say that I am kind of amazed at how little he changed the place over the years. I take it, though, that the nice furniture is from your shop?"

The side tables, lamps, and plush living room furniture all had a similar flare to them, combinations of superior quality wood, honed smooth but not too precious, with combinations of supple-soft leather and to-die-for cushy fabrics. The pieces were made with a level of craftsmanship and uniqueness, blending materials together in unusual ways, that wasn't available in most furniture stores.

It reflected the man himself, she realized as she appraised him sitting in her kitchen, comfortable in his own skin, understated, not flashy, the best combination of qualities, built to last a lifetime. What the heck, she wasn't writing an ad for the stuff, was she? Get a hold of yourself.

"Yes, it is," He looked past her out towards the hallway and living room, as if he'd forgotten the fact that he'd sold it to him, "He used to come over quite often, just sit there visiting with us while we worked. He said the smell of the wood and leather helped get his creative juices flowing." Harris smiled softly and continued, "You know, he used to write some of the most incredible poetry and lyrics. They would just roll off his tongue ...like, well... it was so easy for him. It was fun to be part of that, especially now."

He held her gaze for a moment too long, and she saw tears form in the depth of his eyes before he cleared his throat and looked away.

"He was really special to you, wasn't he?" She could tell that one of her personality defects - the deep-seated insecurity about letting go - held back the warmth from her facial expression, but she couldn't help the emotion in her voice. And, as she heard her voice betraying her, her self-regulating alarms were going off. This guy was getting in past the defenses, and she felt the first sliver of her control slipping away.

"We shared things." Harris spoke then, hesitant and quiet, "I don't know how much he told anyone else in his family about all that, but he shared some important stuff with me. About his mistakes, about his life. I just know that I will be forever grateful to have known him, Mallory." He studied his breakfast then and looked like he was forcing himself to eat another forkful of eggs so that he wouldn't have to keep talking.

"Yes, I've heard that he was going through a self-discovery of some sort right before he died." Mallory conceded, "I guess that's good, you were able to see the fruits of that when he was here. Not all of us were so fortunate."

She finished the eggs on her plate and pushed her stool away from the counter. It was super hard not to drip bitterness from every pore of her body. "Did you say he wrote song lyrics? That's a first, I didn't know that."

At her abrupt change of subject, Harris regarded her with an expression that Mallory couldn't quite identify. Was it pity she read in his eyes?

But, instead of pushing it, he sighed quietly and smiled.

"He did indeed. And they were very good, in my humble opinion. He used to come over, we'd kick back on my deck - I play guitar - and we would come up with a few songs."

A guitar-playing neighbor who would "kick back" and write songs with her aging grandpa? Was this guy for real?

"You play guitar?" She didn't mean to sound so surprised, but the mental image was so out of context from the version of him she had already painted in her mind. He looked like he would be much more comfortable hunting for ducks or pheasants with his dog Penny out there. But, then again, maybe he did that too. He laughed at her obvious surprise.

"I try... and some piano. Since I was a little kid. My father was convinced that music lessons improve one's mathematical abilities. Did I mention my dad is a banker? And that I was a Finance Major in college?"

He laughed slightly as he started to wash off his breakfast dishes in the sink and loaded them in the dishwasher, and again she was struck by how at home he seemed around here. She half expected him to retrieve some dog food and a dog dish from under the sink and feed Penny right there in the kitchen corner and the homey picture would be complete.

"No, you didn't mention that. But, how did a finance major end up making furniture for a living?"

"Well, my mom was in the upholstery business when we were growing up and my dad was into woodworking as a serious hobby. My brother and I both learned to sew before we were teenagers, we helped mom out after school. Paul took to it all right away, he's a super talented designer. I thought I wanted to shake up the business world and doing upholstery in small town Minnesota wasn't going to get me there, so I tried the other route. I worked for a venture capital firm in Minneapolis for a couple years, but when Jackie and I got married, we decided to move back here, thinking we'd start a family. But...things changed, I guess. She left and I'm still here."

He had been straightening up the kitchen counter as he talked, taking her plate away and refilling her coffee cup. After he zipped the insulated bag shut, having stowed the serving dishes away, he stopped moving around, his hands resting on the top of the bag that sat on the counter. It was as if, through his silence, he was challenging her to ask him more probing questions about his failed marriage.

And that's exactly why she didn't ask. Part of her just knew he didn't really want to talk about it. And, the other part of her knew he was still in love with his ex-wife. It was obvious by the way he said her name. Mallory was trying to come up with a mental image of the elusive Jackie but found it difficult. What would prompt someone to leave this guy?

"I guess it's just lucky for Grandpa J that you are here, Harris. It was his good fortune." She realized that she had really enjoyed having breakfast with him and wondered vaguely when she would see him again. "It was really nice of you to bring breakfast, thanks again." She smiled, throwing a look over her shoulder towards the living room, "Is she always such a well-behaved dog?"

"Most of the time, yeah. Except when she smells a pocket gopher. I can't tell you how many holes in the yard I've had to fill back in. She's got an insane sense of smell."

He walked into the hallway and, as if she knew they were talking about her, Penny sat up at attention, her tail thumping against the floor, waiting there until she saw Harris nod his head towards outside and put his hand on the door handle.

"Say, I forgot to tell you, the outside world has finally reached us in Beck's Mill. Someone in town put two and two together about your grandpa, seeing his face on the news and reading his obituary with his real name. I've gotten four texts already this morning from people wondering if I knew the whole time. It's caused quite a stir that he owned a place here and nobody realized who he was all these years. I just want you to know in case you go to the store and someone says something."

He spoke louder, as if talking to someone upstairs, "So there, you old fart. The gig is up, Mike." His laughter, and his dog, followed him out the door.

CHAPTER 7

Later, after putting away the groceries she bought at Beck's Mill Grocery, Mallory stood at the living room window, lost in thought, looking out over the waves of smooth, glittery snow in the backyard.

All morning since Harris left, she had been batting away some of the memories of her summer here a decade ago. Every corner of the house seemed to hold moments that flashed back through her consciousness like an incessant chorus of an annoying 90s pop song.

◆ ◆ ◆

2007

I feel helpless when faced with all the needs I see

She felt the whisper of the cool summer breeze that night as she lay listening to the crickets in the shrubs in the backyard and the mild gurgle of the stream further off. Although most evenings she propped it open to relieve stuffy summer air in the house, this evening she propped the window open with the intent to stay awake. She wanted to hear him when he came back home.

But it didn't work, because she fell sound asleep despite the goosebumps the cool breeze raised on her arms.

Grandpa J had gone out late in the afternoon to "pick up some groceries," which was code for re-stocking his liquor cabinet. Mallory had even asked this time if she could go along, maybe they could see a movie or something, anything to get out of this boring little town. Grandpa J had shut down the conversation right away saying, "There was a reason I had to start my own production studio, Mal. You can't count on the big Hollywood studios to produce anything worth your two hours and your $10.00."

So, she spent the day and night playing games on the internet and reading the latest in the "Twilight" series. It wasn't the first time she'd been left alone, and it didn't surprise her that his trip to Alexandria, only a few minutes down the road, took over six hours.

She loved to read, and her favorite place to do it was in her upstairs loft bedroom, which was really cool with its cozy, cottage-look, whitewashed wood floor and its wood beamed sloping ceiling with a quirky antique chandelier that hung so low sometimes Grandpa J would bump his head on the crystal droplets.

She had finally fallen asleep around 11:00 pm, with the book still open in her hands, when she suddenly awoke to a crashing, banging sound and her grandpa's howling, maniacal laughter as he bounced from one wall of the stairwell to the other and ended up in a drunken heap at the bottom of the stairs.

When she hurried down the steps to help him, he just pushed her roughly away, suddenly angry at her for some reason, and spitting a string of curse words at her - some of which she'd never even heard before. What was she all worked up about? He snapped at her. No problem here! Don't be such a little nag, leave him alone and go back to bed.

A few weeks later, around mid-July, after what seemed like a string of endless days spent walking or biking around town, while

Grandpa J wrote all day and drank all night, Mallory woke to find a note from him. He had tacked it right there by the front door.

"Mal, I will be back in a few days. Charge what you want at the store. You will be fine. Cheers, Grandpa J"

Or, something to that effect.

He had been gone for a week. No calls, no messages - obviously - because there wasn't a landline phone here and he hadn't thought to get her a cell phone yet.

When he finally returned, and she lit into him about leaving her there all alone, she could smell the acrid alcohol on his breath and he snorted his drunk laugh, as he scoffed, "Well, you've heard of Skype, haven't you? And, you didn't die, so what's your problem?"

◆ ◆ ◆

Enough. She turned away from the window and she forced herself to gather the memories, wrap them up in a box and tape it shut. It was over, she told herself, and she had survived it just fine. And, now she just had to sell this place, slough off its memories and move on with her life.

Frowning in concentration, she sat down slowly in the leather-cushioned, rocking banker's chair and pulled it closer towards the nicked and battered hickory-wood desk which still sat facing the windows, looking out over the backyard. The desk's position here, sitting randomly in the middle of the room, didn't fit proper design etiquette, it quite clearly broke all the rules of "conversation groupings."

No, it was abundantly clear that its owner had other things on his mind; his priority was inspiration, not conversation. The life that brimmed outside, in the trees and down the swell of the yard towards the brook, that's what mattered to him.

Ten years had come and gone on the calendar – enough of a lifetime for a person to graduate from high school and college, marry and have children – but this desk and chair sat rooted in the very same spot. They weren't going anywhere. No one knew their significance to JL McMichael's legacy except her, but nevertheless, they too were part of the legend.

While she waited for her laptop to power up, turning the seat of the banker's chair slowly on its pivot, she noticed the worn edges of the wooden desk that had been rubbed to a fine, supple finish where he had rested his arms while typing.

It struck her then – all the hours of incandescent, summer-sunlit afternoons, drizzly autumn mornings and wind whipped winter evenings – if you added up all the hours he spent writing here in Minnesota, how many hours would it be? He'd owned this house for so many years, it had to have been thousands of hours. And still, the family had forgotten that he even owned this place.

As she considered it, though, she realized it wasn't completely surprising they forgot about this house because Grandpa J had created an almost nomadic, vagabond lifestyle to support his creativity.

Often, he would spend months at a time researching his novels in the locations where they were based, or he would stay at one of his other houses. Guillory typically knew where he was, but as far as running the businesses, over the years, her grandfather had gradually shifted the responsibility for day to day management to his children.

Canton had built the publishing company into a reputable agency which published many A-list authors in addition to its namesake. While this was happening, Grandpa J had been off somewhere else writing, so often that they sometimes lost track of where he was.

At the same time, under Jasmine's tutelage, JLM Productions had become a mini-major movie studio (flying under the radar of the major studios with a steady stream of nouveau box office successes), focusing on "movies that matter," as Grandpa J liked to call them. And, while his daughter ran his movie production studio, Grandpa J had been off somewhere else writing.

Grandpa J was a consummate, prolific writer. Spending even an hour with him, it would be obvious that he was *always* writing - if it wasn't with his fingertips on a keyboard, it was in his head.

His two children understood that he needed time away, to burn off the ideas, the characters, the stories that were the inferno in his mind. Often, he would be gone for months at a time - he called these absences sabbaticals - and when he turned up again in New York or LA, they would be the beneficiaries of a trove of new epic novels and tantalizing short stories that spurred award-winning movie scripts.

Mallory had grown up aware that this is how her grandfather lived, but somehow, she lived just outside of his glittery, cultured yet chaotically creative, world.

If asked to put his books and movie scripts in chronological order, try to identify which ones he wrote while here in Minnesota for example, she was embarrassed to admit she couldn't do it. She had never paid much attention to where he was and what he was working on. Their relationship wasn't one like that.

At the end of that first confusing summer, where she drifted lethargically between despair, boredom and depression, Grandpa J told her he planned to make boarding school her way of life until college, like it had been her father's way of life before her. And, while the concept of living the rest of her teenage years 24/7 on the east coast with a bunch of girls she didn't know, was more than a little intimidating - because all she'd ever known was her small school in small town Colorado - it sure beat the alternative. Living with him.

She couldn't imagine spending any more of her life living with her grandfather than she absolutely had to. Partially, it was because he was a creative genius, an artist who thoroughly immersed himself in his work, so much so that he would often forget what day of the week it was and the last time he ate.

But mostly it was because his writing and his drinking were so intertwined; it was rare to find Grandpa J doing one without the other. When he wrote, he drank. When he drank, he wrote. Always, she was the extraneous weight in his life.

She often likened herself to the expensive, oversize luggage that he owned but refused to pack when he travelled because it "slowed him down." He reasoned, that's why you pay people to take care of things for you, like purchase your clothing, pay the electric bills and all the other countless tedious details of living life. He expected to be able to drop in and create; he didn't have time, or patience, to worry about packing and unpacking.

Given this lifestyle, of course having a kid to worry about just didn't work for him. The staggering tuition rates of boarding schools were a small price to pay for his freedom.

So it was no surprise that they rarely spoke except for the occasional holiday or random telephone call. And, because he hardly ever spoke to her - he hardly ever spoke to her about his work, or his dreams. Their relationship, this surface-level, obligatory deference to one another, it left a big hole right in the middle of her understanding of Grandpa J as a person.

What thoughts did he think? What dreams did he dream? She couldn't help but feel when she sold this place, it would seem like those thoughts and dreams and memories had never even happened. Who would speak for them now that he was gone?

Her laptop came to life then and distracted by the task at hand, she started searching real estate agents in the area but quickly figured out that she would need to know how many acres the property was before she could determine what it was worth.

Retrieving the large, brown envelope from her bag, she removed the tattered, yellowed abstract and scanned the document with its lengthy list of owners going back to 1898, the year it was sectioned off from a railroad company.

There, she read that the property was 1.8 acres, which seemed like a perfect size for building a new home, if one would so choose. She started to re-fold the oversized document along its well-worn creases, when she noticed a series of numbers hand-written along the bottom of the first page.

Funny, they weren't a phone number or an address. 25-10-52. Catching her breath slightly, she hoped, could it possibly be Grandpa J's safe combination?

It was! The safe's door whizzed softly open as she turned the dial the last half-turn and she peered inside seeing nothing but a few papers, a few hundred dollars of cash, a keychain with multiple keys on it and a small blue box.

She rolled her eyes at finding the keys inside the safe, of all places. Who puts keys for their house in their safe? She wondered, was Grandpa J getting paranoid as he aged? Just one more facet of his personality that she wasn't witness to, and the thought sat uncomfortably in her mind.

Reaching for the box, curious what other surprises he might have, inside it, she found a black USB storage device and a beautifully delicate gold ring, with a single diamond and two small rubies on either side of the intricate setting.

Surely this had to be her Grandma Camille's wedding ring, why else would he have kept it here in this safe? Her mood suddenly lightened, almost giddy at her find - something that her grandmother had actually worn on her own finger!

Mallory slipped the ring on her left-hand ring finger; it fit perfectly! Rising from where she'd been kneeling next to the safe, she didn't even notice that she was spinning in circles in her excitement. Not caring about the USB, she put the cover back on the blue box and reached for the papers. Maybe there were some old pictures of Grandma Camille in here too, maybe some she'd never seen before.

But, instead of finding any pictures, on the top of the stack of papers, Mallory found three pages of a letter and she swallowed hard over her heart in her throat as she sat down cross legged on the floor in front of the fireplace, her mouth dropping open slightly when she saw it was addressed to her and the recent date on it, just last month:

October, 2017

Mal, my dearest,
I am writing this to you now because, as an old man, I have finally discovered some of life's truths.
But I must disclose to you that I never expected the sunset years of my life to play out quite this way. I always dreamed that my last years would be spent with your grandmother, my bride, Camille. I dreamt that we would spend them sitting on the back patio at the little stone house, watching the birds in the trees and listening to the music of the brook as is flowed alongside us, our laughter bubbling around its colorful mix of stones and across its clear water.
Unfortunately, you were denied hearing it, but let me tell you, your grandmother's laugh was contagious. And, when she shared it with me, I felt like I'd been given a gift, something precious. I miss her laughter and I fear that I have almost forgotten the sound of it. But then, sometimes I wake up hearing it, and my heart smiles at the pleasure.
Recently, Mal, my life has come into clear focus. And, I write this letter as a practice run because I'm a writer and it's how my brain works. I hope you never have to read it, however, because my intention is to share it all with you in person in a few weeks. However, I will practice my admission now, here it goes:

I have been a stubborn, old fool. And, I am profoundly sorry.

If this sentiment was written in a book or script, I could dress it up and package it with more depth and intrigue; but, in the end, it is the essential truth, and this is how I feel. I don't know why I didn't recognize the value of telling you this sooner – because I have always known it – but therein lies the heaviest burden.

I am a weak man, Mal, I simply could not bring myself to submit my pride. Until recently, I have lived under a cloak of self-preservation and a hard, unforgiving heart. It's that simple.

I could not let myself accept my role in the shattered relationship that I fostered with your father and mother and then with you. I have berated myself to no end for the lost years I could have spent with your father, my precious son. If you could possibly see through a window to my soul, I feel like you could understand the depth of my sorrow about this.

Because you weren't here, please permit me to tell you my side of the story. When your grandmother Camille died from cancer, after such a torturous battle, I shut down. And, when I say that, I mean I literally shut down. Physically, mentally, emotionally. There was nothing living inside me, nothing left of me.

Gradually, I realized the only way I was going to deal with this heart-wrenching pain was to wake up my physical body, while at the same time, squelch my life – my memories – with Her.

It's like I turned the lights out on that life, I locked up the doors and set sail for a foreign land. Someplace as far away as possible, into a life that was as unlike my life with her as possible.

The time in Hollywood, the drinking, the other women ... I was hoping that existence – it really wasn't a life, I see that now – I was hoping that existence would bury our time together so far down, that I wouldn't ever feel her again.

The trouble with handling her death this way was that I wasn't alone in my mourning. I had our son.

It's true, I would go days without remembering that Parker was even in the house. I'm sure he told you this, he was ten, so, surely he remembered. Even then, I always had staff, people I could shift the burden of a child upon.

I have such pain remembering Parker, thinking how he must have felt, his father never – not once – allowing him to cry in my presence about losing his mother. It was easier for me to send him away to boarding schools.

Of course, I didn't think about him, I didn't know how to love him, he was absolutely correct when he confronted me with that bitter truth the spring he graduated from high school and told me he wanted to go out on his own. He said he knew that I didn't need him and now he understood that he didn't need me either.

Your father was so much like Camille, his mother. Instinctively, he understood that a university degree didn't validate who he was, and he certainly didn't want my money or status.

And, that, frankly, made me furious. I will refrain from profanity in this letter, but I can assure you I was much less controlled with him at the time.

Because, you see Mal, my entire existence, my very identity, was in what I had built - the life and business - I had created. For him to turn all that away, and to tell me to my face that it didn't really matter to him. Well, that - in my opinion - it was unforgivable.

So, he left. And, after about a year travelling around the country during which I never heard from him, he finally contacted me once he was established in Colorado, having met your mother. She convinced him to reach out to me again and try to mend things, but she didn't know who I was and the extent of my bitterness.

I should have left them alone, I know that now, of course. Here is the truth, please forgive me...but I simply could not stand to see Parker content, and out of my control. What right did he have to be happy when I was so miserable?

I did everything financially I could to entice him back to work in one of the businesses, I berated your mother and her family in the most disparaging ways. I left nothing unsaid or untried to split them up, but he made his choice. And, thank God, he made the choice he did. You were the ultimate result.

But, even given all of that, our love for each other was stronger somehow and over the years we tried to come to an understanding, an acceptance of our differences. At the time of their deaths in that horrible accident, your father and mother and I were finding our way.

For me, it was my way of finally coming to terms with your grandmother's death ten years before. I knew she would have been devastated to know the disastrous relationship I had with her son Parker.

For your father, it was his way of appeasing your mother. Even after all the vicious things I had done and said, Nicole still forgave me and begged your father to do the same. He told me as much. I am eternally grateful to your mother for the loving influence she had on the relationship between Parker and myself.

But, as you know, mourning brings out the worst in me and the loss of Parker, just when we were becoming close again, was like a boot crushing my very soul. I cannot explain it, I've tried so many times through my work to write it down, to reach some peace, but it simply cannot be expressed.

Suffice it to say, when you came to stay with me that first summer after they died, I was existing in a stupor of alcohol and depression unlike anything I've ever known. I was a danger to everyone, including myself. I knew I could never provide you the home you needed.

So, the tragedy of my life continued, and I repeated the very same mistakes with you that I made with your father. Distance, drink and my personal demons run amok...Oh, Mal, I'm so very sorry.

I've said things to you, Mallory, that should never be said. I've done things that should never be done. I cannot remember all of them, but those that I do remember, they scorch my very being, they haunt me. And, to top it off, I most likely would have gone to my grave never addressing this with you fully because I am a coward.

But, recently, a close friend of mine named Harris, whom you've never met but I sincerely wish you could, has been instrumental in opening my eyes. Through his guidance and prayer, I have been experiencing something unexpected, something so deep and soul-wrenching that I have felt like an innocent, wide-eyed child in the midst of it.

I've felt a love that is eternal and vast, yet personal and intimate. This love, it can overcome the past, I know it can. I feel it has started already in my heart and I don't want to ever go back. I want you here with me, Mal. I need you to know this love and see what it has done in me.

I will wrap this up now, I've perhaps meandered too long and down too many paths in this letter, but I want you to know that I have almost finished writing something. Unfortunately, I keep hitting a wall on it.

Somehow, I sense that I need to share it with you, and together, we can finish it. I will discuss in more detail when I see you, but, suffice it to say, there is no one else that I would enjoy more than you to walk along with me as we finish it together.

Always,
Your Grandpa J

Mallory dropped the letter into her lap as if it had suddenly burst into flames, and wiped at her cheeks, where tears had created streaks through her mascara and down her face. The bright blink of her Grandma Camille's diamond, such a happy find just a few moments earlier, was now another harsh reminder of her loss - the loneliness - of it all.

Why was her life such a mess? Why was she left here all alone? No grandparents, no parents - she missed her parents *so much* - no siblings, not even a boyfriend that she trusted. My gosh, if ever there was someone who was left alone on this earth, certainly it was her! And to think her grandfather had it in his power to change much of that, but then he had to go and die before -

Before what, exactly? Mallory stopped herself abruptly, and without realizing it, she crumpled up the letter with an anger erupting so deep inside she felt her body temperature rise.

What would she have said if he had confronted her with these words in person? He's *so very sorry* - she spit the words out loud to the empty room.

She tried her best to picture his face, to actually see his mouth framing the words, but all she could see was the sneer that would form on his lips most of the time, the barely concealed look of contempt she saw much of the time when he spoke to her. As recently as this past January, in fact, when she refused to come to New York to work as an assistant editor at his publishing house - she had seen that look of contempt.

"My job IS writing, it's just not the kind you respect." She'd angrily countered to Grandpa J when he told her to quit wasting her time in advertising - and writing *that blog* - just let go and allow him to help her for once. The message was clear, her work, her life - it was so unremarkable, it was almost nonexistent to him.

So, she reasoned to herself, it wasn't like this "transformation" of his had been fully tested; forgive her if she found it hard to believe it was real.

She wondered how long ago he had stopped drinking, since she'd never heard about him seeking any treatment for it. Addiction was a terrible disease and it made people say and do crazy, erratic things, like they became someone else altogether sometimes.

That was one thing she and Jasper had in common, actually. His mother had struggled with addiction to pain meds for much of his teenage and young adult years, and he had shared many stories with Mallory about the impact it had on his mother's behavior and their relationship.

As she witnessed the struggles in Jasper's family, secretly Mallory had drawn comparisons to her Grandpa J and she tried to rationalize her grandfather's behavior by blaming it on his addiction and depression.

But, in the end, she didn't really know - was alcohol to blame for the way he treated her, or was it the catalyst that took off the mask of civility and allowed her to see how he really, truly felt about her and her father before her?

What religious experience could possibly transform someone so radically that his very core, everything that had motivated him for his entire life, was suddenly shirked away, as if it had never been there? Even his child and his grandchild, people who shared DNA with him, were powerless to change him that way.

Taking a deep breath, Mallory leaned back against the scratchy bricks of the fireplace and stretched out her legs. There was a lot to digest here, way too much to take in with one brief perusal. She smoothed the letter out slowly on the tops of her legs and in a state of disoriented shock, she read through it again, trying her best to keep the negativity out of her mind.

Upon reading it a third time, when she finally felt coherent, these points struck her - 1) he loved her grandmother Camille and never really recovered from losing her, 2) he reminded her that he had started to resolve the differences with her parents, and that reminder made Mallory feel better, 3) he reminded her that he was a complete asshole to her when she came to live with him, Yes, minor understatement there, 4) he was sorry for continuing to be an asshole her entire life, Ok, maybe so, 5) this guy Harris has something to do with this experience - this religious experience - that changed Grandpa J ... oh boy... and 6) he had something that he was writing and he wanted her to help him finish it. What the heck?

A vision of the USB in the blue box cut its way through her stupor and she crawled from where she had been sitting, over to the still-open safe. Holding the USB in the palm of her hand, she read the last paragraph of the letter again. Could his last work possibly be saved on this USB? The absurdity of it made Mallory laugh out loud.

Of course not. JL McMichael doesn't just leave his work laying around on some random USB in some random house in Minnesota...certainly it was safely housed in New York with her Uncle Canton planning for its high-profile release, especially important now that Grandpa J, the literary god, was gone.

Strange that she hadn't heard even a word breathed about it while she was with her family and Guillory in New York. But maybe that was intentional? They had always been very protective over controlling the buzz around his work.

It was curious though, that he put this USB in the safe. Maybe there were some pictures on it, or maybe some of that poetry that Harris said he was always writing. That would be cool to read too, she thought as she inserted it into her lap top and clicked open the single file it contained, one named:

STAND TALL, SON
THE FINAL CHAPTER
(final unedited version.jlm)

CHAPTER 8

... A suggestion for the book club ...

She couldn't believe it, she was shocked - absolutely shocked - that he had started a third, and final, book in the "Stand Tall, Son" series and, from what she could tell, no one else knew about it. Except her, of course.

And, after the momentary shock of discovering it, the dread of the task in front of her descended like a lead weight. She reached for the somewhat crumpled letter and read the last part of the final paragraph again, her breath hitching as his final words now became clear:

Somehow, I sense that I need to share it with you, and together, we can finish it. I will discuss in more detail when I see you, but suffice it to say, there is no one else that I would enjoy more than you to walk along with me as we finish it together.

The novel that had started all the hype, written over ten years ago already, was a moving account of two friends set in the 1930's. One boy, the lead character Shep, was the son of an African-American rural-Georgia sharecropper who raised his one son and three daughters on his own, in a simple country farmhouse after losing his wife to cancer.

Shep's life was one of financial hardship, strict discipline, respect for hard work and his elders. And, while his father Ray loved them deeply, he was never openly affectionate towards his children; he was from a generation where you demonstrated your love by making a better life for your children than you were given. And, by God, Ray was determined to see Shep succeed so he didn't end up living hand to mouth like Ray had his entire life.

The way Ray figured, anything - or anyone - who stood in the way of this goal would sorely regret it. This included the spoiled white kid - whose banker father determined the fate of the farm by controlling the purse. That kid, who didn't care about his reputation or his future, the one who was destined to be a reckless failure his entire life, if he messed up Shep's future, *he* would sorely regret it.

That kid - the other boy in the novel named Reilly - was the only child of the recently promoted small-town bank president and his cultured, genteel wife from Charleston, South Carolina.

While, on the outside, Reilly's family seemed very respectable to the members of the small, close-knit community, behind closed doors, nothing was quite what it seemed. Reilly's family hid things - secrets that went back generations - things like substance abuse, adultery, high stakes bank fraud and money laundering schemes, and even murder.

The first novel followed the two boys, as unlikely friends as there ever could be, through childhood, with various escapades and their dreams of escaping their respective suffocating home lives.

Over the years, they faced various hardships due to racial and family divides and on numerous occasions, when their two worlds collided in ways that revealed some of Reilly's family secrets and put serious strains on their friendship, they struggled to reckon back to their childhood bond.

The first novel left them as they graduated college: Reilly, having his ivy league college degree and a new wife, pregnant with their first child, was living a life full of lies and deception. Shep, meanwhile, was pursuing his interest in aviation in Virginia, but missed his friend dearly and had a deep desire to resolve their differences and gain back their friendship.

The highly acclaimed second novel hit bookshelves just as the movie of the first novel - produced by JLM Pictures, of course - hit theatres.

Grandpa J, Aunt Jasmine and Uncle Canton - the business enterprise known as JL McMichael - was in full-on, epic mode. The movie even surpassed the action hero sagas and spy thrillers at the box office that summer.

Who would have dreamed it possible? A literary saga striking a chord with both middle America and coastal elites? But, that's what it did, according to the literary and movie critics, and high school English Lit teachers who, by including the novels in their curriculum, virtually assured a ready and willing audience for the next book and movie in the saga.

The second novel, "A Young Man's Pride," which followed the young men through the ravages of World War II and the respective hardships of returning home, injured physically and mentally, was a blockbuster full of drama and adventure.

But it was also quite obvious that it was a bridge to More. There was more to their story; it was still unfinished, and everyone knew it. The world had been waiting to hear how it ended. And, now... here it was, sitting right in front of her, on her computer screen.

She started reading the first few paragraphs, recognizing the characters and the imagery as if they were alive and were members of her own family. But, as she continued to read, she had the sense that some things didn't make sense. It became clear that the story picked up mid-stride, as if she had arrived late to the movie and was beyond frustrated because she was too late to understand the storyline.

She scrolled through the book quickly to find what chapter she was reading and finding that she was in chapter six and the last chapter she saw was chapter thirty-three, most likely close to the end, she frowned in frustration. What had he done with the beginning? There was only one file on this USB.

She looked again at the little blue box, certainly nothing else was in there. She reached back into the dark corners of the small safe, feeling around for any loose USBs, and found nothing. The single drawer of his simple wooden desk was almost empty, except for a few pens, some loose change and a pack of dental floss. Shaking her head, she swore at him under her breath, what was he thinking, not putting the whole novel in one place?

But, curiosity overwhelmed her desire to read from the beginning, so she plopped down in the comfortable, overstuffed chair, stretched her legs out on the matching leather ottoman, and set her computer on her lap, ready to read The Final Chapter.

A couple of hours later, a brief whir from her laptop confirmed that the symbol that had been blinking for the past ten minutes would not be ignored and the screen went black as the battery died completely. She scrambled to retrieve her power cord from her work bag sitting next to Grandpa J's desk, but now would have to wait for the computer to reboot.

Turning on a few lights along the way while reading a few texts and checking social media on her cell phone, she wandered into the kitchen in an aimless attempt to find something to eat. Find something quick, she told herself as she opened the refrigerator and reached for a bottled water, something that wouldn't require any prep time, she wanted to keep reading. Even though it appeared that this was the raw, unedited version, she was already completely entranced by the story.

As she took the break, searching the refrigerator contents for something appealing, the knowledge that she was expected to finish this somehow was sending her into a complete panic. How would she ever do that? Who was she to even try? What was he thinking?

And, before she knew it, she shut the refrigerator door again, with only bottled water in hand, and returned to the big chair. She had better things to do than make lunch, she had to keep reading.

CHAPTER 9

"Hey, Harris, I brought you some tortilla chili. Do you mind if we eat up at the house though? You guys don't have any bowls down here." Carissa called towards Harris's office noticing he had just hung up his phone. She turned back towards her husband Paul, now wearing his jacket, ready to leave.

"You look especially beautiful today. I like the new hair style, babe." Paul walked around the sewing table towards his wife, taking in how pretty she looked with her short box braided black hair held back with her winter-knit headband, "Is the chili spicy?" Paul smiled a teasing smile and wriggled his eyebrows suggestively, as he pulled her closer, kissing her smooth cheek.

"Maybe." She laughed at him and hugged his waist in response. Harris walked out of his office, ready to leave for the day, and noticed that Paul's wife Carissa was alone with Paul in the workroom, their six-year-old son Peyton, nowhere to be seen.

"Chili sounds awesome. Thanks, Carissa! Yeah, let's go up to the house. Where's Peyton?" Harris followed them out the door, switching off lights and locking the door behind them.

"He's around somewhere. He took Penny outside - for a walk - he said." She glanced around the yard, seeing tracks in the snow leading around the building and down the street towards the little stone house. "Uh, oh. I think he's visiting your neighbor Mike."

She pointed in that direction, seeing her son following Penny up the stone pathway towards the front door.

"Oh, that should be interesting." Harris smiled a wide smile, laughing a little. "But, it's not Mike living there now. Paul, why don't you guys just go up the house, get started with dinner. Tell Carissa the story on Mike. I'll go get Peyton."

He strode towards the little stone house, realizing that he would enjoy talking to Mallory again if she was home and wondered how her day searching for real estate agents had gone.

This reminded him that she was here with an express purpose, to sell this little house and get on with her life, with that guy, back in Baltimore. If only his financial situation was more secure, and he could figure out a way to purchase the place. But given the timing of this business deal with Will's shop, it was unlikely he could make it work.

"Hi! Penny likes coming over here. Where's Mike?" Peyton asked with a bright voice, looking up at her expectantly from the front step.

From his position on the street, Harris saw Mallory standing in the open front door, her glossy, dark hair pulled back today under a white bandana, the waves falling forward on her shoulders. And he couldn't help but notice that she looked great in the faded blue jeans she was wearing. Of course, remembering their breakfast earlier in the day, he realized that she looked equally attractive in her flannel pajamas.

Peyton, bundled up in his winter parka and snow pants, was trying to hold onto Penny's collar as she urged him forward towards the interior of the house, her tail bobbing back and forth excitedly against his legs.

"Well, hey, how's it going? Yes, she sure does like coming over here. I know her name is Penny, but who're you?" Mallory spoke to Peyton, a bemused, humorous smile on her lips.

"My name's Peyton. Where's Mike? Penny wants her treat." Peyton looked up at her, a serious, no-nonsense expression in his deep brown eyes as he pushed his blue and white striped knit stocking hat up further on his forehead.

"Well...Mike isn't here right now. I'm his granddaughter Mallory. What treat does he usually give her?"

"It's in that can by the fireplace. I can show you, I know where it is." He walked past her into the house, the dog quickly falling in step behind him, as if to say, See I told you, this is my house too.

"Hey, Peyton, buddy, hold up a minute. Sorry." Harris jogged up the rest of the snowy walkway, with an apology in his voice, watching the boy in his snow boots and his dog traipsing through the hallway and into the living room. Mallory just laughed and waved her hand at him.

"Pshht ... no big deal. Dog's gotta have a treat, y'know." She turned to watch as Peyton stood on his tip toes and took a brightly colored can off one of the bookshelves near the fireplace and retrieved a dog treat from inside. Penny sat at attention on the braided rug, her tail thumping happily, waiting for her treat.

"See, told you, she knows she always gets a treat and then she lays here while Mike writes. She likes it here." Peyton knelt by the dog, running his fingers through the thick red fur under her chin and around her ears.

"Yes, she does, but she can't stay today. Mallory has things to do." Harris turned to Mallory, as if to explain, "You remember I mentioned my brother Paul's wife Carissa, and Peyton? This is Peyton."

He cleared his throat and turned back to the boy, "Say goodbye now, Peyton. Your mom's got dinner ready over at my house." Harris reached out his hand for Peyton and walked to the door, Penny dutifully following them.

"Well, thanks for coming over, Peyton. It's nice to meet you." Mallory said as they reached the door. Once there, Peyton turned suddenly, looking up at her expectantly.

"Are you coming over to Harris's house too? Mom made chili and it's really good. See ya!" And, with that, Peyton dropped Harris's hand, ran out the door and headed down the walk, his snow boots making a heavy clomping sound while Penny bounced through the snow in the front yard, sending sprays of snow high into the air.

Harris turned slightly, embarrassed at the second intrusion on her in one day. She must think we are the most socially awkward, overbearing people she's ever met. Well, now what could he do? He had to invite her over. To eat another meal, with two other complete strangers.

"Well, of course, you're invited to come to dinner, if you'd like. I have to say though, we're not usually this - well, I don't know. Forget it. Yes, we are. We are those people." He laughed and stuffed his hands in his jacket pockets, looking at her from under his brows, wishing this whole awkward situation was history.

"Well, I don't know quite what you mean by ... those people, but sure. Who's all coming to dinner? Will I meet the whole family?"

And, then, as simple as that, Mike's granddaughter slipped on her boots and her wool coat and walked into his life. And Harris felt something move inside him. Something - a feeling - that he hadn't felt in such a long time, he'd forgotten what it was.

Mallory wiped her hands on the towel and hung it back up on the hook next to the sink, checked out her reflection in the mirror, and smoothed her hair neatly under her white bandana. She squinted into the mirror, brushed away some stray mascara and tried to listen - if she wasn't mistaken, someone was playing the piano and she thought she heard the faint strum of a guitar.

They said - and this was her forewarning - that their family dinners typically ended with someone playing a musical instrument of some kind. So, now would be the time to make your escape if you thought that kind of thing was insufferable.

Dinner had been delicious, and the conversation had been easy and relaxed. Harris's brother Paul was super chill, with longish blonde hair and a beard that complemented the vibe of his throwback 70s-era energy. It was obvious that he was crazy about his beautiful wife Carissa and his precocious, adopted six-year-old son Peyton, who had the most endearing wide-eyed gaze and sweet smile.

Mallory was embarrassed to admit, she was surprised by the fact that Carissa and Paul were an interracial couple living in rural

Minnesota. True, it was much more common to find interracial relationships in the cities where she had lived the past ten years, but that didn't excuse her pre-judging people living here. Of course, love didn't see skin color, she knew better. Why would Paul feel any differently just because he had grown up in a small town? Obviously, Harris hadn't thought it important to point it out to her, so it was not a big deal to him either. Lesson learned.

She was grateful that they all tried to make her feel welcome and, with the addition of Peyton, who provided a source of comedic relief unique to children, she found herself thoroughly enjoying the evening.

They even navigated a moment of awkwardness when Peyton brought up Mike and asked again when he was coming back home. Mallory wasn't quite sure how - or if - to tell Peyton about Grandpa J's death. Luckily, before she said something, she saw the look Carissa threw her and she deferred to the mother who deftly changed the subject.

It touched her, seriously touched her, when a few minutes later, Carissa called Peyton into the kitchen and he emerged a short time later, promptly walked over to her and hugged Mallory tightly. Like only little children can do to perfect strangers.

With a heartbroken little voice, he said, "Mommy just told me about your grandpa going to heaven. You are probably sad, but I know he will think Jesus is pretty cool."

Mallory felt her eyes tear up instantly, his innocence struck her so intensely, and she hugged him back, feeling a warmth seep over and through her. As she hugged him, she glanced up and noticed Harris had a fleeting smile, but he didn't say anything to shorten the moment. He wasn't embarrassed by the emotion or uncomfortable with the vulnerability, which made Mallory feel both uncomfortable and at the same time, very safe somehow.

Appreciative of the special moment and these new friends she'd met, she left the bathroom and walked through the hallway back towards the living room where they were all sitting.

Her attention was diverted again by how charming Harris's house was. The mahogany floor and wooden built-ins all had a high gloss shine, giving the home a stately, grand look, but the flat rock fireplace in the living room and the open layout, including a generous, open stairway leading upstairs, made the home welcoming and comfortable.

And, of course, he had furnished it beautifully with custom hardwood and leather furniture, lamps and mirrors. It was obvious, this was a house for a family, not a bachelor pad, and Mallory wondered again, what had happened between Harris and his ex?

"– so, what did she say to that? Man, you could have at least waited until we were done with her built-ins." Paul was saying something to Harris as Mallory walked back into the living room and sat down to finish her after-dinner drink. She still had a lot of reading to do tonight, she thought to herself, just finish this drink and then she would have to leave.

Harris glanced over at her from where he sat on the piano bench, looking very uncomfortable, and Mallory wondered belatedly, did she interrupt a family business discussion? She thought they were just hanging out, playing music, but obviously she walked in at an inopportune moment.

"Sorry...did I interrupt something? I can go-" Mallory looked from Harris to Paul and back again, while starting to shift out of her seat.

"No, nothing. Don't go. It's fine." Harris spoke up, glanced at Paul who just laughed as he started strumming a few chords on the guitar, humming a tune and started to sing, impromptu.

"It's nothing, sorry to say... No sparks, sorry to say ... Not gonna happen ... there's just no way..." He drifted his tune off with a laugh in the direction of his older brother, winking at Carissa who sat curled up in a chair next to the piano, with Peyton on her lap and Penny contentedly sleeping at her feet.

"Really?" Harris rolled his eyes at his brother and turned to Mallory as if to explain, "He thinks he's funny, this is why we don't encourage him to socialize. We keep him locked in the shop most of the time." Harris turned back to the piano and played a few chords.

"No, you don't, Uncle Harris. You don't keep him locked in the shop." Peyton spoke up from where he sat on his mom's lap and shook his head solemnly, prompting laughter from the room.

"I don't? Maybe I should though, what do you think?" Harris laughed at the doubtful expression on the little boy's face, "Oh, okay. We won't do that. But, you keep an eye on him. Make sure he behaves himself."

A few songs later, most of them ad lib, unscripted and funny, the exchange was forgotten. Mallory stood to leave along with them when Carissa urged Paul and Peyton out the door because, "They had school tomorrow."

As they walked towards the front door, Harris reached for Mallory's arm and asked if she minded staying back for a minute, he wanted to talk to her about the house.

His question took her by surprise, and his touch through her cotton blouse, set off some anxious butterflies inside. Suddenly, she didn't feel prepared to have this conversation, the discovery of Grandpa J's novel having erased all thoughts of her original intentions for coming here in the first place.

"Please come back and sit down. Can I make you a cup of coffee? I have de-caf. Or, hot chocolate?" Harris offered as he walked into the kitchen and reached into a cabinet for a can of cocoa.

"Sure, cocoa sounds fine, I guess. I can't stay long though, I have something I'm working on." Mallory pulled a counter stool out from under the marble topped island counter, sat down and watched, her chin in her hand, as he poured milk into a pan and fired up a burner on the gas range.

"Oh? Good. I'm glad you have the internet working so you can write."

Mallory noted his comment with renewed dismay, he assumed she was talking about her freelance copywriting or her blog. He didn't know the half of it. Yeah, she was expected to write, no doubt. As in, try to finish a novel that a world-renowned author was unable to finish before his untimely death. Yeah, no pressure there.

"Well, actually, I do have some writing to do. Turns out that I found some interesting items in Grandpa J's safe today."

As she studied him, she wondered if she should bring up the letter and the mention of Harris in it. For some reason, she had difficulty accepting the friendship between her grandfather and Harris, and grudgingly she acknowledged that, while she was curious what had transpired that seemed to have left such a mark on her grandpa, it seemed rather private too.

After all, how well did she really know this Harris guy anyway? Maybe it wasn't her business to know what had happened between them.

"I found that he was working on the third in series of "Stand Tall, Son," it seems to be the final chapter of their lives." Even to her own ears, she finished the statement sounding like it was a death sentence.

Harris put down the spoon that he was using to measure the cocoa and stared at her with his mouth open in surprise. "No way. You've got to be kidding. He was writing *that* while he was here?"

"I guess so, or at least the last part of it from what I've found so far. What's confusing to me is that the beginning of the novel isn't on the USB that I found in his safe."

"Hmm, that is strange. You think his assistant in New York knows anything about it?"

"Maybe, but I think Guillory would have mentioned it to me if he knew anything about this novel being this far along." She shook her head in confusion again, trying to work through the puzzle of it. "And, that's not all. I found a letter too. A letter that he wrote to me."

Harris stopped stirring the hot cocoa and looked at her intently, his deep dark brown eyes almost searching for something from her.

What was he thinking, she wondered as she lost her equilibrium, a dizzying buzz making the room seem electric. He waited for a long, stretched moment, probably wanting her to share first, and then asked, "Do you want to tell me what was in the letter?"

And just like that, Mallory knew that she didn't want to discuss the personal contents of the letter with him. It was such ancient history, and it was a tortured history, nothing that concerned him.

"It was just his mea culpa, in true Grandpa J form." Mallory's voice came out flat, emotionless. "We had some unresolved issues, I guess that was bothering him."

Why was he still looking at her like that? Mallory was beginning to sense that Harris knew more than he let on, and it was starting to bug her that he acted like he could understand. He wasn't there, how could he understand?

"Anyway," She continued with a sigh, "That's whatever. He also mentioned this novel in the letter. He said it wasn't finished and that he wanted me to help him finish it."

"Oh, okay." Harris turned away after a moment, started stirring the cocoa again before looking up, "And, that's a good thing, right? I mean he must really trust you, and believe in your writing skills, to ask you to do that."

"Well, sure, if he hadn't gone and died on us, maybe we could have done this together. But, things didn't quite go according to his plan, did they?" She felt the frustration seeping out in her voice, "I don't think you're quite understanding the gravity of the situation, Harris. It's not like he's a kid in Comp class asking me to help on an assignment. This is JL McMichael, it's the third in a trilogy. I'm sure there are contracts for publishing rights, film rights and promotion plan ... what am I supposed to do ... oh my gosh ..."

Speaking it out loud to another person made it all so real, and she put her head in her hands, rubbing her temples to relieve the pressure of the headache she felt just below the surface. She had no alternative, she would just have to pass this off to Uncle Canton, he could arrange a ghost writer to finish it. That was the only solution that made any sense.

"Mallory, it does seem like a huge responsibility and I really wish Mike was still here to explain all of it to you. But, obviously he trusted you. And, you have other people, like Guillory, who can support you through it, right? It doesn't seem like you're completely left on your own with this."

Harris's voice was soft, but sure, and Mallory had the distinct feeling that if he hadn't been on the other side of the counter, he would have taken her into an encouraging hug. He was just that kind of guy. The kind who wanted to make you feel better, the kind who always tried to see the bright side.

"Yeah, I guess. You're trying to tell me to look at it as a glass half full kind of thing?" She laughed a short laugh when he made a show of pouring a half cup of hot chocolate from the pan and pushed the cup towards her across the counter.

"Well, yes, I guess I am. Now, is that cup half full or half empty? *Of course, it's half full*, because I know there is more in the pan. And, there's even more if I make another batch." He laughed and hesitated for a brief second before saying, "And, just so you know, I'm down with that. I could drink hot chocolate all night, if you want."

He laughed, but the statement left Mallory wondering what he meant by it. As she took a sip of the warm cocoa, she mused again, was he flirting with her? He sure didn't seem like it, but he was hard to read.

"No, that won't be necessary, I'm overcoming my fears as we speak." She paused, giving herself a moment to think about it, "You're right. I will call Guillory tomorrow and we will figure out what to do next. In the meantime, you said you wanted to talk to me about Grandpa J's house?" She tried to focus on his face but was distracted again by the ring he wore on his left hand and she found herself wondering again about his ex-wife, the one for whom he bought this house.

"Yes, I was curious how many acres it is and where the property line actually lies. Mike and I never really cared about it, we just had an agreement that I mowed both yards together as one."

"It's 1.8 acres, I looked at the abstract this morning. But, I didn't look close enough to see the property line. I could go get it and you could look it over, if you like."

"Don't worry about it. I can look at it tomorrow. Did you find any real estate agents yet?" Mallory tried to gauge his interest but wasn't sure if avoiding eye contact and looking into his cocoa cup was part of his negotiating game face.

"No, I didn't really get very far on that. I take it that you're maybe interested?"

"I am, but honestly, the timing isn't the best for me because of this business deal." Harris took a drink from his cup, his brows turned down slightly as he thought through the situation, "I'm still trying to figure out a way to make it work. But, I understand you need a decision quickly, you want to sell it and move on with your life."

When he said it like that, Mallory couldn't help but feel a little sad. Of course, he was right. But, she was starting to realize that this little piece of earth, the one her grandfather left her, should somehow end up with Harris. Something about that just felt predestined.

CHAPTER 10

"Hi, Guillory, I was just thinking about you this morning. How are things going in the city?" Mallory answered the ringing cell phone the next morning, plopped down and pulled her knees close to her chest as she settled into the comfy big chair (quickly becoming her favorite chair ever) next to the crackling fire she lit earlier.

As she talked on her phone, she was a bit mesmerized by the scene outside the living room windows; snow was fluttering out of the dove gray sky, the ample, fuzzy flakes drifting lazily down until they disappeared on the brick patio, so water-filled and dense that they left little puddles on the bricks as they melted.

"Things are good. Suzanne and I are considering meeting with a few real estate agents for your Grandfather's home, either to sell or to rent it out. Speaking of Suzanne, she wanted me to tell you that you're invited to Thanksgiving here next week, but I told her you were in Minnesota and I wasn't sure how long you were staying. How is Minnesota, by the way?"

She looked around the relaxed, homey room with its wood beamed ceiling and rustic-edged bookshelves lined with her grandfather's books, standing there like an army of soldiers, the only uniform thing about them was their hard covers, but otherwise they were a happy mix of different colored spines, with a host of different sizes and thicknesses. Everything from poetry and gardening to philosophy and the Bible, which she found sitting open on the bottom shelf, with a series of faith-searching books behind it. She pondered briefly, if a man's library reflected the man, what did this one say about her Grandpa J?

"Just fine. Grandpa J sure didn't change much around here in ten years." Well, that's not exactly true, she continued her internal conversation, she didn't remember seeing a Bible around here ten years ago. "But, what's up with you?"

"Oh, I was just checking in on you. And, also, I told Canton I'd call you to see if you found what he's looking for." Mallory's heart hitched slightly as she glanced at her laptop in front of her on the ottoman, the cursor happily blinking after the words The End.

After reading late into the night, she had finished what was stored on the USB this morning. And, although the novel was enthralling, full of rich characters, with an intriguing plot and a completely satisfying conclusion, reading it through to the end left her with more questions than answers. Questions like, why were the first six chapters missing and what did he want her to finish?

Because, it was already finished. He even sealed its fate with those two words every author wrote with a mix of emotions running the gamut from euphoria, to anticipation, to apprehension and sometimes... melancholy, as Grandpa J told her once.

He said writing The End was like putting someone in the grave. Once buried, while you could continue to experience that person's spirit through memories, you could never really touch them, never really live with them in the moment, ever again. Fate was sealed when you wrote The End.

"Oh?" Mallory nonchalantly questioned, trying her best to be casual, "What is Uncle Canton looking for?"

She felt genuinely guilty about not coming clean with Guillory about her find. Honestly, she hadn't considered exactly how she would unveil this novel to the outside world.

But it didn't really matter, she told herself, they don't really need to know when I found it, not the exact day anyway. For all they know, it's still safely ensconced in his little safe over there, for Grandpa J's eyes only.

"Yes, well, it turns out that your grandfather was close to finishing the third "Stand Tall, Son" novel. At least that's what Canton and Jasmine believe. They said he spoke to them about it over the past few months but refused to give them any details on his progress and he wasn't uploading anything onto their server like he always has in the past. Canton is extremely upset about the fact that they cannot locate the manuscript, especially because now the two of them are in France for that literary in film award your Grandfather received. They won't be back until after Thanksgiving."

"Oh, yes, that's right. Hmm. Did Grandpa J say anything to you about a third novel?"

"Not specifically, no. Your grandfather was acting very strangely – not in his usual routines - this past year or so. He didn't check in with me as regularly, he didn't ask me to arrange his travel, he started paying his own credit card bills - just things that I have always done for him - now he wanted to do for himself. He told me that he was trying to retire, he wanted to go off-grid." Guillory laughed into the telephone, as if to say, like that was ever likely, given his lifestyle and the business enterprise his life had become.

"Huh, yeah, that doesn't really sound like him at all, does it? I wonder why the big change."

"Well, you know how I feel, I shared it with you. He told me that his world view had changed, he was a new person. I think the way he was acting had more to do with his transformation than him trying to retire and take it easy. Quite the opposite, really. He acted like he had just started to live, like he had a new lease on life. He was done with his old life."

Mallory felt the words float through her mind and settle down somewhere south of her heart. Guillory's words so clearly echoed the words of his letter, that she felt them pressing on her spirit somehow. She looked again at the old wooden desk where her grandfather had probably sat just a few weeks ago, writing that letter and she glanced at the open Bible on the book shelf alongside her. He was done with his old life. Yes, so he said.

"Yeah, I think I'm starting to see that, Guillory. Thanks for calling, it's good to hear your voice. Let Suzanne know that I'm bummed, but I won't be able to help her make the green bean casserole this year, I don't think I will be back to the city by Thanksgiving. Give the fam hugs for me though, ok?" She smiled into the phone, remembering the warmth of the holidays spent with them, "Oh, and I'll let you know if I turn up anything that's of interest to Canton or Jasmine, ok?"

"Okay, Mallory. It's always good to talk to you, and please consider spending time with us over Christmas if you're back by then. We will keep in touch."

"Mallory left it for you earlier this afternoon, when you were at Cindy's with the guys." Paul spoke up from behind his computer screen as Harris regarded the yellow envelope in his hands, his name written on a blue note in hand-writing that he didn't recognize, "Now that the mantle is installed, I suppose that's the last we will hear from Cindy?"

Harris looked up from Mike's abstract, a question furrowing his brow, "Why would you say that? She still wants the built-ins done, same as I discussed with her originally." Harris paused, his brow turning down into a full frown, "You are making this a bigger deal than it really is. It's not like we were seriously dating or anything."

"Well, maybe you don't think so, but I wonder what she considered it. Just sayin', I pity the poor woman."

"I don't think she would appreciate your pity. Or need it for that matter. She was cool with it all. Just drop it, ok?" Harris shook his head, wishing his family would lay off the constant matchmaking for one hot second.

He and Cindy had "the talk" the other night, and, even though he had initiated it, she seemed to agree with him. They enjoyed each other's company, but that was all, nothing more. They would remain friends. No harm, no foul. Case closed. He had tried to put himself back out there in the dating world, but, when it's all said and done, another dead end in the relationship department.

Pulling his chair away from his desk, he sat down heavily, set the envelope on his cluttered desk and looked again where she had written his name in bold black letters.

Harris was disappointed that he hadn't been here when Mallory dropped it off; seeing her seemed to lift his spirits and he found her sense of humor refreshing. Besides, she was a connection to Mike, and that made her feel like a friend already.

But he acknowledged to himself, there was also something else about her. He couldn't put his finger on it, just a sense he had. Maybe they would keep in touch once she left? But, then again, maybe not. After all, there was that guy she mentioned, back in Baltimore.

He opened the envelope and started to look over the old abstract, flipping through the pages. He was disappointed that he would have to tell her his decision to pass on purchasing the house but knew there was no way around it. Given his decision, it was even more important he knew where this property line sat. As he scanned the legal description, he noted the various owners with some curiosity and reviewed the abstract drawing. Oh, that's where the property line is. Not far off from what he and Mike had discussed.

As he was folding the abstract back into place, he noticed a small piece of JLM monogrammed note paper stuck towards the back of the abstract. Freeing it from its place, he wouldn't have thought much of the numbers that Mike had written because he had no context for them, they weren't telephone numbers or addresses. But the name written alongside of them left no question who the note was for and what the note detailed:

For Mallory: Minnesota - The Hills - The Ranch   all 25-10-52

This looked like a list of safe combination, and suddenly Harris's mind filled in the blanks of Mallory's mystery. Could it be that he left USBs in safes at these other places he owned? And, maybe one of those had the complete novel instead of just the last part?

He was so excited to get her the information, that he instinctively picked up his phone, and then realized with frustration, that he hadn't asked for her telephone number yet.

Well, he thought as he grabbed his coat from the back of his chair, I will bring it over there. Might give me a chance to ask her again about the letter she found. While tantalizing to the rest of the world, the final chapter in the "Stand Tall, Son" series paled in comparison to what Harris suspected was in that letter.

CHAPTER 11

Mallory typed the last words of the "The Twenty-Something Dreamer" blog with a sense of satisfaction. There. Done. Finally.

Today, she shared on her blog what she had been feeling for a while and had set in motion over a month ago. It was time to move on, past the electronic connections to people she didn't really know, towards something more tangible. Towards relationships more authentic. No offense, peeps, just need to get more real with people. With *real people*.

She had started the blog five years ago, while in college, just for fun, with a couple of girlfriends, Mel and Chris. The other two had long since moved on to careers and marriage, while she ...well, she was still here.

It was basically a day-in-the-life-type blog - she focused on travelling on a single person budget, the best books to read so you have "first rate, first date convos," fast fashion so you look the part, and work life minutiae, all spun with a sense of humor. For the most part, she enjoyed writing it, but the shine was starting to wear off, the content was feeling a little forced, so she decided it was time to cede the platform to another voice. And, while there had been some impact with the few advertisers and promotional deals she had picked up along the way, she knew this was the right move.

Her phone buzzed with an incoming text, startling her out of her reverie, and she frowned slightly when she saw Jasper's name come up again. His text read:

Ok, you win. I've texted you four times, no reply. Five is the charm. Remember, you said it.

She couldn't help but smile at his reference to one of the old blog posts about handling a relationship argument. Mel had said, let the guy text you three times and then – only if you want the relationship to continue – give in and text him back. Mallory had said, make it five, then you'll know he's truly sorry and truly interested. So, because it was a matter of principle, she picked up the phone and called Jasper instead of texting him back.

"Oh, my gosh, it worked!" He laughed into the phone, "I know you said not to call or text, you would contact me, but I couldn't help it, I got swept up in the moment. I just drove past that place we went last summer where we heard that phenomenal blues musician, you remember the place?"

He must have been driving up to one of their Philadelphia dealerships; the quaint restaurant featuring live blues music on their outdoor patio was located in a Chester, Pennsylvania neighborhood, just off the Delaware Expressway. Mallory remembered the weekend well, they met up with a few of his college friends, and had a lot of fun at that little place and a few others. It was just one of many fun times she had with Jasper over the past two years. They both loved music. And Jasper, no dummy, often softened her resistance after an argument with tickets to one of her favorite shows.

"Yeah, I remember the place. And, I hope you're using voice text if you're in your car." He had an exasperating habit of texting while driving when he was on open highways.

"Yes, Mother, of course." He took the rebuke in stride, knowing full well she was right. "But, I just stopped to fill with gas and saw your blog post pop up. So, that's a surprise. What made you decide to do this now?"

"I don't know, I guess it just feels like the right time. I've probably said all I can say, it's time to be quiet for a while."

She looked across the living room thinking to herself, *plus* I might need to focus my writing skills in another direction, and since I feel my skills are severely not up to the task, I need to be on my A game.

"Wow, ok. But, what will you do? Have you found another job yet?"

Thanks, Jasper, for your support and way to go, boosting my confidence like this. She stood up and walked into the kitchen to retrieve a bottled water from the refrigerator, completely annoyed by his question and the condescending tone in his voice.

"No, I haven't found another job yet. I'm doing some freelance copywriting for Bradford. And, FYI, I'm doing fine, no need to worry 'bout me."

"You know what I mean, it's just that I've never known you to be so...I don't know –"

"Rudderless? Clueless? Without direction or motivation? Take your pick of these, or I can keep going–" Her voice rose a little and she felt her stomach tighten in defense of something she didn't understand.

"Mallory, whoa, slow down. Forgive me for asking! I'm just concerned, that's all. It's just, well, you seem different - not in a bad way - just ... different." Jasper let his voice drop off like he was struggling to voice what he knew to be true but didn't want to keep grasping for the words.

Mallory took a drink of the cold water, and slowly put the water bottle back on the counter, while trying her best to assess what she was feeling.

He was right, of course. She did feel different, but she couldn't explain or define it, certainly not to Jasper after what they'd been through. She couldn't even trust him to remember to feed her cat. If she had a cat.

"Listen, Jasper, this "difference" in me, it's got nothing to do with you. I'm trying to sort through things, I need to work on one thing at a time. Like I said before I left Baltimore, I need you to give me space."

A flash of a person passed the kitchen window and she looked over towards the front door just as she heard the heavy clack of the door knocker announcing a visitor. She walked towards it, hoping she could cut this telephone call short, and opened the door just enough to see who it was.

"I know. I know you need that, but it's really hard for me-" In a strange, unsettling juxtaposition, Jasper's deep, silky voice spoke into her ear at the very same moment Harris's smiling brown eyes washed over her.

Immediately, she felt the heat rise in her cheeks, as if she had been caught taking the last cookie from the cookie jar. "...you know I love you, hon. Why don't you just come home?"

Mallory could hear the sugar sweet drip in Jasper's voice and, because her cell phone volume was turned way up, she was pretty sure Harris heard it too.

Leaving the door open, hoping he would he take it as an invitation to step inside, she turned quickly away and stepped towards the kitchen for more privacy. She had to finish this call with some degree of dignity and try to keep it quiet since Harris was standing right there in the next room.

"Jasper, we've been through this." She whispered, "I have to be here to wrap things up. We will have to talk about this later, I have to go now."

As she hung up the phone, she realized that she was cutting him off, not even giving him a courtesy Goodbye or Love you, on every conversation they had recently. Part of her felt bad about that, but part of her really could care less what he thought. Was that a sign it was over between them? If so, then why did she feel this sadness every time they spoke?

She drew in a deep breath and exhaled slowly while watching transfixed out her kitchen window as a bird flitted between the shrubs amongst the craggy oak trees, searching for something in the snow. Did birds even eat acorns, she wondered numbly.

Bottom line, her mind refocused again, she was shot, completely used up, admitting to herself that this thing with Jasper was toxic. She had to figure out what she felt and take a step in one direction or another. But, she was helpless in her indecision, she just felt too overwhelmed right now to trust herself to *do anything* about *anything.*

"Mallory?" Harris spoke up quietly from the hallway and she turned to take in the sight of him, standing there so comfortable in the surroundings of this cozy house, all tall, dark and handsome and just...nice. With the abstract in his hand. She shook her head a little to clear the cobwebs of confusion and tried her best to be present.

"Yes, hi. Come in, come in. That was just-" She threw her hands up and laughed a weak laugh, rolling her eyes, "That was my -that was Jasper, from Baltimore. He's just, well, he's -"

"Yeah, sorry to barge in on you." He nodded as if he understood and held the abstract out towards her, "I brought this back to you, but I don't have to stay. You can call him back." He stepped over towards the kitchen counter, set the abstract down and turned back towards the door.

"No, you don't have to leave, unless you need to, I mean, go ahead then. But, I'm not going to call him back just yet. He and I, well, that's just very confusing right now." She turned to the refrigerator and took out a bottled water and held it out to him. "Can you stay awhile?"

Harris regarded her with a small smile turning up his mouth and for some reason, Mallory felt the heat rise again in her face. There it was again, that feeling that he was flirting with her. It would be beyond embarrassing for her to assume he was, but, if he was, he had the most disarming way of doing it.

"Sure, I can stay awhile." He walked over closer to her to take the water, sending her nerves on high alert, and then he reached for a stool, pulling the abstract towards him across the counter, convincing her that he had not been flirting, he was indeed here with a different purpose.

"I found the property line," Harris said, "It cuts from that group of maple trees in the front yard back to that group of evergreens by the stream in the backyard."

"Oh, ok, good to know." She sat down across the counter from him and thought, I could care less where that property line is right now. She was hoping he would just buy the house and then she could be done with all this.

"Have you come to any conclusion on buying it?" Mallory raised her brows with the question, "I know I should give you a price, but, honestly, I'm just not sure what it's worth." She scowled in mock severity, "Now, don't be all intimidated by my hard-charging negotiating skills on display here."

"Yeah, that might not be the best way to open a negotiation. But, it doesn't matter." She saw the bright white of a small smile at the joke, but he seemed sad, and she realized something was up. "I'm sorry, Mallory, but I just don't think I can buy it right now. This business merger will take care of any extra funds I have, at least for the time being. Things could look very different in a year, but right now, I just don't have the money that I know you could get for it."

Disappointment waved over his expression and Mallory felt a wave of it herself. For some reason, she just felt like this place was meant to be his. This idea - someone else moving in here, someone who didn't even know Grandpa J - that just didn't seem right. And, even though she could sure use the funds in her bank account, and she really didn't need to own a second property that she could never inhabit, she didn't want to make him feel worse by dwelling on it. She could tell it hurt.

"That's okay, Harris, I understand. Let me think on it." She looked down at the time on her phone and noticed that the afternoon had slipped by and she was uncomfortably hungry. "Do you have plans for tonight? You wanna go get something to eat?"

An hour later, Harris pulled his pickup truck out of his driveway and Mallory jumped in the passenger side from the walkway in front of Grandpa J's house.

At first she thought she would feel awkward with him, like they were going on a date or something, but immediately Harris started talking about the property and the trees he had planted for Grandpa J and how they would go for walks with Penny on the bike path leading west out of town, all topics of conversation probably designed to put up safe boundaries on the evening. And, for that, Mallory was grateful.

Given the Jasper telephone conversation earlier, the one Harris had certainly heard in detail, Mallory sensed that he was being careful to be respectful of whatever this was she had going with Jasper. It was best to keep things simple in Minnesota, she had enough trouble in Baltimore.

Once they had settled into the same booth at the sports bar from the other night and ordered burgers again, this time with pepper jack cheese and mushrooms, Harris reached into his jacket pocket and brought out a small piece of paper.

"I have something to show you. I think you will be very excited by the latest clue in Mike's mystery." He spread out the note paper and slid it across the table towards her, and she was sure his eyes were twinkling, or maybe it was the lighting from the Coors lamp hanging low over the table.

She recognized the notepaper immediately, having used some of it just this morning when taking down some notes from Bradford for a new product line he was working on. It was Grandpa J's handwriting and it was written to her, with the names of his LA home and Wyoming ranch alongside the safe combination.

"What? Where did you find this?" She couldn't believe it – how lucky would she be if one of those two safes had the complete novel in it? This must mean he had similar safes in these other two homes.

"It was stuck inside the abstract. So, you're thinking what I'm thinking?" He smiled wide and raised his eyebrows.

"Ah, yes, I think I am. For some reason, he left the first part in one of the other homes. He *must* have. Still, I just don't understand why he used USBs and not the server. It seems like so much extra work and such a risk that something would be lost."

"Well, it maybe looks like that to you now. But, remember, he didn't know he was going to...you know ... die so suddenly." Harris glanced down at the table as if he still had a hard time speaking about Grandpa J in past tense.

"True." She paused, considering the situation as it presented itself, "Well, this is interesting. Trouble is, my Aunt Jasmine and Uncle Canton are both in France right now, accepting an award in

Grandpa J's name, otherwise they could check to see if he left anything in those safes."

She debated about calling them to see what they wanted to do about it, since these were technically their homes now. But, something held her back. What if he really did leave the front end of the novel unfinished and expected her to help write it. Even though she felt hopelessly unqualified, was it right for her to ignore his wishes?

She looked at Harris intently, wondering what he would think of the absurd plan that was forming in the back of her mind.

"Or, I suppose I could just go out to see for myself. I found a set of keys for his homes in the safe. Since Jasmine won't be in LA and no family even lives in Wyoming where he has the ranch, I don't suppose it could hurt to go check it out-" She dropped her sentence off mid-stream, waiting and holding her breath to see if he would think this was an absolutely insane plan.

"Wow, that's a great idea! I think you should totally do that. I'm pretty sure that Mike would want you to chase this down until you figure it out."

Over dinner, between laughs about living the local life in Beck's Mill, they discussed his work, and they discussed her work and the recent demise of her blog. They talked about his family and they talked about her friends and *Guillory's* family.

No offense, Harris seemed like a really nice guy, but, over the years, she had gotten accustomed to not talking about her family. Really, she didn't talk about them to anyone, not even Jasper.

After her parents' death, and then the next few years with Grandpa J where she felt like a complete burden to him all the time, she often pretended in her mind that she was not even from the same family as them.

As the waitress took away their plates, the conversation had stopped a bit awkwardly on Paul and Carissa's plans to have a baby in the near future and the fact that Harris's mom was excited about the prospect they would give Peyton a brother or sister, and she would get another grandchild to shower with her attention.

Mallory noticed the closed look that shadowed his eyes and the slight hesitation in his voice as he told her, "Yeah, that was supposed to be my role. You know, first one married, first grandchild."

He looked down at his water glass and toyed with his phone on the table in front of him. She noticed again the ring on the middle finger of his left hand, and for some reason, after tonight's relaxed conversations, she felt comfortable enough to venture out.

"Well, for what it's worth – from what I know of you in just a couple days – she's clueless, or severely lacking in good judgement." Mallory smiled as he glanced up, seemingly surprised by her comment, "But, I have to ask, what's up with the ring? It's really cool... is it your wedding band?"

Harris studied his hand and twisted the ring around slowly on his finger, thinking about what to say, how to tell her in a way that would keep the conversation open, so it wouldn't shut down. He just didn't know Mallory very well yet, he didn't know how she would react.

"No," He replied, "That ring went to the jewelry liquidator the day the divorce was final. I needed to put the period on that sentence. But, I won't lie, it's hard. I still think about her sometimes. I think about us together, I guess."

He stopped twisting the ring as he slipped it off his finger and held it out towards her for a closer look, "I made this with a friend of mine who does cool work with metals. It's made of mahogany inlaid into a titanium band and clear coated for wear. Do you like it?" She looked at the ring closely, appreciation lighting her bright blue eyes.

"Yeah, it's so unique." She rubbed her finger over the small titanium cross that was inlaid into the mahogany, "I've never seen anything quite like it." She handed the ring back to him with a friendly smile, tucking some of her dark curls behind her ear.

"Thanks. I wear it to remind me of my priority. Life can get so full of other stuff, it's easy to drift off course. I find that my faith keeps me grounded." Harris watched her cagey expression, wondering if she would ask any questions about her grandfather.

"Yeah, when I was young, I grew up going to church, but after my parents died, it was just easier to put that in the past, like so many other things." She paused slightly, shifting in her seat a little, "Let's just say, Grandpa J was not the church-going type."

"True, from the sounds of it, he wasn't." Harris paused, watching her carefully, "Until the end, that is. Even though he might still tell you he wasn't the church-going type, I know where his heart was. So... I know where his soul is."

Her cagey expression of a moment ago had turned to outright skepticism - it was written all over her face - and it permeated through the hesitant smile that turned up her mouth but didn't reach her eyes.

"Yeah, right." Mallory scoffed, "It's statements like that, that make me wonder, how do you *know*? You sound so sure of it." She turned her glass around in the ring of condensation it had left on the table, her eyes avoiding his, "I don't really know what I believe about life after death, like heaven. And, I am having a *really* hard time believing that Grandpa J actually bought into it."

"Oh, he did, I can assure you. I was there, I saw it."

"What?" She looked back up to him, laughing derisively, "Okay. Like a meeting with God where a light came out of heaven and an angelic chorus started singing and all that?" She smirked as she rolled her eyes and took a drink of her water.

"No. Nothing like that."

Harris tried not to let her words bother him, she had no way of knowing what the moments with Mike were like, how profoundly Mike had been changed.

"He felt something shift, he said it's like he felt something heavy suddenly lift off of him, opening up a part of him that he didn't know existed." Harris did his best to recount the exact words Mike used, she needed to hear the truth – the authentic truth – of what happened to Mike if there was ever a chance that she would believe it was real.

"Hmm, I guess." As she looked off towards the table behind him, distracted by her thoughts, he watched her deliberate and noticed again how similar her eyes were to Mike's. They were the exact same shade of light blue, almost lavender in color, with darker blue flecks around the edges. In addition, hers were framed by the most captivating long dark lashes.

He reluctantly averted his eyes to stop from staring at her as he thought – There, he had laid the truth of Mike's life change out there for her consideration. The ball was in her court, she had to decide how to play it.

"Well, I guess it can happen to anyone then. Even guys like Grandpa J."

She looked him deep in the eyes with her comment, almost challenging him to prove it to her – she didn't really believe it – and Harris wished again that things were different, that she could have experienced it herself, to actually witness the changes in Mike.

"Funny you should say that, 'cause I think *it*, as you call it, happens most especially with people like your Grandpa J, the ones who think they have nothing to lose – they feel so far gone – and suddenly they find they have the world to gain."

CHAPTER 12
... A few days later, Day One of my journey ...

"Yes, yes, I hear your horn, lady, but I don't think I stand a chance in a battle with this UPS truck in front of me, so seriously, just take a chill pill." Mallory fumed out loud to the driver behind her who laid on her horn again while they both sat immobile in the long line of cars waiting to make a left turn at the stop light. Glancing into her rear-view mirror, Mallory watched with bored amusement as the woman scowled from behind her designer sunglasses while her little dog crawled all over her lap and jumped up to lick her face. No wonder she was ticked off, that dog would drive me nuts too.

Okay, this traffic was officially insane. There was no other way to describe it - or the people that chose to live here - she thought, as she willed herself to find that last sliver of patience and sympathized with the plight of the poor Californians who had to deal with this every day.

Her flight on day one of her adventure, had been delayed out of Minneapolis because of snow and ice, go figure. And, then there was a problem at LAX with the flight crew on the airplane currently stationed at their gate, so they had to sit on the tarmac with jet fuel fumes clogging the cabin air for an extra forty minutes. And, when she turned up at the rental car counter, she heard that her car hadn't passed through the cleaning process yet.

Gina, the slightly harried-looking and no-nonsense rental car associate behind the counter, took her job very seriously. When Mallory tried to joke around with her saying she didn't care that it wasn't fully cleaned, certainly it was cleaner than her apartment, Gina wasn't having it. Maybe she checked her sense of humor the moment she punched the time clock, because all Mallory got was a tight mouth and a cranky command to wait for ten minutes over there by the potted plastic tree.

Of course, the ten minutes she promised turned into thirty. These many delays and slight inconveniences all contributed to Mallory's position, now stuck in rush hour traffic that afternoon, with her Google Maps app blinking crazy with a constant stream of Traffic Slowdown notifications. This was definitely not going as she planned.

Her plan? Arrive in L.A. early in the afternoon, get to Grandpa J's house, check things out, stay at a hotel near the airport and then tomorrow take a flight to Jackson, WY and drive out to the ranch.

As far as she was concerned, the sooner she could see L.A. disappearing beneath the clouds on her flight out of here, the better.

It's not that she necessarily disliked the city with its many excesses of money, fame and power players, it was more that the memories of this town were laced with a loneliness that haunted her as a teenager and into her early twenties. If she was truly honest with herself, it still haunted her today.

The light finally turned green, and Mallory urged the rental car along with the stream of other impatient drivers past the restaurants and shopping districts and finally into the curving, winding streets of the Hills. The climb became a bit steeper and, as she wound her way through the neighborhoods, the traffic finally subsided to a trickle, the busy, teeming streets replaced by perfectly manicured high hedges and ornamental trees and the occasional resident out walking their dog along the pristine sidewalks.

And, finally, there it was. The Hills House, as he called it. But you couldn't really call it house, by Mallory's standards of what made a home.

From the street, what you could see of it behind the gate, it looked like an art museum with floor to ceiling plate glass windows, brushed concrete and metal surfaced walls with touches of redwood trim. The three-story home with its gleaming concrete basement garage, was built into the hill it perched upon, blocking the view of the city on the other side. That view was reserved for the elite few people that were allowed through the gate and into the house. She had met a few of them. They weren't so special.

She pulled the car into the short stone-paved driveway and felt again the apprehension she had been trying to overcome since she hatched this plan.

Who was she to even be here? She didn't own this place and she hadn't even spoken to her grandfather more than three or four times a year in the past three years. This was his house - scratch that - this was Aunt Jasmine's house.

She supposed that she was breaking any number of laws with this plan. Yes, she was most definitely breaking laws with this plan.

Heaving a big sigh, she regarded the set of keys nestled in the drink holder of the rental car, focusing on the one with the blue tag with The Hills written on it. This better work, or she had just wasted over a thousand dollars on airfare.

She opened the car door, glancing surreptitiously over her shoulder, but this stretch of the street didn't have houses on both sides, making it even more exclusive and very unlikely anyone was watching her.

As she tried to recall the gate security code, she rationalized, if he had changed it, the worst that could happen would be a random jogger would report her to the police when they spied her trying to scale the brick wall over by that tree. Really, how bad could Beverly Hills police detention be?

But, thankfully Grandpa J was a creature of habit and liked to keep things simple, because the gate clicked open the second she finished punching in the code. She laughed out loud at the fact that she actually remembered the combination of dates which included his birthday and her grandparents' anniversary. How ironic that she could forget entire sweeps of time spent with him here in L.A., but still recall that security code.

As she walked the short distance from her car to the expansive concrete steps leading to the front door, it occurred to her that the cleaning service might be here today, but there wasn't another vehicle in the driveway, so it was unlikely.

She knew from experience that Grandpa J hired a cleaning and gardening service for this home, he had never hired a full-time housekeeper because he didn't spend much time here.

When he was in town, he spent most of his time at the studio or out with friends and business acquaintances at night. He called these evening extracurriculars "work." But, Mallory had never witnessed much work getting done amongst the party crowd and the parade of women in his life.

Mallory rang the doorbell and tried to peer through the smoky glass side lights along the redwood double doors. After ringing the bell twice more, she felt reasonably confident she was alone. The key worked, and, with a deep breath, she pushed open the door and braced herself for the memories - the worst of which she was sure would barge their way back into her consciousness.

◆ ◆ ◆

2009

Now I understand ... and I mourn my innocence of a moment ago

It was summer break, the summer before she began her Junior year at the second boarding school she'd attended, the one in Delaware. She was sixteen, turning seventeen in September, and was doing her best to feel part of something - anything - that she could call a life.

She had just gotten her driver's license, she had a pseudo-boyfriend from the boys' school across town (mostly texts and Facebook PM's, but it was something) and she had a few girlfriends who she hung out with at school. It wasn't much of a life, but it was hers.

She was livid that summer when her grandfather told her that she had no choice, she had to come out to California instead of New York where three of her friends also lived. He said absolutely no way could she stay alone at his place in New York and he couldn't ask Guillory to take her because Suzanne was recovering from pancreatitis and was not able to take on the extra burden. Because, of course, that's what she was. A burden.

When she arrived in LA, still mad at him for forcing her to come out here, she didn't have much of a choice but to accompany him to the studio most days. He said too much time spent sitting around his backyard pool would age her skin and dull her mind.

It always felt so weird to her, seeing her grandpa working with directors, actors and musicians; he was like a different person altogether, not the sullen, cranky grandfather that she knew him to be most of the time.

When he wanted to, he had a way of adjusting, truly belonging, to the world he was in at the moment, never seeming out of his element. She remembered distinctly wishing that *this* grandpa - the one who was relaxed and funny, sharp-witted but kind - she wished *that* grandpa would chill with her all evening when they got back to his house in the Hills on those infrequent nights when he didn't have plans with his entourage.

But, most of the time when they entered the sprawling glass house behind the gate, her grandpa would return to his body. The Grandpa J she knew would tell her the caterer had left some pasta in the refrigerator so "don't be shy," then he would retire to his study with a bottle and some ice, and she wouldn't see him again until the next morning.

That was the routine for the first few weeks that summer, until an especially memorable day that opened with a conversation Mallory overheard between Grandpa J and Aunt Jasmine. They were in his office at the studio, and the door was slightly open. Mallory would have walked in unannounced, but held back when she heard her Grandpa J say in that condescending tone of his–

"Why can't Mallory just stay with you this summer? You have the boys around, certainly they can try to keep her company."

"No, Father, I've told you before, that's not going to work. They have their own lives, you can't expect them to babysit her."

Mallory heard her Grandpa J's derisive laugh, as if he agreed with her, before he resumed, his voice pleading.

"Oh, come on. She's not so bad."

"Well, then you keep her..." Jasmine had countered sarcastically, there had been a slight pause and then her aunt continued, "Oh, wait. Of course, I understand now. She's cramping your style – she's putting a dent in your social life – is that it?"

Her grandpa had laughed at the inside joke, and Mallory heard the familiar sound of ice hitting a glass and liquor being poured. Then she heard Grandpa J say, and even though his voice was low, she clearly heard his words, "I just feel so inept around her. *I just didn't know how to love her.*"

That was enough. She didn't need to hear any more. And, as she faded away from his hallway, finally wandering into a quiet corner between two sound stages to spend the afternoon secluded away from everyone around her, she started to realize just how alone she was, now that her parents were gone.

The thoughts that raged inside her that afternoon took her on a wild ride resulting in waves of nausea and pain. It was an abysmal, aching feeling.

Heartache. She remembered identifying it that day, like it's a real thing, not just something they talk about in country music songs.

Looking back on that day, analyzing it as if it happened to someone else, Mallory recognized the traumatic impact it had on the awkward, insecure sixteen-year-old girl, as her already shaky self-image took another hit from the words of her grandfather.

Unfortunately, the day that started bad, had even worse things in store for her later.

◆ ◆ ◆

Shaking her head as if that would shake the memory away once and for all, Mallory took in a deep breath as she stood in the foyer of the Hills house and surveyed the polished concrete floors and elegant marble accent walls.

Every element in the house was set up to maximize the views of the valley below and the city in the distance. Decorations were kept clean and minimal, and the furniture, while grand in scale and texture, was low line and subdued in color.

When you stepped through the foyer and gazed over the massive living room and out the seamless wall of windows, it was as if you could fly right through the house, over the infinity pool, and off the side of the hill, floating above the valley that housed the city beyond. It was a breathtaking view to be sure.

She quickly turned away from the living room with its marble and stone fireplace and the blonde wood doors which hid a full liquor cabinet and wine cooler, feeling the hair raise on her neck. Best to keep moving, just get this done.

"Hello? Anyone here?" Mallory called as she walked through the kitchen which sat to her left and glanced down the wide hallway into the dining area. But, the house felt eerily quiet, like no one had been there in weeks. She swept her finger along the marble countertop, marking a line in the fine layer of dust.

Huh, no one coming to clean? That didn't sound like Grandpa J at all.

She pulled open the double door refrigerator, remembering that he never had more than the essentials for food here. Today, while it lit up cheerily when she opened it, the refrigerator was completely empty.

She left the kitchen and continued down the opposite direction past the open stairway with the "floating" wood and metal steps, one set of stairs led upstairs to four guest rooms and baths and the other set of stairs led downstairs to the screening room and game room, the sauna, and a wine cellar, along with the bedroom and en suite bath she used when she stayed here. She didn't miss it, no need to see that again.

She followed the hallway towards Grandpa J's study, where he did most of his writing while he was in L.A., it was the set of doors just before the doors that led to the spacious master suite. She turned on the lights in the study, trying to remember if he had a safe in there, but drew a blank because she had hardly spent any time in the room when she stayed here. It was off limits.

The large windows looked over a pretty part of the lawn, quiet and peaceful, with a small bench sitting outside on the brick patio that connected to the large pool patio just to the left of it. She remembered the antique metal and glass liquor cart, now empty, that sat in its spot next to the walls of built in bookcases and the massive, modern edge desk without drawers. But, she didn't see a safe.

After trying a few of the doors in the built-ins along the south wall, she found the safe, an exact duplicate of the one in Minnesota. There it is! Quickly spinning the combination, she opened it and found a bank bag which held some cash. Aunt Jasmine scored again, she thought as she reached under and around the safe, focused on finding a USB. And, finally, she found it and held it in her palm, smiling with satisfaction.

Not finding any other USBs in the safe, she shut the door, making a mental note to text Aunt Jasmine the safe combination. She might need that cash. Yeah, right.

Mallory walked out of the study and glanced hesitantly at the stairway leading to the basement. Don't do it, the cautious voice told her. You don't want to go there.

But, something inside her wanted to face it, stand up to it already. You're a big girl, you've moved on.

She stepped onto the stairway and then sat down midway down the flight of stairs, scanning the open great room in the basement with its own bank of windows. The way the house was built into the side of the hill, this floor's view was limited to the far south side of the property with the uncanny feeling that if you stepped outside and weren't careful, you might just tumble down the hillside. The sunken open room had couches that were so wide and deep they looked like beds and, of course, a well-stocked bar area. Funny - there weren't any bottles on the gleaming glass shelves anymore.

The spare bedroom she used was off to the right, with access to the outside and near the door to the garage.

It was all so familiar, and it was all so dreadful.

◆ ◆ ◆

2009

We all have to grow up sometime, don't we?

On the drive home from the studio that evening, unaware of her new-found knowledge of his utter disdain for his granddaughter, Grandpa J asked her what was wrong, she seemed extra quiet today.

She shrugged, didn't say a word and looked out the window at the traffic. As usual, he let the subject drop because, God forbid, he should care enough to delve a little deeper into her feelings on anything.

He went on to say that he was going out to dinner with a few people and afterwards he would be hosting a little "thing" at the house. Maybe she wanted to go hang out with that neighbor kid who they saw jogging the other day, the one who lived down the street a few houses?

No, thanks, she'd said, she had never even met him, for all she knew, he could be a serial killer. He had laughed at that but had a dismayed look on his face that said he wished she was just a little more adventurous, it would make his life *so much* easier.

While he was at dinner, Mallory walked the neighborhood and ended up at the juice and smoothie place about a mile of winding streets down the hill. There she sat, enjoying her smoothie, and struck up a conversation with some other kids from the neighborhood. Although she had never met the three girls and neither of the two boys were the jogging boy from down the street, they all lived in the neighborhood and they knew her grandpa's house well.

They killed some time just chilling in the park nearby and, as it turned dark, one of the boys - was his name Dillon? or Dalton? she couldn't remember any more and it didn't matter - had offered to walk her home, asking her if he could check out her grandpa's pool. Supposedly his parents were building a new infinity pool and he said he was curious. Sure, what a line, she'd thought.

As they came upon Grandpa J's house, it was obvious the business dinner had turned into a full-blown party - the house was all lit up, loud music blared with the dull sound of a booming base and multiple cars lined the street and overflowed into the driveway that snaked around the house and down to the garage.

"Your grandpa must be cool, he's having quite a party," Dillon/Dalton said with a laugh and looked like he was excited to get in on the action. Within an hour or so, Dillon/Dalton, who couldn't have been older than eighteen, was drunk and hanging all over one of the many young actresses in the living room upstairs.

That was the thing with Grandpa J's crowd, they came in all ages, and while a sober Grandpa J might have had some qualms about serving alcohol, and other illegal substances, to underage kids, this Grandpa J was too far gone to notice.

Most were surprised to hear that JL even had a granddaughter, but if she thought that would be off-putting to people, she found quite the opposite. In this town, if you were young and well-connected, the expectation was that you were game for anything.

After dodging the wandering hands of a creepy, 40-something set designer and outright ignoring the overt sexual demands of a 50-something studio talent director, she finally decided to call it a night and tried to disappear to her bedroom in the basement.

Once in her basement bedroom, she plopped down on her bed, not even changing out of her shorts and top, turned her back to the door and pulled her headphones on attempting to drown out the music and half legible conversations of the people in the basement great room and outside on the patio.

She was laying still in her dark room when, over the music in her headphones, she heard the sounds intensify briefly and light flashed as the door opened and closed quickly.

The hair stood up on her neck, was someone in here with her or did someone mistakenly open the door and leave again?

She turned and squinted into the dark, trying to make out a figure that she was sure was standing there in the inky darkness. Her heart started pounding at the intrusion, was she imagining it? Was someone there?

As she tried to roll out of her bed to flip on the bedside lamp, she turned hard into him, hitting her temple on his hip just as he bent over her and she felt his knee drive into her stomach as he fell on top of her.

Then suddenly, before she even had time to think, his hand was over her mouth and she felt the intense panic of a trapped animal. She remembered the sudden motion knocked her headphones off, leaving her ears terribly sore where they were torn from her head.

Over the wrenching and flailing of arms and legs, she smelled pungent alcohol on his hot breath and heard him drunkenly telling her to hush, shhh, hush, as if he was surprised by her struggle.

Somehow, even though she was batting at him with all her might, he shimmied his body more fully over hers, burying her into the pillows on her bed, leaving her with increasingly limited space between his heavy, dead weight chest and hers. She remembered the fleeting thought she had – like she was caught inside a grave, buried beneath the casket.

And, while she was physically there, on the bed underneath him, her mind was a million miles away, thinking in rapid fire. How could she get out from under this guy? Who *was* he? She couldn't see anything in the dark room, why did she pull the blinds? Did anyone see him come in here? Where was her grandpa?

Then, he paused, with his big hand still over her nose and mouth, trapping her breath and voice within her, and in the dim orange glow of her alarm clock, she saw him staring at her, only inches away.

He was holding his breath, as if trying to read her reaction. She forced herself to stare back at him, realizing vividly that she didn't remember him from the party. He was young, twenties she guessed, he had longer hair with a beard and mustache but, in the darkness, she couldn't really tell what color his hair was.

The thought danced around the back of her mind, if he thinks you like him, he will make a mistake. Just lay still.

He fell for the ploy. As he shifted his weight slightly, finally removing his hand from over her mouth, there was just a sliver of time. Just enough time for her to pull her leg up hard between his legs.

With a shocked moan of pain, he doubled up and she rolled out from under him and off into the darkness of the floor between her bed and her door. She half crawled, half ran to the door, pulling it open to the raucous noise outside.

Frantic now at what could have happened, she stumbled through the downstairs rooms, looking for her grandfather. But each room was full of strange faces; she could feel people staring at her and she could hear them laughing at her when she asked where JL was.

As she took the stairs towards the main floor – where she was sitting right now, ten years later – she saw the guy stumble from her bedroom hallway into the gathering room, where he was met by an older guy in a suit with a scowl on his face.

Mallory watched as they talked together and then the older guy scoffed and stormed out the patio door. The young guy half walked, half stumbled over to a group of people at the bar, glanced drunkenly around, probably looking for her to make sure she wasn't broadcasting what he had tried to do.

It could have only been the span of a few minutes, but it felt like time was standing still as she searched for her grandfather among the people upstairs. Finally, she located him sitting by the pool with his current girlfriend Esme, an actress twenty-five years younger than him, chiseled in between him and two other men on the outdoor sectional couch.

Mallory's heart sank when she recognized one of these two men was the scowling older guy from the basement, who now wore a slithering smile. She remembered stopping at the sliding door, doubting herself, wondering should she even mention it? Grandpa J's eyes were glazed over, and she could hear his drunk laugh at the joke they were sharing ... and, the worst of it was that guy was sitting there, obviously he knew something about what had just happened.

She thought, maybe she should find one of the two security guys who were hired for the evening. Grandpa J always hired undercover security guards who would bartend or act as bouncers at his parties, just in case the event the party got a little rowdy. This was Beverly Hills, after all, no one wanted bad publicity.

But, she reasoned, no need to find the security guys, this was her grandfather's home, he was sitting right here and certainly he would confront the guy. She stood up straighter and walked out onto the patio, heading over to the group who all turned to look at her in unison, as if the punch line had just been dropped and she was the butt of the joke.

"Well, Mallory, there you are!" Grandpa J called out loudly, "Come here, come here!" As she covered the short distance between the house and the couch, she was formulating a plan to get him alone to tell him.

But, before she could say anything, he continued in his slurred speech, "I hear you've met Tristan? Quite the heart throb from the Land Down Under, and, as luck would have it, he can act pretty well too."

The group around Grandpa J all laughed, and Mallory was left to wonder what had just happened - what was he talking about? *I hear you've met Tristan ...*

Her sixteen-year-old mind didn't put two and two together until she noticed the shiny shoes and the expensive suit the older man was wearing - the uniform of a Hollywood agent - and she took in the confident smile he smiled up at her from the couch, daring her to contradict whatever story he had just woven before she arrived on the patio.

But, at sixteen, she hadn't learned the lesson yet, she still harbored some starry-eyed delusions that life should be fair. Tears pricked her eyes and her voice had an annoying shrill tremor when she found her words.

"Oh, you mean the guy who just burst into my bedroom and tried to attack me? Funny, he didn't take time to introduce himself."

Mallory remembered being really mad at herself that her voice was shaking, it made her sound so weak. She wanted her grandfather to instinctively believe her - to jump to her defense in a rage of righteous anger - but there was a small voice somewhere deep inside saying, "Don't count on it."

Her worst suspicions were confirmed when her Grandpa J looked up at her with a doubtful crooked smile and waved his hand at her, as if brushing her away like a fly.

"Pshhtt, kid. You always take things the wrong way. He just likes you... Spencer here is the kid's agent. Isn't that what you said, Spence, that he wanted to be introduced to my Mallory?"

Grandpa J was leaning over Esme, and somehow got distracted by her short skirt and long legs, because when he looked back up at Mallory, it was as if he forgot what they were even talking about.

"Yes, he did tell me that he would like to meet your granddaughter." The snake in the suit hissed up at her with a victorious smile lighting his beady black eyes, "And, now that I have had the pleasure, I can see why."

It took every bit of nerve she had, but she ignored the snake, focused on her grandfather and tried one more time.

"Grandpa J, did you hear what I said? He tried to attack me. *In my own bedroom.* Aren't you going to do anything about it?"

To her dismay, she felt the tears now tumbling out onto her lashes and her heart was starting to race inside her chest, the first sign of the panic attack that was just below the surface, itching to be released. She knew better than to believe he would defend her, even before he replied, but knowing this didn't make it any easier to hear his response.

"You need to lighten up, kid. Seriously ... why doesn't someone just get you a drink?"

CHAPTER 13

...Day Two of my journey: I'm disappointed with this travel experience, can I get a refund on my ticket? ...

That morning as Harris collapsed in his office chair, tired from a busy morning of work-related emergencies, he checked the time again and raked his fingers through his hair, concern for Mallory taking precedence over his work thoughts again.

Having secured her phone number before she left, Harris had been checking in with Mallory over the past few days. Her search for the missing piece of Mike's puzzle had been fruitless in L.A.; she told him the USB she found in the safe there had the middle chapters eleven through seventeen on it, all of which were duplicates of the ones she found in Minnesota.

She was paranoid that security footage of her visit to Beverly Hills had reached her Aunt Jasmine and she was frustrated beyond belief at her failure to find the missing chapters. In her text from LAX, she said she had started to "question her faculties" as she boarded her flight to Jackson, Wyoming.

And, now that she was at the second home, a 90-acre working ranch, south of the Jackson, WY airport nestled up against some foothills with the Tetons in the distance, her last text from an hour ago sounded a bit ominous:

At the ranch now. I see someone else's car here at the house though, so not sure how this will go. Thanks for checking in. I'm glad I have your number, you may need to bail me out if I am forced to make the acquaintance of the county sheriff.

And, then a second text followed up moments later:

Or, I might be greeted with the barrel of a Remington. This is Wyoming after all.

Even though the words were startling, he smiled despite his alarm, her sense of humor was so sharp and soft at the same time. He hadn't stopped to question why he was becoming so wrapped up in her quest, it was just so easy and natural to think about her, with each day that passed, she engaged more of his thoughts.

He hadn't even realized how often he spoke of her until this morning when Paul asked if she would be coming to Thanksgiving at their parents' house later this week.

No, he'd replied to his brother, why would you think that? He'd felt himself tense up with the question and Paul's nonchalant shrug and laughing eye roll had annoyed him even further. But, as he turned back to his work, he realized that he really would like to ask her to join them for Thanksgiving. It wouldn't seem awkward at all to him. He wondered if she would feel the same.

"Mallory, what a surprise! You're about the last person I expected to see at the ranch." Mallory's cousin Geoffrey greeted her at the front door of the Grandpa J's ranch home, coffee cup in one hand and cell phone in the other.

She smiled her most winning smile and inched towards him, trying to send the message that she belonged here as much as he did.

"Same here. Surprised to see you too! How's it going, Geoffrey?" She pulled her rolling bag after her and walked past him through the wide double doors. He turned slowly on the heel of his expensive leather shoe and watched her with raised eyebrows.

"It's going well." Geoffrey said slowly, confusion in his eyes, "I'm sorry, but were they expecting you? No one mentioned it to me, and I just spoke to Rhett earlier this morning, when I told him I was leaving."

Mallory mentally kicked herself that she hadn't somehow contacted Rhett, the ranch manager and residence keeper, after she landed and drove out here. But she didn't have his number and felt confident that she could rely on his good nature to let her into the house. Finding Geoffrey here wasn't in the plan.

"Oh? You're leaving? That's a shame. I was hoping when I saw a car that I would have some family company during my stay here this Thanksgiving." She bluffed boldly, sending her gaze over the expansive room with its log walls and massive river rock fireplace in the center of the room. She desperately needed to pull this off or he would be on the phone to his father in a hot second and her ruse would be blown.

"Yes, I've already been here a few days. Dad wanted me to go through Grandfather's things, straighten things up with Rhett and prepare to sell it."

Going through his things? Did that mean he found the rest of the novel already?

"I guess it has to happen. Kind of sad to think it will be sold though, right? This place is really special." Mallory let her voice trail off softly as she sat down in a comfortable leather chair next to the crackling fire and glanced at the mantle with its complete set of Grandpa J's novels prominently displayed alongside some large elk antler sheds.

"If you like horses, cows and country music, I guess." Geoffrey muttered as he joined her in the large open living room. He watched her carefully from the chair opposite her, waiting for her to explain her sudden arrival.

"All of them an acquired taste, I suppose." She agreed good-naturedly, "But, I love it all. This was my favorite place of Grandpa J's. I wish I could have spent more time here."

This much was true. Well, truthfully, she was surprised to admit to herself that she was starting to fall in love with the little forgotten house in Minnesota too.

"Well, sorry then, that he didn't pass it on to you. But, I suppose Dad wouldn't mind too much if you spent a few days here before he sells it. He said he never understood why grandfather bought it in the first place."

"Huh, yeah. Grandpa J once told me that it reminded him of his childhood dreams and now that he'd made enough money, he could afford to make his dream a reality. I guess every little boy has dreams of being a cowboy, right?" She smiled at him, hoping somehow Geoffrey was like other little boys at one time in his life.

"No. I wanted to be a superhero. Spiderman specifically." He laughed a little and shrugged lightly, "You know, because he got the girl."

"Ha, yeah. All that other superhero business - like saving the city - it's so overrated." She looked out the large wall of windows, drinking in the view of the snowy meadow and dark black-green swaths of evergreens that reached higher and higher until they disappeared into the craggy peaks of snow-covered mountains.

"So, how are you doing with all this?" Geoffrey glanced down at his shoes then, evidence that he meant the question rhetorically and, not waiting for her reply, he continued quietly, "I know I've had a rough time since he died. I think it's finally starting to sink in that Grandfather is gone."

"Well, yeah. For me too, I guess." Mallory finally managed to find her voice and crossed her arms in front of herself, suddenly feeling chilled for some reason, even though the fire spit and sparked right next to her.

"Listen, Mallory, I'm sorry that things have been...strained...between us over the years. I've been taking stock of my life since Grandfather died, thinking about what kind of person I want to be." He stopped abruptly, and sighed heavily before continuing, "I realize that I've been a real horse's ass to you in the past and I want you to know I'm sorry for that."

Mallory turned back to face him slowly, not sure if she dreamt what she just heard, it shocked her so much. His confession came so out of the blue that she blinked and self-consciously smoothed her hair down her shoulders trying to internalize his words and accept his apology without reservation. What would be the reason to hold on to the bitterness after all? Where would that get her in the end?

"Well, thanks for saying that, Geoffrey. I want things to be different between us too." She hesitated briefly and plunged forward, "Do you have to leave today? Maybe you could stay an extra day and kick back with me here?"

"I wish I could, Mallory, but I have to get back to Florida for a big fundraiser tomorrow." He smiled though as he hurried on, "But, hey, will you be in New York for Christmas? Dad and Aunt Jasmine will both be at the office Christmas party on December 23 and then everyone is going to spend the holiday at Dad's in Connecticut. You should come." He looked like he meant it, but Mallory's instinctual response to pull back reared its head.

"Well, I'll see. I'm not sure where I will be for Christmas." She tried to hold his gaze but couldn't quite do it, focusing instead on the fire again.

"Sure, I understand. I heard that you're looking for a job? How's that going?"

"I'm still looking. It's okay though, I'm doing some freelance writing and I've got the house in Minnesota to work out."

"Yeah, how is that place? I've never been there. I don't think Dad or Aunt Jasmine have either. He seemed to keep all that rather private for some reason."

"It's beautiful, it's small, but really peaceful, a great place for him to write, I'm sure. I am probably going to list it with an agent when I get back there."

Geoffrey hesitated briefly, probably hung up on her misstep reminding him about Grandpa J's writing, but he didn't ask, and Mallory let out a sigh of relief when he spoke.

"Yeah, listing someone else's place isn't a whole lot of fun. So many details. The list here for the movers is almost a whole notebook. It's weird seeing his personal things and wondering what to do with them. I wish Dad would have just come out here, but he said he already went through all this at his New York place and that was hard enough."

"True. It must have been hard for him." She paused slightly and then continued, "I've always wondered, was your dad really close to Grandpa J, other than business, I mean?"

She wasn't sure he would answer her, maybe she was pushing this newfound friendship with her cousin too far, but she was so curious to know how others learned to love her grandfather, despite his faults. Geoffrey just looked at her with a slightly confused frown creasing his otherwise perfectly smooth, tan forehead.

"Well, yes, they were. I suppose like most father-son relationships. Why?"

"I just never witnessed it. I never saw him close to my dad. Before my dad died, I mean." Mallory stood up, this was getting too personal and rejection was burning inside again, why did she push it? Why dredge up what was in the past? And, what good could come out of it, talking to Geoffrey, of all people?

"I forgot that, Mallory. I'm sorry about that." And, his eyes looked like he meant it as he continued, "But, at least *you* got to spend time with grandfather. I know he thought highly of you. He was always telling Dad that he was trying to convince you to join the business, but he said you were a maverick and he gave up trying to tame you a long time ago."

The comment didn't make sense to her. If Grandpa J felt that way, why did he continue to pressure her so much about joining him in his business? Saying one thing to them and something completely different to her? Nothing about that made any sense, except that the man was obsessed with control. And look where that got him.

A while later, as she stood on the front porch, she watched Geoffrey's car turn around the bend and then reappear for a moment before he passed through the Grandview Ranch gate and disappeared beyond the hill.

She had to admit, she was sorry to see Geoffrey leave. But she wasn't completely sure if it was because she wanted more of his company or less of her own. Left to her own devices, Mallory knew she would keep replaying his comment in her mind in a pointless attempt to reconcile it. And this pilot-light resentment she felt towards Grandpa J, this ever-present gnaw that seemed to burn low just under the surface, a resentment that was never quite extinguished, it was starting to really wear on her.

A cold breeze blew across the porch and shivering, Mallory pulled her coat closed over her chest, as she was reminded again how remote this house was. The mountains behind her, while teeming with life up close, stayed silent from this distance and the cattle in the pasture bordering the driveway were quiet today as well, they were too busy rooting out what they could find in the few patches of green that were still accessible between the tufts of white snow.

Grandview Ranch was owned by three brothers and managed by Rhett, the brother who lived nearby and took care of the house for Grandpa J. The brothers were a bit of a local legend, with stories a mile long of bear fights and bar fights, and they had the scars to substantiate most of the stories were not complete fabrications.

The house Grandpa J bought – this house – was their childhood home. The tale about the purchase of it, possibly embellished a bit, was that Grandpa J was in Jackson fifteen years ago, renting a place while he conducted his search for a mountain vacation home, and crossed paths with the brothers one summer evening.

While in Jackson, unlike in Minnesota, Grandpa J wasn't shy about living his life as JL McMichael, the renowned author and movie maker, possibly because the area had already seen its share of celebrities, and the locals were somewhat accustomed to sharing their beautiful city and mountains with outsiders.

One night, after making the acquaintance of the brothers during a local bar skirmish over the attention of a woman who was also the extramarital love interest of brother Marcus, the group of them returned to this house for a friendly game of pool (in some macho way to prove who was most deserving of the woman's attentions, according to Marcus's telling of the events afterwards.)

Grandpa J won the pool game. And, although he didn't believe the pool game swagger was anything more than too much whiskey and too much testosterone, he found the local woman's attention suddenly diverted to him nonetheless. He proceeded to date, then unceremoniously dumped, the woman and after a few more weeks of whiskey-laden nights that frequently ended in pool games, the brothers and Grandpa J became fast friends.

A few months later, when Marcus's marriage headed towards divorce and he wanted to divest quickly, Grandpa J convinced him to sell him the house and a portion of the ranch. Their friendship with the famous author added to the brothers' local legend, but for all its turbulent moments, Mallory knew that it was a true friendship - as evidenced by all three of the brothers, cowboy hats and all, attending Grandpa J's funeral in New York.

Mallory walked through the heavy double doors back inside into the cozy warmth of the living room and surveyed the open-layout, wood and leather Wyoming-styled home, recognizing that this would likely be the last time she would see it. Although she hadn't spent much time here, her memories of this place were mostly happy ones. Grandpa J was a different man, more real somehow, when he donned his cowboy hat and pulled on his boots.

While in Wyoming, he wrote a lot and spent many weeks at a time riding horses around the ranch and hiking in the mountains. On a whim suddenly, she walked down the expansive hallway over to a closet near the garage door, and glanced inside, looking for his snowshoes. Yup, there they were and alongside them were the other ones with the slightly smaller sized shoe openings- the shoes he bought her for Christmas the one winter break she spent here with him her senior year of high school.

That had been a good holiday break. She remembered it distinctly because by the time the next winter holiday break came around, he brushed her off again to Guillory's family, leaving her wondering just what she had ever done to make him dislike her so.

Further down the hallway, Grandpa J's study was cordoned off by a heavy white oak door on which was carved a strikingly beautiful scene of a Native American chief in full headdress atop a horse. As she pushed the door open, she noticed that his study was neat and rather empty. Inside the built-in cabinet on the north wall, Mallory found the safe that she was looking for.

After the disappointment of Beverly Hills, she didn't hold out much hope this safe would hold anything too exciting. And, besides, Geoffrey probably had the combination and had checked it already. If the entire novel was here, it was most likely in his hands now and that's the true reason he was rushing back home - to share it with his father.

Well, that's okay too, Mallory thought, already conceding defeat in her mind. Just as well, they would know better how to deal with it.

She gasped in surprise, however, when the safe opened. In it, she found rows of thousand-dollar packets of cash stacked at least ten high on the top shelf. There was easily over fifty thousand dollars here!

She knew her Grandpa J always kept some cash around him, but this amount surprised her, and obviously Geoffrey hadn't been able to open the safe because one would think he would have figured out some way to deposit this before leaving. After finding cash in Jasmine's L.A. home, now she would have to tell her Uncle Canton about finding cash in his home too. She would sure have some interesting confessions to make to them at some point.

The rest of the safe was empty except for some papers regarding the sale of the ranch and a few papers having to do with his investments and the sale of his Palm Beach house. Underneath the papers, she found three USBs. Why three, she wondered as she walked back to her rolling bag to retrieve her laptop. Now, finally, this could be interesting!

Just as her laptop was whirring to life, her cell phone buzzed with two texts and a voice mail notification, reminding her that cell service could be spotty in this area of the mountains.

Jasper's text asking if she planned to come home for Thanksgiving just annoyed her, she had already told him she would be in Minnesota.

Harris's text stating that a Remington was nothing to mess around with and to text him back if she was okay, made her smile and she promptly typed her reply–

No Worries, checking things out now.

The Colorado number on the voice mail was most likely Maggie Sherwood, confirming that Mallory was still planning the annual winter pilgrimage to her parents' hideaway outside Ouray, CO. The remote mountain cabin – her parents' utopia, now their final resting place where she had spread their ashes – along with a few photos and videos and a modest life insurance policy, was all she had left of her life with her parents.

Maggie, and her husband Don, the owners of three successful outfitters in the area, had grown close to Mallory's mother after they first gave her a retail sales job and eventually promoted her to manage their stores. It was in the Telluride store that her mother met her father. That fateful day, the handsome young drifter came in to purchase a pair of skis and left with the pretty shopkeeper's phone number.

Now, many years later, Maggie and Don still kept in touch with her. In exchange for the use of Mallory's mountain place for occasional hiking weekends, the Sherwoods kept the grounds up and the generator operational.

Her computer finally clicked open the USB - showing that it was blank. A wave of disappointment washed over her, and the hint of a headache accompanied the inner voice that was busy berating her - way to go, just how much money did you spend on this little adventure again?

The second USB had a few files on it marked PERSONAL and she hesitated before opening them, feeling guilty, even though Grandpa J was long past caring about who read his personal matters. She debated, would he put the novel in one of these files to hide it somehow? Overcoming her misgivings with a glance towards heaven in case he was up there somewhere watching her, she opened it.

But, all she found were statements recording his investments and some files that related to mundane legal work done on behalf of the movie studio.

Pinning her hopes on the third USB, she found no text files at all, they were all photos. Tons and tons of photos. Her breath caught, and her headache disappeared as she clicked through them, finding many of them were snippets of his life with her grandma that

Grandpa J must have digitized in recent years. The photos memorialized a life of laughter, adoring glances in random moments, sweet photos of beach sunsets and sunshine-dappled mountain hikes. And so entranced by the photos, she forgot her original mission and the renewed disappointment that none of the USBs had the novel on them.

Later that afternoon, Mallory drove the few miles over the ridge to Rhett's ranch house, and they enjoyed a beer together, sitting in the sunlight on his back deck which overlooked the most spectacular mountain stream. Rhett was one of those quintessential Wyoming ranchers, the type who found it more enjoyable to sit outside when company came over, even during the winter months. He said he'd much rather listen to the rushing stream and the birds that sat chirping in the lodgepole pines, than sit inside listening to the clocks tick. Unless it started snowing, then he'd make an exception.

They had a thoroughly enjoyable afternoon and evening, as he recounted numerous stories of her Grandpa J and the wild, sometimes hair-raising, times they had throughout the years. Mallory had heard some of these stories before, but many were new to her.

As she listened to all of these memories, and tried to picture her Grandpa J in them, she found herself feeling strangely distant; she *wanted* to be engaged in the conversation, mostly because she really liked Rhett, with his big, booming voice and his broad mustache and toothy smile, but still, as she drove back to Grandpa J's house after their dinner together, she felt disengaged. Like she wasn't fully present. This disjointed feeling was really starting to bother her. And, she wondered, when would she begin to feel normal again?

CHAPTER 14
... Holidays are often some of the most difficult days ...

Harris held the door to his kitchen open and Penny trotted past him from the garage into the dark, quiet house. Switching on the kitchen light reminded him that he needed to replace a bulb in one of his under-cabinet lights and in his mind he made a mental shopping list adding the other things he needed, like dog food, milk, coffee - but no other groceries - he didn't think he'd need to eat anything else for at least a week after the Thanksgiving dinner he'd just eaten at his parents' house.

Holidays were always a big deal for his mother, who would wake up before dawn putting the finishing touches on the preparations she had started days before. The table was always set just so, the dinner was always four or five courses, with coffee served in what she laughingly called her "parlor," which had a working fireplace and doubled as an office and music room.

Harris knew holiday dinners always ended there, not because it had a fireplace like his mom used for her rationale, but because it had the piano and no television to distract his father who liked to kick his stockinged feet up on the ottoman in their great room and watch old westerns on television if he had his way. But, they all indulged their mother's love of music on holidays, so after cleaning up the kitchen while she sat at the counter at their insistence, they would all "retire to the parlor" for a few songs and lots of laughs.

Coming back to his quiet house after a day like today always left him feeling a little empty inside. And today, especially so.

He had put himself out there, he knew it when he texted her, but it was as if he couldn't help himself, he had to ask Mallory to join them for Thanksgiving dinner. But, really, was he surprised by her lack of response?

Yes. He thought they had gotten past the potential she'd "ghost" him. You know, when someone you've been talking to somewhat regularly just, without warning, drops off the face of the planet. It hurt that she ignored his invitation and it hurt that she could so casually ignore him, even after he thought they had developed something of a friendship.

And, No. He admitted he wasn't completely surprised by her lack of response. He was beginning to wonder if Mallory was even capable of letting people get close to her. It was the most unnerving thing to watch her duck and dodge in conversations if they got too personal, and the walls of isolation she put up with other people were so obvious that he felt her pain, even though he couldn't understand it.

Shaking his head, both at his own naivety - who invites a girl you just met to your parents' house for Thanksgiving dinner? - and at her inability to accept the fact that some people (namely him) really liked her, he picked up the guitar that was leaning against the piano as he passed through the living room and walked out into his screen porch.

The past few days had been unseasonably warm and, even though it was early evening, the temperature was still in the high fifties. The snow that had covered his and Mike's lawns a few days ago, had almost all disappeared already. Taking advantage of the anomaly of a warm evening so late in November, he sat down and started strumming, his only audience his dog Penny, who eventually strolled in and laid down, her chin resting on his left foot, promptly falling asleep.

He would often play randomly, letting his mind wander, just talking to Jesus about various things, but tonight after playing for a few minutes, one of the songs that he had written with Mike came to mind.

The first night of their collaboration happened a couple of months ago, when the two of them were sitting together out here in the screen porch. After grilling some burgers that night, they were just hanging out talking while a Twins game played in the other room. Mike had asked him to play something on the guitar, and after a few popular songs, Harris started picking the tune that had been playing around in the back of his mind all afternoon. It was a rhythmic, quiet riff, kind of pretty in its lilting way, but he didn't think it was all that special. Mike instantly connected with the random bars and asked what it was.

"Nothing really, just something in my head." Harris remembered he was self-conscious playing it for him then, because he'd noticed it. Because he'd liked it.

When he tried to switch to another song, Mike shook his head, crinkled his eyes at him when he smiled and said firmly, "No, Harris. Go back to that other one. There must be more."

So, feeling a little embarrassed, but also secretly pleased, he played the guitar and hummed the melody through to the end of the passage, until there was nothing else left.

"I love it!" Mike smiled enthusiastically when Harris stopped playing, his eyes dancing electrically, "Have you written lyrics yet?"

"Ahh, no. I don't have the gift. I can barely cobble together a sentence, in case you haven't noticed." Harris said as he laughed at Mike's excitement. He knew Mike enjoyed poetry and loved to read, but still, he was surprised by his intensity.

"Well, I would be honored to take a stab at it," He sat forward in his chair, he hands on his knees, as if he wanted to dig in right that very moment, "If you're ok with that, of course."

"Sure, be my guest, Mike. Write away." He'd laughed at the notion, making light of it in his mind and even thought derisively about the semi-retired hotel manager's attempt to write song lyrics, I'm sure this will be interesting.

Looking back now, he shouldn't have doubted Mike's ability; the lyrics he wrote fit the melody perfectly. It soon became evident that Mike had the uncanny genius to turn words around on a dime, link them together with striking clarity, giving voice to the internal musings of the soul.

As he sat here now, strumming the tune for that first song they wrote together, Harris wondered, if he'd only known who he was dealing with – if he'd known who Mike really was - how would this moment, this memory, have been altered?

He started humming the opening bars, and he fought back tears at the memory of Mike first lacing together the heart-wrenching lyrics for this song:

As I look into that mirror
At the reflection of who I am
It becomes clear that I am longing
For the innocent boy, not the man

I can only see what I've done
All the pain and the sorrow
Hurt is the mark of yesterday
It devours today and tomorrow

This is how I see me
This is who I am
I cannot see it differently
This is who I am

But You say that mirror is broken
You tell me that I am free
You hold my hand in yours
And tell me that You love me
No matter what I've done
No matter what I've said
You say that I am Yours
And that you've always loved me

Mallory stood frozen in spot outside his window, the dampness of the water-soaked ground permeating the thin soles of her suede boots. Just then a cool breeze shifted the dogwood bushes alongside Harris's house and startled her so much she nearly gasped aloud. Giving away her position - lurking here in the flower bed next to his screen porch - would be very embarrassing, and she didn't know what kind of logical excuse she could even concoct to explain it.

Why *was* she here anyway, creeping outside his window in some kind of semi-hypnotic state, entranced by his music? Hadn't she already done enough damage to whatever friendship they had been building?

She had eagerly kept him up to date on the progress, and disappointments of her trip, even confessing to him that finding the trove of pictures on the last USB in Jackson provided a ray of redemption on the otherwise futile trip.

She had taken Geoffrey's offer and stayed those extra few days at the ranch, and, when the only return flights available were on Thanksgiving morning, it hadn't bothered her in the least. After all, aside from Guillory's family in New York, she didn't have any family celebrations to attend anyway.

His text invitation had come so unexpectedly, she didn't know what to do or how to react. Even though she knew that he only invited her as a friend, she felt a cold protective shield of indifference take over inside of her. A dinner with his whole family? To become more connected to people that she wouldn't ever see again after she sold this house? What did he want from her?

He was so unexpected. Everything about him...he just didn't fit her constructs of what men were like. He was just so *different*.

So, feeling all weird and awkward about it, she had walked over here to offer some kind of apology. But now all she could do was stand here listening as he repeated the song, the words filtering through the screen and out over his yard.

And, the words of that song though. Something about the words of that song stirred things inside her too, making her legs feel wobbly, like she was standing on uneven ground.

This was too much. *He was too much.* Time to go, she would apologize some other time. Maybe then she would know what to say.

She turned and trying her best not to step on any twigs to blow her cover, or in any puddles left by the melting snow, she walked across the yard. Back over to Grandpa J's house, to her forgotten house.

CHAPTER 15
... I am not suited for this job, you will need to find someone else ...

A blank canvas, that's what it was. A massive white, soul-less, 8.5" x 11" wilderness that measured as far as the eye could see and the mind could imagine. And, panic. Racing heart, unnerving sweats and a tension headache blinding her from deep within her skull, suddenly shooting ice picks through her eyeballs.

Mallory squeezed her eyes shut so she wouldn't have to look at the paltry few paragraphs on page one of The Final Chapter and pushed away her laptop in frustration, heaving her thousandth heavy sigh. Rationalizing to herself that the last few dry, uninspired days must be due to her "writing routines," today she had started with some different music.

But, unfortunately, jazz wasn't any better than indie rock at inspiring her. She had tried not lighting a fire today, equating coziness with laziness, but all she got for it were some cold toes and slightly numb fingertips. And, tea instead of coffee ... well, she had never understood, nor appreciated, the supposed health benefits of tea. She would choose a strong cup of Columbian java over green tea any day.

Since her return to Minnesota on Thanksgiving, she had tried to attack the novel from every angle she could think of. She had tried envisioning Grandpa J sitting here, at his desk, writing it. But she would get distracted by the view outside, and once actually found herself tracing some rather interesting animal tracks in the recent light dust of snow, the tracks leading in a zigzag pattern from her back patio until they ended down near the stream under a bunch of broken branches and cat tails. But, alas, at the end of the trail, she didn't find an animal. So, while she was immensely grateful for the distraction, it was a complete waste of time.

She tried writing elaborate character profiles, using the previous novels as her basis. And then, in her mind, she tried layering them into what she knew was predestined to happen in this third novel. But, that didn't work either. It was just a lot of noise. It didn't help her move them to action, they didn't come alive.

So, she tried writing an outline of the chapters, thinking she could bluff her way through it, just get them busy living. But they stayed dead. And the page...well, it was still blank.

Erasing the few paragraphs with the swipe of her delete key, she closed her laptop and reached for her phone. The missing chapters weren't going to be written today. Not even a word was going to be written today. Ughh.

She knew it wasn't right. It wasn't fair. Actually, it was borderline mean, but she dialed Jasper's number anyway, telling herself she wasn't using him as a crutch, she really missed hearing his voice.

"Hey, Jas. How's your Sunday going?"

"Hi, hon. Everything is great here, I'm just heading out to meet father at the club for lunch. But, you don't sound so great. Are you feeling okay?"

"Not really so great. I'm stuck on something I'm writing, thought I'd call you for a little distraction."

"Ahh, I see how it is. Come on, you can admit it. You miss me." He laughed a low chuckle into the phone, "I'm like your - what do they call it - oh yeah, I'm your muse, right?"

"If it makes you feel better, you can think that." Mallory laughed, but it came out weak, she knew better. Even if he was an inspiration to her, it was unlikely to be enough to help her out of her current predicament.

"I missed having you with me at Thanksgiving, Mallory. Mum says hello, by the way. And, she wants to know if she can count on you to help with the gala again this year? She said she emailed you the details for your table, but you didn't respond." He paused, making it obvious that he agreed, that she was seriously lacking in proper etiquette.

For several years already, Mallory had worked alongside Jasper's mother Katharine, and various others, raising funds in support of inner-city childhood literacy. Katharine had always enjoyed the celebrity appeal, and the generous donation, that Grandpa J brought to their gala event through Mallory's involvement. But, this year, Grandpa J was gone, and Mallory knew that the cache he lent to it, and the affluent donor friends, would be gone. Sorry to say, she just didn't have too many $10,000-per-chair friends to fill her ten-person table.

"Mallory," Jasper continued, thankfully not caring enough to wait for her response, "I know I sound like a broken record, but when are you just going to come home so we can move on with our lives?"

"I am moving on with my life, Jas. This is my life." She paused, working up the argument inside her mind, ready for the debate.

"Well, I hope you're finding whatever it is you're looking for. Because while you're out there in the woods in Minnesota, I'm still here, waiting for you to come home. I miss you, I love you and I just want you home."

He paused again, and Mallory heard the car door pinging and the sudden quiet as he closed it behind him. She pictured him in her mind, the picture so clear she felt like she was next to him in the secure warmth of his newest luxury sedan. Jasper was central to her world back there, as cool and comfortable as a life could be, right? And, mostly, when she was with him, she felt his sincerity, even though it was often obscured by his wandering eyes, and sometimes it felt a bit needy, his dependence on her.

"Okay," he continued, "I will stop groveling now. But, please tell me that you're coming back for Christmas. I want us to talk. Really talk, Mallory. About our future."

It felt good to be wanted again, she realized as she gazed up at the rough-hewn beams of the living room ceiling above her, focusing on the many gouges and imperfections in the wood. A little like her life - very imperfect.

"Yes," she found herself replying, "I will be back for Christmas. And, yes, Jasper, we can talk about our future then."

Later that day, it started to snow again. By evening, they had gotten at least 4" and her walkway was completely covered. Bored out of her mind by a totally engrossing, but unproductive, Sunday watching HGTV on her streaming service, Mallory opened the door to the garage in search of the snow shovel. Certainly, Grandpa J must have one somewhere in here. He couldn't have expected Harris to shovel his walk for him too, could he?

She found the shovel hanging on the wall next to the black Jeep that she had discovered the day after she arrived. Pleasantly surprised to find it, she had tried to think of a way to use the Jeep, but the nearest rental car return for the service she had booked was in a town over an hour away. So, she decided it made the most sense to return her car when she left for Colorado next week and take an Uber back out here when she returned from her trip.

Just because she was curious, she opened the door, and noticed there weren't any keys in the ignition or under the floor mat and made a mental note to search around the house for them.

Later, after she finished shoveling the walk and the driveway, she pulled off her mittens, blowing on her frozen fingers. After fumbling with the lighter, she finally got a fire crackling and poked around the house looking for his car keys, but to no avail. The thought of asking Harris if he had them had come to mind at least twenty times and each time it did, she searched harder, hoping that she wouldn't be forced to ask him.

Finally, she admitted defeat and picked up her phone to text him. But, what to write? Do I just ignore the fact that the last time we communicated, he asked me to Thanksgiving with his family? And, I – like some immature little brat – just ignored him? Oh, just get over it! Call him.

The phone rang twice before he picked up.

"Hey, Harris. It's me Mallory, your next-door neighbor." Really? That's the best you can do? She rolled her eyes and looked out the window towards his house, with its friendly lit windows and puffs of smoke coming from his chimney.

"Yes, I know. How's it going, Mallory? Do you need something?" He was keeping this very cordial, she thought.

"Well, yes, actually. I was wondering if you knew where my grandfather kept the keys for his Jeep?"

"Oh. Sorry. He had asked me to bring it in for a recall notice on something, but I forgot. You know, with everything going on. It's ok to drive though and I have the keys here. I can bring them over if you want."

"No, that's okay. I can come over there if you're home."

"Sure, of course, just come on over."

As she neared his front door, Mallory worked through her apology in her mind. Just be cool about it, admit you are a moron and tell him that you struggle with meeting new people. Well, that's not really true, don't say that. You know you enjoy meeting new people. Okay, the truth is, you struggle with meeting new people who are exceedingly nice. Well, actually, you struggle with meeting new people who are the *parents* of exceedingly nice guys. As in, this nice guy standing in front of you.

"Hello, neighbor." His hair was a comfortably messy, and he was wearing a white thermal-knit long sleeve t-shirt and faded blue jeans that fit him just right. She looked down at his feet encased in leather moccasin slippers, just like her dad used to wear. There he is again, she thought - being all likeable like that - and his small, teasing smile said that, on some level, he must know how stupid she felt.

"Okay, I'm just going to apologize straight up." Mallory felt the momentum of thoughts coming out of her mouth, "I don't know why I didn't respond to your invitation. Of course, it was very kind of you to invite me to your family's Thanksgiving." She sighed dramatically, frustrated with trying to explain it when she didn't know how. "Harris, I'm just not good with families. What I mean is, I'm basically socially awkward with normal, well-adjusted, loving families. I guess I just haven't had any practice."

"No need to apologize. You don't do families. Got it." He opened the door further, the grin widening into a full smile, "But, are you okay with just me? Want to come inside or I could leave you standing on the porch, whichever makes you feel more secure?"

That night, her visit to pick up the Jeep keys turned into watching a Sunday night football game, but soon they were talking, and he switched the television to a music channel, so she could tell him about her trip to California and Wyoming.

While she shared her frustrations about not finding the novel, and her concerns that her aunt and uncle would wonder what she was doing rummaging around their houses, he just nodded and smiled, telling her not to worry, he was sure it would work out.

When she shared her frustrations about the daunting writer's block she was having, he just nodded and smiled, telling her he was sure it would work out. She found herself wondering, does this guy ever freak out about anything? Why does he always have that serene smile drifting around his mouth?

A few hours flew by and, in the end, she agreed to have Harris keep the keys and bring the Jeep into the garage for its repairs this next week since she had a rental anyway.

Still, she was glad that she had come over to see him, things felt resolved again between them. She walked home that evening with her spirits feeling lighter than they had in days, thinking, *now there's a nice guy.* And, while they might not be a dying breed in Minnesota, in her world, they were almost extinct.

CHAPTER 16

"Yeah, see you two later, have fun!" Harris shifted the knit stocking cap down further on Peyton's head and fist bumped his mitten as the boy followed Paul out the door for a Saturday shopping trip in search of a Christmas gift for Carissa.

But before he leapt up into the backseat of Paul's truck, Peyton stopped in his tracks and swung around to face Harris with a warning scowl on his little face, "Now, remember, uncle Harris, she doesn't know what we're doing, don't tell her our secret!" Paul threw a knowing look towards Harris and laughed as he hoisted Peyton up into the booster seat.

"Don't worry about him, bud." Paul said as he strapped him in, "He's a steel trap, she won't get anything out of your Uncle Harris." Paul leaned in and kissed the boy's cheek before saying, "Now. If you're worried about her getting our secret out of anyone, you should be worried about me. She knows she can get anything she wants out of me."

Harris laughed at the startled, worried expression in Peyton's eyes, but Paul quickly told him, "Don't worry, bud, just teasing you...I got your back."

Harris closed the office door behind them, reminded again how Carissa and Peyton had filled up his brother's life in so many ways.

Harris remembered a time when Paul seemed almost listless, no real direction in his life, getting in and out of relationships with women so often, his parents became concerned.

Even while Paul was searching though, Harris was always confident that someday he would find a very special someone that would understand him, and accept his laid back, casual approach to living life. Carissa, with her wise presence and loving spirit, was the perfect fit for his brother. And, Peyton...well, that little boy had captured his whole family's heart immediately. Now, no one could conceive of life without the two of them in the family.

Just as he was sitting back down at his desk to review next month's orders, he heard the office door open again. Moving his roller chair over and glancing around the door, he was surprised to see Carissa with her arms full of fabric samples. Wow, she just missed them, Harris thought, although it probably wouldn't have mattered, she most likely already knew what they're up to today. Somehow, mothers always knew these things.

'Hi Carissa, so you've decided on a fabric for that ottoman of yours?"

"Yes, I had to wait to come over here until the boys were gone. You know, I'm not supposed to know what they're doing today, but I suspect it has something to do with buying me a Christmas gift?" She smiled as she pulled off her scarf and unzipped her ski jacket. Harris shrugged noncommittally and laughed when she jabbed his arm.

"Hey," he replied, "Don't interrogate me for information! I've been sworn to silence by the little man."

"Ha, ha. Okay, fine." She smoothed out one of the rich, denim and chenille damask swatches. "This is the one, it's heavenly and so unique!"

"Oh, good. That's a nice one and it will look great with your leather sectional, especially with those leather accents along the bottom of the ottoman." Harris picked up the fabric swatch and laid it over a leather swatch that was similar to the leather in Carissa's ottoman.

"That's what Paul said too. You and your brother are so good at this." She turned away, looking at the empty coffee pot sitting over in the kitchen area. "Do you mind if I make some coffee? I didn't have any at my house this morning and I'm dying for a cup."

"Be my guest, I could use a cup too."

A few minutes later, as she poured them both a cup of coffee, Carissa asked with a knowing smile, "So, have you seen much of your neighbor lately?"

"Yes," Harris tried to reply casually, thinking over the past week and the almost-daily occasions where Mallory stopped over or he dropped in on her, "I've seen her around. Why?"

"Oh, no specific reason. I'm just curious. You know, you mentioned that you asked her to come to Thanksgiving dinner, but then...well, I was just wondering."

"Yeah, I think that invitation really spooked her. She's just...well, she's just a little skittish about people. But, she's alright." Harris looked past Carissa's shoulder, out the window towards the little stone house where Mallory probably sat right now writing the missing chapters, or at least she was trying to write them.

"Harris, come on. You can be honest with me. There's something there between you two, it's obvious to us. Can't you see it?"

"Oh." He squinted at Carissa, suddenly finding it difficult to focus on her face.

Had he really considered what was happening with Mallory? No. He hadn't really acknowledged it, even to himself. All he knew was that he enjoyed seeing her, he felt *buoyant* around her somehow, he felt another level of purpose again, excited about the future. But, was Carissa correct? Had he started down that path – the one where he gave everything – without even realizing it? The debate he was having with himself must have been written all over his face.

"Yeah, Harris." Carissa nodded sagely over her coffee cup and when he stayed silent – standing there in a stupor, thinking over the situation – she put down her cup and patted his forearm reassuringly. "It's obvious. And, it's about time, God knows it's your turn."

"But, this can't be the same thing." He searched Carissa's face, in some way trying to talk himself out of something that could prove dangerous. He didn't even know Mallory and she had another guy in her life. This wasn't *that*, what Carissa was thinking, this wasn't at all what he knew from before. "With Jackie –"

"Harris, please don't even finish that thought. These past few years, we've watched you compare every relationship, every woman, to Jackie." She shook her head slowly as she held his gaze, "You know that's not fair."

"I know. You're right. But, what I mean is, with Jackie, I just knew. We both knew. It was obvious we were into each other right away."

He looked at the house, almost wishing she'd walk outside right now, maybe it would be clearer to him how he felt if he could see her. He shook his head sadly as he looked back at his sister-in-law, "I don't know, Carissa. This feels different. Mallory is - well, she's broken."

"And that frightens you?"

"No," He replied quickly, before he thought about it, but then recognized it wasn't that simple, "Well, yeah, I guess it does a little. She's very complex. It seems like she's haunted by things, and people, in her past. I don't know, it's hard to explain."

"Well, if you ask me, I think it has to do with the loss she's experienced in her life. Imagine losing your parents when you're fourteen, you're an only child and you don't have any family to help you through it. She had to navigate it all on her own. Makes me sad just to think about it."

"I know. She doesn't talk about it though. She closes up real tight when the conversation even gets close to that. And Mike told me - even though he felt he had a lot to be regretful for in his life - his biggest regret was with Mallory and not helping her recover from the loss of her parents."

They sat in silence for a moment until Carissa spoke up suddenly, "Harris, do you ever wonder why God brought Mike here?"

"No, I guess I haven't thought about it, why?"

"What if it's for Mallory? And, you might be part of the story too."

"I guess you've lost me -"

"I'd be willing to bet that Mallory hasn't ever really grieved the loss of her parents, or the loss of her grandfather. She probably has never really shared how any of it makes her feel. With another person, I mean. She probably hasn't allowed anyone close enough to share that."

"Well, there is that other guy she's mentioned, you know, the one in Baltimore." Harris noticed his jaw tightened just thinking about this other guy and the thought of "how close" she felt to him made him a little queasy.

"Yeah, maybe." Carissa nodded and took another sip of her coffee, clearly lost in thought, pondering "God's plans."

As far as Harris was concerned, however, even if she was right about Mallory never grieving these losses with another person, it was unlikely that Mallory would ever let her guard down enough to share it with him.

CHAPTER 17

Whew – see what he has to say about this! – Mallory thought with satisfaction as she sent her last email of the day to Bradford that Saturday evening. She had written enough on-line catalogue copy to meet his requests for at least a month. In fact, Bradford had been so impressed, that he sent her some social media projects for two additional clients and she was so energized that she finished them up today instead of waiting to send them to him on Monday as he requested. She wanted to get as much work done as possible because, in a few days, she would be leaving for Colorado and internet service was sketchy at best in the mountains.

As she hung up the Skype call with Bradford, where they celebrated her productivity with a glass of red wine, she realized that she was starting to miss her friends back home. Her other friends from work were busy with their lives and Bradford had told her he was planning a night out with his new girlfriend – the one that came as a two-for-one deal when he took home a new dog from the animal rescue center where she worked.

Mallory reminded him that he didn't like dogs. He laughingly replied, you never know what you'd do for love, until it's too late. She'd laughed along with him, but inside she thought, I've never done anything like that for love … and the realization left her sad.

She was sad much of the time lately, when she thought about it. It was becoming clearer to her everyday how *generally sad* she was. Why this fact was more evident here in Minnesota than anywhere else, completely stymied her. Maybe it was the solitude, these endless days of early winter ... soft snow, then shimmering sunlight, then drifting snow, followed by brilliant sunlight again. The crackling fire in Grandpa J's fireplace, the comforting sounds of people coming and going from Harris's shop up the street. All of it made for a sleepy, dream-like world, a world completely set apart from the other world that she knew was living just outside of this bubble. And, it lulled her to sleep.

In this world, in this comfortable dream bubble, she was able to write. In fact, she was an accomplished writer, just like Grandpa J expected her to be. The words flowed with abandon, sometimes so fast her fingers couldn't keep up with the bubbling stream.

And, the characters. They were real - so real she could touch them - she could feel them from the inside out. She had to slow down to paint them for the reader in all their complexity, but she was able to do it. And, when she would review what she had written, it was a - well, it was a masterpiece. Something like Grandpa J would have written.

There. She wrote it, the novel was done. The End.

And, even though she made those keystrokes with bated breath, she had a shy smile of satisfaction on her face. Everything was as it should be. It was complete. Now, she could show him, and she knew inside her very soul how pleased he would be. He would tell her how sorry he was for saying those things before and how he loved her unconditionally because she was a part of him. He would admit his faults and she would forgive him. Who was perfect, after all? He was her grandfather, part of her dad.

And the dream that brimmed with warm accomplishment gave way to a memory, somewhat less idyllic.

◆ ◆ ◆

2015, Spring

She pushed open the double doors of the upper East side restaurant, after skirting Central Park for a few blocks, and scanned the room for them, finding Guillory, Suzanne and Grandpa J seated at their favorite table by the window. She breezed past the hostess with a confident swagger, "I see who's waiting for me."

As she neared the white clothed table, she found herself so excited she could barely feel her feet hit the ground. They were there to celebrate her, after all. She had a college degree and had accomplished what she set her heart on!

"I'm ready, Grandpa J. I'm ready to do this!" He was facing away from her, so she touched his shoulder from behind in her excitement, not even recognizing the strained smiles on Guillory's and Suzanne's faces. "I got the job! I'm moving to Baltimore!"

She knew it was a bit demonstrative for him that she touched him, especially in a public place, and she felt a bit out on a limb because she usually didn't invade his personal space, but certainly, this was an exception.

He turned then, slowly, his head bobbing irrationally, as if he couldn't focus on who the ill-mannered, annoying fan could be that would so outrageously interrupt his private lunch.

"Well, there you are, you little ingrate. It's about time you get here, seems like we've been waiting here for hours. Why are we here again, anyway?" He swayed back to face Guillory for clarification, but Guillory's eyes were locked on Mallory and he was shaking his head slightly, that same familiar look that said, he's gone, nothing can change this now, best to just keep the peace.

"We're here to celebrate Mallory's graduation and the exciting news that she has to share with us." Suzanne patted Grandpa J's arm lightly, like one would do with an elderly person with severe dementia, trying to coax him back to this world and the people who were trying to live a reasonably pleasant life in it.

"Yes," Guillory found his voice and pulled out a chair next to him, patting the seat for her, "Mallory, please sit down and tell us all about this exciting news."

She did as she was told; she didn't try to defend herself. She followed instructions because that's just what you did. It was no use fighting, he always won. He was in control of the people around him, including her. But, as Guillory and Suzanne looked at her expectantly, she was lost somewhere in her mind, searching for that feeling, the one of two moments ago, the one that felt something close to happy, where had that feeling gone?

"I'm sorry, I didn't realize that I was late." She offered, but Guillory shook his head again, trying to communicate with his eyes, but she didn't understand what he was saying.

"Well, anyway, yes." She mumbled her exciting news, "I have a job. It's in Baltimore, I have an apartment lined up, and I start next week."

Tentatively, she looked from Guillory and Suzanne and then over to Grandpa J. He was slipping from his chair slightly, one leg half dragging on the floor and his expensive looking sweater pulling off his shoulder haphazardly. With her statement, he turned a fiery gaze on her, not even trying to hide the disdain in his bloodshot blue eyes.

"What did you say? You took a job with someone else? After all I've done for you, that's how you treat me?"

He reached for his drink tumbler, which was empty except for some melting, watery ice cubes. Frowning, he turned around searching for a waiter as if he had capsized in high seas and was in desperate search of a life preserver. One suddenly appeared, of course. The wait staff knew Grandpa J well at this restaurant. Soon the young man had another fresh vodka at the ready, whisking the offensive empty one away without a word.

"It's in advertising, Grandpa J, not publishing. You remember." She said it, knowing she had told him about her plans a few months before graduation, but was sure he wouldn't really remember. It was her way of hurting him, making him feel less than iconic, if just for a moment. "It's what I want to do."

"I don't give a damn what you *want* to do. You owe me –" Grandpa J took a long drink from the iced tumbler, and then focused his gaze on her, the bloodshot blue eyes suddenly narrowed and burning with intensity, her heart stopped beating for a moment in the blinding intensity of those eyes.

"Mallory, you are no better than your father. He was an entitled little brat too, sometimes I wondered whose son he really was - NO!" He pounded his glass and his palm on the table, looking at no one in particular, when Guillory tried to silence him, "I'm going to tell her, someone has to tell her."

He focused on her again and spit out his words, *"Don't you understand? You owe me.* You would be one sorry, lost, little *nobody* if I hadn't stepped in to take you when those parents of yours were so careless, and utterly stupid, getting themselves killed like that. Who would choose to live in Colorado anyway, and raise a child there, in the backwoods mountains, of all places? When I wanted to give him everything. *Everything*, Mallory! He could have had all I had."

Grandpa J slurred into a hiccup and stopped then, long enough to take a drink, long enough for Mallory to secure in her heart that she hated him. If ever she felt the seething, boiling notion called hatred, it was at that moment and it was directed towards the only living person that she knew that shared her bloodline. Well, they may be blood-related, but in no other way did she share anything in common with this worthless piece of human flesh.

"Well, now, JL," Suzanne spoke up quietly, trying to instill peace over the eruption, "You know you don't mean these things. Mallory, please. Your grandfather-"

"Don't speak for me, Suzanne. I know exactly what I'm saying, and she knows I mean every word. He used me - your father - he used me just like you're planning to use me. You don't care about me either, I can see it in your eyes. I've always seen it in your eyes. So, if that's the way you want it - just go, be on with your life, on your own. See if I care, you ungrateful stupid twit."

He turned in his chair, and for a moment he paused. Mallory wondered, as stunned as she was, would he apologize for this latest tirade? But, then he stood up unsteadily, and taking his glass with him, he headed for the doors, his shock of thick white hair disappearing amongst the people on the busy Saturday sidewalk outside.

They sat in stunned silence, Guillory, Suzanne and her. The tears that were coming down her cheeks felt like hot acid and the tightness in her throat was suffocating. She knew that Guillory was saying something to her and Suzanne had moved over to the chair Grandpa J had just vacated and she was trying to pull her into a hug, but Mallory pushed her away, feeling the drowning sensation that had overcome her before on many occasions. She needed air. NOW.

She wound through the people waiting for a table in the foyer, and pushed the double doors open, gasping for air. She had no clear destination in mind when she reached the sidewalk, just anywhere that was the opposite of where her grandfather was. If she was to continue living, she had to stay as far away from him as she could possibly get.

◆ ◆ ◆

The painful memory scorched her and her subconscious valiantly took over, protectively softening the edges, blurring them back into her dream as she thought, Perhaps, she could just get on that streetcar, sitting there on Park Ave. Funny, she didn't recall ever seeing streetcars in New York before. Maybe she could just ride this streetcar to Baltimore and start her new life?

The bell was ringing, and she could see the smiling, laughing passengers on it through the half-open windows. Yes, that's what she'd do. But, she didn't have any money! She searched in her purse and thought, maybe I have some money in my pockets? But, she noted in horror, she was wearing her yoga pants, why was she wearing yoga pants for this graduation celebration lunch? Maybe that's why Grandpa J was so disappointed in her, she never did know quite what to wear, or what to say, or what to do. Yes, that's why he was so disgusted with her all the time. And the bell on the streetcar just kept ringing, they were waiting for her ....

CHAPTER 18

Mallory sat up, startled, in a panic, where was she? This wasn't her apartment in Baltimore. She pushed her feet off the ottoman, searching for the cell phone that was furiously ringing and vibrating against her thigh. As the fog of the dream cleared, she answered her phone, groggily looking at the time that blinked on her laptop sitting open next to her in the oversized chair. Wow, 9:34 pm! That glass of wine earlier must have relaxed her so much she fell sound asleep.

"Mallory? This is your Uncle Canton. Is it a bad time for me to call?" His voice sounded very far away, and his phone was crackling, like he had bad reception.

"Ah, no, it's fine." She pushed her hair out of her eyes, trying to wake up. "I can hardly hear you though."

"Yes, sorry, the reception isn't always good here, we're at Lake George visiting some friends this weekend." Despite her trepidation about his obvious reason for calling, she had to smile at his comment. Even her Uncle Canton had friends that he hung out with and she tried to picture him in some primitive cabin on Lake George on the edge of the Adirondacks, but she was reasonably sure he would only have friends that owned a multimillion-dollar mansion. It would certainly come complete with a swimming pool, for those who just couldn't handle the fact that live creatures made their home in lake water.

"Mallory, I wanted to talk to you about something. I understand that you've recently visited your grandfather's homes in L.A. and Wyoming. Of course, your Aunt Jasmine and I understand that you've lived in these homes while father was alive, so you probably have attachments to them, maybe you have personal items stored there. If you wanted to retrieve any of those things, we could have made arrangements for you." He paused, the scolding tone of his voice coming through loud and clear, even with the poor cell phone reception.

"Well, yes, I'm sorry I didn't clear it with you first." Inside, her conscience was burning with guilt. Even though she didn't find anything of consequence in either of the houses, and in fact, her house had the most revealing find of them all, she still felt like she owed them this secret. This novel was so much more theirs than hers.

"What's done is done, I suppose. Did you find what you were looking for?" He left the question hanging in the air, just waiting for her to tell him.

This was her chance to be rid of this burden. But, instead of a clear way ahead, it seemed murky. There was still something she had to do, she just wished she knew how.

"No, I didn't find anything. But, I guess I don't really know what I was looking for."

"I'm sorry to hear that, Mallory." He paused, as if searching for the right words, "We are all dealing with his death in our own way,

I guess. Now that he's left us, we see clearly his ubiquitous influence. He was simply - everything - to us."

She didn't know if by *us* he meant his wife and children, or her Aunt Jasmine, or Guillory or any of the hundreds of people who had worked for Grandpa J, all who must have had a completely different experience with him than she had. Again, the fact that she stood on the outside of that group of people was starkly evident as the dredges of her dream gnawed at her. And the memory of her "college celebration" lunch almost three years ago, yes, she wished that had been a nightmare, but, in fact, it was very real.

Without much more to say, a few minutes later, they hung up. He didn't ask about a potential novel and she didn't share anything about finding one. But, it was becoming clearer in her mind every day. She would share it with him. Soon, she would share it with him.

The following Monday morning, after making an appointment with the real estate agent she had chosen to sell the house, Mallory spent the morning washing windows and cleaning the upstairs which had become dusty from nonuse. As she dusted the quirky chandelier with its ornate burnished gold metal appendages and glass droplets, she wondered if Grandpa J ever even stepped foot up here the last months he was alive.

After finishing the chandelier, she took a rest on the top rung of the step ladder, and looked around the cozy bedroom with its simple, wrought iron single bed and antique, robin's egg blue armoire. She had to admit, for all the pain she experienced that first summer with Grandpa J, there were some good memories in this house too.

For instance, she remembered one night when Grandpa J stretched out beside her on her quilt covered bed and told her about his parents, and that he was adopted. And, about how he knew, even as a child, that he would be a writer. From an early age, he told her with a hesitant, half-smile, he created entire worlds in his head, full of people, places and adventure - he was certain all he had to do was live long enough to write them all down.

She remembered long rainy afternoons where she would lie on her bed and he would sit in the cushioned rocking chair over there by the window and they would both devour books for hours on end. Sometimes, he would read aloud from the novel in his lap and he would ask her what she thought of various passages. Offering his accolades and criticisms, he would point out the nuances that she had missed. With time, it became clear to her that nobody lived and breathed for the written word like Grandpa J.

She also remembered the first painful attempts she made to talk about her parents' death with him, her way of trying to make sense of the senseless tragedy, now that a few months had gone by and the acute pain had passed somewhat. With each attempt, however, he would block her out. At first it was with stern looks and stoic replies about needing to "move on, let them lie in peace." Gradually, it became ambivalent indifference saying things like he "didn't have any answers, so stop looking to him to provide them."

As those first weeks passed, she noticed that he started drinking more regularly, and in her fourteen-year-old mind, it seemed his need for alcohol coincided with these conversations. When the grief about her parents would overcome her, she would remove herself, get out of the house for a walk or hang out upstairs in her bedroom, hoping that if she didn't talk about the dark sadness anymore - if she didn't force him to dwell on the loss of his son - the drinking would stop. She was wrong.

Mallory hefted the water bucket into the shop sink in the garage, watching as the gray water drained away. There would be a lot more cleaning to do before she was done, but finishing the upstairs was a really good start. She had the simple white curtains and cotton sheets in the washer, she had shaken out the down comforter, and the colorful quilt that laid atop it was drying next to the fireplace.

Now everything would smell fresh when the real estate agent came by tomorrow for the initial walk-through. Hopefully, the agent could find a nice young couple who wanted a starter home out here in the woods, next to the stream. Mallory really wanted Harris to have good neighbors.

Thinking of Harris, she wanted to find out when the Jeep would be done. Somehow, she would need to return her rental car when she flew out to Colorado, but how would she get back here, well over two hours away from the airport, when she returned? If she could manage that, she would use the Jeep until the house sold, possibly just driving it back to Baltimore with some of Grandpa J's books and personal items. Unfortunately, she would have to sell the house furnished, leaving her favorite Harris Original chair next to the fireplace. Even if she could afford to have it, and the other furniture, moved, none of it would fit in her small apartment.

She'd better check with Harris on when that Jeep would be done at the garage and noting that it was a beautiful sunny day, and she could use a break, she thought she'd walk over and see what the brothers were up to today.

"Hi, Mallory." Paul turned in his office chair, away from his computer as she opened the door to their shop, "Sorry, but Harris is upstairs working on an order that has to ship today. I can let him know you're here though-" He picked up his cell phone as if to call him.

"No, that's okay. I was just wondering if he heard back from his mechanic friend on the Jeep. He didn't give me the guy's number."

"Yeah, he heard from him this morning. Turns out it won't be ready until late next week, something about waiting for parts."

"Okay." She bit her lip, she was unaccustomed to being so far away from conveniences like airports with no ready means of transportation, "Well, I will be in Colorado for a couple of days next week anyway ... so no worries. I'll just return the rental and take an Uber out here from the airport when I get back."

"Well, you could try that. I thought Harris told me you just got back from a trip?" Paul hit the send button on a file and turned, giving her his full attention.

"Yes, I did. He probably told you about the quest I've been on?"

"He just said that you were taking care of some business that Mike - I mean JL - left unfinished."

"Ha, that's right, just a little unfinished business." She paused, reflecting on the thought that he had kept her secret private, even from his brother. "And, it's okay to call him Mike. That's his real name."

"Ah ha, yes, that's right. Did Mike have a house in Colorado too?"

"No." She paused, trying to summarize the story of her Colorado childhood in her mind, "I lived in Telluride and then outside Ouray, Colorado until my parents died in a car crash when I was fourteen. I go back in December each year to a cabin they had in the mountains. It's where I spread their ashes."

"Wow, I'm sorry to hear that, Mallory." His brown eyes, so much like his brother's, filled with sadness for her, "Do you have other family that still live there?"

"Nope, no family. Just me." She paused, noticing his expression saddened even further. Of course, he would react that way, he had a well-rounded, loving family, he probably couldn't imagine a life without them. Kind of like the family she had. Before the accident turned her life upside down. "But, that's okay. I like the solitude."

"Mhmm-"

"Hey, Mallory! How's it going?" She heard Harris's voice as he jogged down the steps from the production area upstairs into the basement office area. Dressed in comfortably washed dark jeans and a soft-looking, navy blue sweater with the collar of a bright white dress shirt peeking out, she wondered again, why wasn't this seriously gorgeous guy dating somebody? What's his deal anyway?

Before she could answer Harris, Paul interrupted-

"Hey, Harris! Mallory was just telling me that she will be going to Colorado for a couple of days next week. Weren't you planning to go see Connie sometime in December? You guys could travel together, 'cause Mallory's planning to return her rental. You could share rides back from the airport and stuff. I don't think Mallory would have much luck getting an Uber to come all the way out here."

Ignoring his brother's stare, he turned to Mallory, "How far is Grand Junction from Telluride? We have a client who lives in Grand Junction and she said she wanted Harris to come out there before the holidays." He explained, ignoring the rather stunned look on Harris's face.

"Well, I actually go to Ouray, which isn't far from Telluride. But, it's about two-and-half-hour drive from Grand Junction. I guess it's not very far away." Mallory turned to face Harris, wondering what reaction she should have to this bold intrusion to her life.

When she travelled there each year, she usually flew into the Telluride airport because of the convenience to Ouray, but Grand Junction was certainly doable. She couldn't believe she was even considering flying along with him. This annual visit had always been a solitary affair, she wasn't sure she liked the idea of sharing it with someone else.

"Oh, I don't know." Harris spoke up hesitantly, his hands on his hips, glancing down at the floor, "I don't want to put you out like that. I wasn't sure I'd make it out there in December anyway. I could just wait until after the first of the year-"

"Yes, you could," Paul interrupted him, "But, remember she said that she wants to see our ideas for Patio before she leaves for that spring/summer show she goes to in Vegas in January."

He turned back to his computer and clicked some photos into position on their website, "I'm just sayin', strike while the iron's hot, and all that."

"Well, yeah." Harris looked up at Mallory from under his brows, like a little kid waiting for a reprimand from his teacher. "I remember you telling me your parents had a cabin in the mountains there, but, I really wouldn't want to be in your way, Mallory. Are you planning to visit friends or some relatives while you're there?"

"No, I was just telling Paul that I go each year at this time. I stay at the cabin for a few days, just hang out, hike if the weather's good, maybe do some skiing, you know - mountain stuff."

A blubbering idiot, all because she didn't have the guts to tell him she didn't want him to come along. While at the same time, she admitted there was something about the idea that tempted her in an odd way. She assessed him standing there across the room and wondered, what was on his mind? He couldn't possibly think this was more than a few days with a friend, right?

She threw up her hands and laughed away her paranoia, "Sure, you're welcome to come along if you like, Harris. I will forewarn you though, the accommodations are rustic, to say the least. But, there are hotels in town a few miles away, if you'd prefer."

"Oh, okay. I was thinking I'd just stay in Grand Junction while you went to your place." He smiled easily at her idiotic assumption and Mallory felt her cheeks flame up. Oh my gosh, what a fail. I am such a complete imbecile. "But I would love to see your place, if you're okay with that. It sounds like fun. What day did you plan to leave?"

CHAPTER 19
... I have something I want to show you ...

Well, now that they rented a car, they had indeed spent the day travelling by planes, airport *trams* and automobiles, Harris joked as he shifted his duffle bag and briefcase into the back seat of the rental car a few days later. It had been a rather long day already and Mallory was tired, but he seemed completely refreshed and ready to sell something.

Their flight into Grand Junction was ahead of schedule, the skies had been crystal clear, and now they were headed over to the office of his client, who owned six high-end home boutiques spattered across the state of Colorado. While on the plane, Harris told Mallory that they had been selling furniture to this client for a few years and just recently she asked to see their new outdoor living and enclosed porch concepts, including some of their new cabinetry.

He was certainly in his element when he proudly showed Mallory their new designs on his tablet computer, and she was fascinated listening to him describe the design process and the wood crafting involved in making their products. Something about his enthusiasm was contagious, and extremely attractive, if she was honest. More than once today, she had found her attention diverted by his smile, or a look on his face, and her imagination wandered dangerously into that zone, the no-go zone.

Harris said he was perfectly comfortable having her come along to the meeting, but she insisted he drop her off at a coffee shop nearby, she was in dire need of some caffeine to reboot before they drove to the cabin tonight. As she shifted out of the passenger side door, he waved a short wave and smiled brightly, saying something about wishing him luck and Mallory thought, if you smile like that, no worries, you could sell a surfboard in a Telluride ski shop.

So, as she sat waiting for him to finish his appointment, drinking her cup of coffee and munching on biscotti, she contemplated how crazy it was that she was in Colorado with an almost-stranger, yet she felt more comfortable with him than anyone she could remember in a long time.

If it wasn't so dark, he would feel a lot better, Harris thought a few hours later as he looked out the Jeep's passenger side window, taking in the deep shadows in the trees under the clear starry night sky. He glanced over again at Mallory, a dark blue knit stocking hat pulled down low over her long curls, while she nonchalantly chucked through another drift on the mountain road as if this was part of her daily commute.

"Okay." He said, willing himself to relax, as he struggled with the lack of control of all this - being the passenger instead of the driver on treacherous roads - it was driving him nuts. But, he admitted, she seemed to know what she was doing. "Now, I'm seriously impressed. You really are a mountain girl, aren't you?"

He flinched and grabbed the door handle as they hit a particularly stubborn drift on a curve in the winding mountain road and the tires gripped at the snow pack under them.

"Ha, yeah. Well, I was only fourteen when I last lived here, so I didn't do much driving. But, I guess it is true, snow doesn't really scare me. You get used to it." She laughed lightly, "It's not much different than Minnesota. Except for the absence of seventy mile an hour winds and arctic cold."

As he laughed at her exaggeration, Harris looked out his window again trying to make out the shapes of the dark mountains all around him, but everything seemed cloaked in an endless inky shadow.

It had been dark when they reached the breathtakingly stunning town of Ouray (which had dubbed itself Little Switzerland because of its location perched amongst some ruggedly steep mountains.) And, once they had traded their rental car for the Jeep at the Sherwood's house, they left the twinkling lights of town behind them, and turned on a dirt, snow-covered road a few miles out. It was then all signs of human life had disappeared.

He was just beginning to experience an uncomfortable deja vu - the Jeep's lights bouncing around the endless trees and the cold, empty road ahead of them reminding him of a scene from a horror movie he was sure he had watched at a critically impressionable point in his childhood - when suddenly the headlights glanced across a driveway, it was covered in snow, but it obviously was a driveway.

"Well, this is it." Mallory announced, "But, don't be alarmed by the isolation. Maggie told me they were just up here two days ago to check things out before they left for their vacation. They turned up the heat, checked the water and left plenty of fuel for the generator. They take such good care of me, it makes it easy to have this place."

The driveway wasn't long, but it curved around some trees and down a small hill, hiding the house from the road. When the lights finally spidered their way back up the snow-covered hill again and illuminated the yard, their movement set off the motion-sensitive security light above the center door of a three-stall carriage house with guest house over it. With towering evergreens and hip-high snow drifts all around it, the dark stained house with its rustic carriage garage doors and paned windows stood silently in the Colorado night, as seamlessly a part of the mountain landscape as the spruce and aspen trees huddled around it.

Using the garage door opener clipped to the Jeep's visor, Mallory pulled into the middle stall and the door opener light illuminated a spacious garage with knotty pine covered walls and ceiling. Harris noticed outdoor gear occupied the space of one stall of the garage including winter parkas and snowsuits, boots and skis stationed on one wall with a mountain tread snowmobile and a new UTV parked alongside each other.

Mallory had mentioned that this area was well-known for its UTV trails, she said you could travel on trails for days and still find new ones, and the sights would be some of the most stunning you were ever likely to see. As they drove through town earlier, he found himself planning in his mind to come back again in the summer sometime to see it for himself.

The third stall of the garage had a utility sink and a small seating area around a brick fireplace with cords of dry wood neatly stacked in custom-built shelving against the wall. The simple wooden bench and comfortable looking chairs facing the fireplace looked like the perfect place to warm up after a wintry afternoon enjoying the snow. Someone sure had a vision when they built this garage, he thought with admiration, and it intrigued him to see the rest of the house.

"This is all so cool, Mallory! Your parents built this place?" Harris asked as he followed her up a set of stairs, carrying their two rolling bags while she carried the bags of groceries they had picked up in town.

"Yes, they did. And, when I say that, I mean they *literally built* it. My dad worked as a landscaper in the summer and ski instructor in the winter, but he wasn't afraid of jumping into things, so he and mom built this with a few of their friends, one of the guys was a full-time carpenter. Their plan was to build this guest house as a test run for the permanent home they planned to build someday after they had saved enough money. I think I was twelve the summer we lived in a camper they parked in the driveway as they finished this place."

After unlocking the door, she flipped on lights and walked over to set the groceries down on the butcher-block covered center island in the small kitchen.

"Well, they did a fantastic job, it's beautiful and so well thought out." He admired the rock fireplace on the same wall as the one below, sharing a massive chimney. Cords of wood were stacked in the lower shelves on either side of the fireplace with bookshelves hugging the chimney on either side all the way to the beamed ceiling.

"It's small, only two bedrooms and one shared bathroom, but it was home. I loved it here." She glanced around with a smile on her face. "Lots of good times."

She turned away to put a few groceries in the small refrigerator and Harris wondered what was going on inside her. It must be difficult for her to come back here each year, and always alone. He really wanted to open her up about it, some things should just not be kept locked up inside. But, instead of finding the right words, he glanced around the living room, thinking he would start a fire, maybe she would share some of it later.

"I can light a fire, if you want. Looks like you have plenty of wood here." As he walked around the comfortable-looking overstuffed chairs towards the fireplace, he noticed a cased guitar sitting propped in the corner. "Hey, wait. Mallory, have you been hiding something from me?" He laughed at the surprised look she had on her face.

"Ahh, no, I don't think so. Why?" But, her guilty-looking expression was comical, leaving him thinking maybe she was hiding something? He wondered vaguely, what could that be?

"Do you play the guitar? And, maybe you just forgot to tell me?"

"Oh, that." She laughed sheepishly, turning back to put some eggs and orange juice in the refrigerator, "No, not me, although I've tried a few times over the years. That guitar was my dad's."

"Cool. Do you mind?" He asked with raised eyebrows as he picked up the case.

"Please. Be my guest. It's probably in need of a tune though."

Harris removed the honey colored guitar and dropped the strap over his shoulder; as he strummed it he noted that it was indeed badly out of tune.

"Well, I'd be happy to tune it for you. But, it might take a little while, probably should get the fire going first to warm the place up a little."

They busied themselves around the cabin, first starting the fire and then eating the grilled cheese sandwiches Mallory made on the electric skillet. As they cleaned up afterwards, Harris asked which bedroom he could use, saying he was starting to notice it had been a long day and that he was rather tired, he would probably make it an early evening.

More than once today, she caught herself dwelling on the thought of him staying here alone with her. But, really, the fact that she felt uncomfortable about him staying there thoroughly annoyed her.

They were adults after all, and she had many male friends, including Bradford, who she considered one of her best friends. It was ludicrous to be concerned about Harris. There had been absolutely no signals that he considered her anything other than a friend. You told him he could come along, after all. Don't make this all awkward now, she chided herself.

So, she laughed when she told him that he was "absolutely not allowed" to sleep in her old room, with its pink ceiling and queen size bed, because the mattress had a pillow top that she had special ordered for it and she loved that pillow top. He instead must sleep in her parents' room. With his height, he might prefer that king size bed anyway. Of course, he agreed without any awkward overtures.

Later, as she brushed her teeth and washed her face, she heard him tuning the guitar, methodically picking the strings until his strums sounded perfectly in tune. Opening the door quietly, she intended to just say goodnight and disappear to her bedroom, but the sight of him sitting there made her stop cold.

He was bent over the guitar, partially facing away from her looking into the fire, lost somewhere in his mind, sitting where her dad used to sit when he played guitar. The song he was playing - that song sounded strangely familiar, but also foreign, she couldn't bring it to mind, and almost protectively, she didn't know if she wanted to. And, those slippers. He was wearing those moccasin slippers again. No fair.

"Hey, you got it tuned." She walked over and sat down on the couch next to his chair, drawing her legs up underneath her. What could it hurt to sit with him for a little while? Obviously, she wasn't looking all that attractive - no makeup, her hair in a loose side braid and wearing an extra-large Ski Telluride flannel hoodie. He certainly wouldn't get the wrong idea with her looking like this hot mess.

"Yes, I did." He turned to face her, and lifting the strap from around his neck, he propped the guitar carefully against the wall. Leaning forward in his chair, he looked down at the floor for a moment, then up to her with a serious look on his face and suddenly Mallory wished she had just gone straight to her bedroom, this conversation felt like it was going to require some honesty.

"Mallory, I have been wanting to ask you something."

"Okay. What have you been wanting to ask me?" She met his serious tone with one of her own, teasing him. But, after his mouth turned up in a slight smile, undaunted by her pseudo-serious expression, he continued.

"Well, you've told me that you and Mike had some major issues and I don't know what they were, he never told me, but I know that he was really sorry for them, whatever they were. I really want you to know that he loved you very much and that he realized that he needed to ask you for your forgiveness and try to heal your relationship."

He said it all while looking at her directly, his gaze never drifting away, he seemingly was perfectly comfortable having this heavy conversation with her, an almost stranger.

"Well. That's a whole lot of something-you-wanted-to-tell-me." She sat there for a moment, kind of going numb in her mind and she felt the barriers of protection raising up for a battle.

But, really, she told herself, her battle wasn't with Harris, was it? He was an innocent bystander. It was probably time to shed some of this weight.

"Harris, it might surprise you to hear me admit this, because I know I've been pretty hard on him, but I see that Grandpa J meant a lot to you and you're trying hard to deal with his death. I'm sorry that I've been so - I don't know – cold about him. It's just that every time you talk about him, I feel like you're talking about a stranger, someone I don't even know."

Mallory felt everything she was saying was coming from deep within her soul, but still she couldn't quite believe she was saying them out loud. Immediately, however, she knew she wasn't as strong as him, she couldn't force herself to confront her vulnerability in Harris's soft brown eyes, so instead she took comfort in staring at the fire that crackled in front of them.

The brilliant yellows, oranges and reds were mesmerizing, and as she watched the flames, her eyes became noticeably sore and tired and her body yawned with a general ache all over it. But really, she concluded, as she sat there evaluating what she was feeling, it was her *spirit* that was weary. Weary of everything. It was as if she was trying to climb a rock cliff and she was stuck midway up the surface – too far up to go back down and yet too far down to see the top. She was just stuck there. She knew she needed to move on from here. But, how?

A heavy sigh came from deep inside and she forced her eyes from the fire, back to meet his gaze. Was this what real vulnerability felt like? Well, it sucked. She felt an overwhelming nervousness, letting go of this, with him. She didn't really know him, did she?

Still, he was so easy to talk to, even now, he just sat there listening to her, seeming like he really cared. He must care, right?

"Okay, here's the truth, Harris. I'm starting to realize that I do have that kind of memory of him too – good times, funny things he'd do, moments where we really connected – those memories have just been hidden under the bad memories for so long, I tend to forget them. I think I've thrived – it's like I've *survived* – on the bitterness or something. Doesn't that make me sound really shallow and selfish?"

To her utter horror, she felt tears pricking her eyes. Could this get any worse? She wiped at her eyes roughly with her palms, "Okay, now I'm crying. That's just great."

"Hey, that's alright. I won't tell anyone, I promise." He joked with a soft smile and Mallory could feel in her bones that he was holding back from hugging her, because he was just like that, and she was the polar-opposite of that. To break the tension she felt, she moved even further out into the vulnerable zone. She knew it was time to show him.

"I have something I want to show you." She uncurled her legs, resolutely pushed herself up from the couch, and walked to the kitchen counter to retrieve the letter from her purse. For some reason, she had carried it with her since the day she found it in his safe. It had been their secret, hers and Grandpa J's. Until now.

Harris sat back suddenly, she rose from the couch so fast that she almost checked him in the face. He was trying hard to let her feel her way through all this without him butting in, obviously, it was a lot of stuff. But, the abrupt change in her mood was like a dive into an ice-cold lake. It left him feeling so completely out of his element that he started praying again as he watched her cross the room with a piece of paper in her hand. God, just help her feel this, not run away. Help her through this.

"I found this the day I opened his safe. I want you to read it, but I am going to bed now because I'm exhausted. It will explain some things." She stood over him, holding the slightly crumpled letter out toward him, this letter that he knew existed, that he had suggested Mike write, and that he had wondered about for weeks now.

But, in this moment, he was struck instead by her beauty, with her long dark hair falling out of its braid and over her shoulder, a few loose curls curving along her neck and around the hood of her flannel top. He knew he was staring uncomfortably at her and he had all he could do to stop himself from reaching up and combing his fingers through those soft-looking dark curls.

Luckily, she turned without seeming to notice him staring, and without another word, she went to her bedroom, closed the door softly behind her, and left him in front of the fire to read the letter alone.

His eyes were moist, the tears on his lashes burned and his chest felt tight, like someone was sitting on him, as the multitude of emotions passed through him, and in a daze, he laid the letter onto the cushion of the couch where she had been sitting, just moments before.

He noticed his hands were literally shaking under the white-hot, righteous anger he felt towards his friend Mike. How could he have done that to his granddaughter? An innocent young girl, *who had just lost her parents*, and treat her like that?

At the edges of this anger, he felt a deep force taking over him inside, an empathy he'd never experienced for another person, but now, with Mallory, it was *so real*, as he imagined how she must have felt completely alone then, and still alone even now as an adult. And, as if it was the most natural thing in the world, he felt an overwhelming tenderness for her, instinctively knowing that he would say whatever he could say, do whatever he could do, to try to make up for this pain in her life.

But, as he gazed into the fire, even as all these emotions were kicking violently around inside him, they were slowly being quieted by a calm, peaceful sense of Grace. These were the demons that Mike had faced down earlier this fall, that night in his screen porch when their laid-back evening of music and talk turned into a serious conversation of faith.

These were the dark memories Mike couldn't shake, and it brought him back to that night months ago, when Mike cautiously opened the door on the conversation:

"Harris, I can't imagine a life like yours. This Jesus you know. I can't see how it works for a guy like me. You have no idea what I've done." Mike had said this with desperation seeping through his words and he ran his fingers through his white hair in nervous frustration, putting his elbows on his knees and his head in his hands.

As he watched his friend, Harris had lumbered around in his mind for words - he wasn't prepared for this conversation, he couldn't think of any eloquent way to answer him - so finally, he had just winged it.

"That's the thing, Mike. We all sin. It doesn't matter what I know or anyone else knows." Harris had reached out from behind the guitar resting on his knees and put his hand on Mike's shoulder, "What matters is *He already knows*, and *He still loves* you."

That night Mike had gone on to share with Harris many of his demons but most of these - the ones relating to Mallory - he had not. But in the end, it didn't matter how many regrets there were. It didn't matter what regrets they were. Mike had met Jesus that night, and the lens shifted in his life. He walked as a new man. And, he vowed that night that he, and the people in his life, would never be the same for it.

That's what Mallory needed to know, Harris resolved, all the way deep into her soul, securely locked into her heart, she just needed to know this. He glanced at her closed bedroom door, imagining her laying there on her pillow-top bed, sleeping like the young girl she had once been. The girl who had been happy at one time - just cheerfully living a carefree life like young girls are supposed to live - in this cabin in the Colorado mountains, with two parents who loved her unconditionally.

CHAPTER 20

This. This was her happy place. Mallory turned in her bed, away from the bright sunlight coming from between the wood slats of the shutters on the window, fluffed up her pillow and snuggled into it until her neck was perfectly positioned. I feel like I could sleep for at least four more hours, she dreamt lazily. And, why not? It was Saturday today, right?

But there was a sound coming from the other side of her door, it sounded like - sizzling. She pressed her hands against her eyes. What time was it? Sitting up in her bed suddenly, she realized it was not Saturday, she remembered where she was and who was standing on the other side of her door, busy making breakfast by the sounds of it. Well, time to face the music, she thought as the memories of the reading material she'd given him last night filtered through her sleep haze.

Pulling herself out of bed and her hair out of her eyes, she glanced at the mirror that hung on the closet door. Remembering the breakfast he made her the first morning she was in Minnesota, she felt a strange sense of familiarity about the whole situation, the fact that she was here at her childhood home, on her most intimate of life experiences, and Harris, her neighbor, was making her breakfast. Was she smart to trust him with all this?

She scowled at her reflection in the mirror as she admitted she was starting to feel guilty because she had never even trusted Jasper enough to bring him along with her to Colorado. This, even after he said he wanted to come and, bargaining with her like he always did, he'd told her he would just ski while she "had her moment in the mountains." For some reason, that had made her want to invite him along even less.

Mallory opened the door to bright sunlight, dimmed slightly by the haze of sizzling ham.

"Hey there neighbor, good morning. Something smells good." She spoke to his back, noticing that he was already dressed in jeans and an untucked, soft light blue flannel shirt. His hair had that messy morning-look to it again, still glossy wet from a shower. "Did you have enough hot water?"

She walked to the coffee pot and poured herself the cup that he had set out on the counter with a creamer pack next to it. He already knew how she liked her coffee. Was that a good sign or something she should be worried about? Oh, don't be paranoid, she told herself, he was with you last night when you bought groceries, it doesn't take a genius to guess you take cream with your coffee.

"Yes, I did, thanks." He turned from the skillet where he was frying some ham and casually leaned back against the counter, holding a couple of eggs in his hands. "This morning you have a choice when I make you breakfast, how do you like your eggs?"

"Over easy, please." He nodded and turned back to a frying pan he had on the stove. "Did you sleep well?" She asked as she pushed the toaster button down for the bagels that he had already set inside it. When he didn't answer right away, she thought he must be focusing on the eggs that were bubbling in front of him.

"Yes, I did, thanks." He repeated himself, smiling a teasing smile at her. What? She wondered, was he laughing at her attempt to make small talk? He sighed then, speaking slowly, "Mallory, honestly, no. I didn't sleep very well at all last night."

He easily flipped the eggs and sprinkled them with salt and pepper, busying himself with the pan, leaving her wondering what he could mean. She hadn't slept in her parents' bed for at least a couple years, but Maggie had never said it was uncomfortable— "And, it had nothing to do with the accommodations, before you ask." He slid the eggs onto a plate and turned to face her, "I couldn't sleep because I kept thinking about Mike. And, you."

His approach to this discussion of the letter took her completely off guard. She didn't know how they would talk about it, but Mallory thought he'd at least wait until they had breakfast on the table. Then perhaps he would make it a casual conversation, maybe lightly brush over it and be on with his day. You know – how most people would react. He had his own life, after all, not much time, and certainly no desire, to delve into hers.

"Well, I don't know what to say–"

"Before you say anything, I want you to know that I appreciate you showing it to me. I'm honored. That took guts."

He laughed a small laugh as he brought the eggs and ham over to the small table that he had already set with glasses of orange juice, plates and silverware. Mallory followed him with the bagels, feeling a little shell shocked already.

"You are one gutsy girl, Mallory. And, you were right when you said it would explain some things. But, I find that having read it, I want to know so much more. Does that scare you?"

She caught herself blinking in surprise and couldn't think of any appropriate response.

"Yes, actually. That scares the living you-know-what out of me." She looked down at her plate, suddenly not hungry at all. Why would he push like this?

"Okay. Just wanted you to know that I care." He stabbed into his eggs and took a big bite, looking as if they were discussing the weather instead of her crazy, monumentally messed up life. "But, of course it's your decision. You decide when - or if - you're ever ready to share it with anyone."

"What "it" are you talking about, Harris?" This conversation was pushing all of the alarms inside her and a flash of anger came from out of nowhere, shocking her so much she couldn't keep it from erupting out of her mouth, "Do you want to know more about my life with my narcissistic, alcoholic, neglectful grandfather? Or, my lonely, pathetic teenage years? Or, maybe you're interested in my current pitiful existence, without a job, clueless and without direction? Which of these would you like to know more about?"

She sat back in her chair, crossing her arms over her chest like a spoiled teenager - she was sure that's what she looked like - but really, come on! Who was he anyway? She didn't even know him, why did he pretend to care? What was he after anyway? Treating her life like it was some "New & Interesting Find" on Amazon!

They both just sat there for a stunned moment, the steam from their breakfast rising in the air between them. He was quiet – so very still – and, although he had blinked at her eruption, giving her some satisfaction that he was shocked by it, he didn't fire away in defense of himself. He just sat there, looking at her peacefully. Frankly, it was a look of something, kind of like ... well, honestly, it looked like love in his eyes.

"All of it, Mallory." He spoke softly, but his voice was confident, "I want to know all of it."

With his words out there, spoken so plainly, she had no alternative but to answer. Maybe it was the timing of his question, or maybe it was the look in his eyes, but Mallory suddenly had the strange sensation that a wall, like a dam, gave way inside her. And once the flashes and emotions of the memories swirled around her, she finally abandoned her battle and let herself be carried away by the current. She was powerless to stop it.

◆ ◆ ◆

December 2006
and the fog diminished the intensity of the sun

She will never forget the thought she had – She's here for *me* – when the school secretary Ms. Reigns came to Mallory's biology class that December morning. She saw Ms. Reigns peek in through the window in the classroom door with a strange, cautious look in her eyes, and catching Mallory's glance through the window, Ms. Reigns smiled at her as she opened the door and walked quietly towards her desk, the third one back, the row nearest to the door. But, it wasn't her normal, "Good morning, Miss Mallory" smile, the one she greeted all students with. That smile was always broad and uninhibited, and she made it a point to remember your name and added either Miss or Mister if you visited the office for a hall pass or to pick up the gym shoes your mom dropped off because you forgot them at home.

"Mallory, please come along with me to the office." Ms. Reigns bent low and whispered softly, settling her hand gently on Mallory's shoulder. Why do I need to go the office, she wondered? I don't think I forgot anything at home today. I don't even have gym this semester.

But, she's here for *me.*

"You may leave your things at your desk, someone else will take care of them for you." Why would she say that? What's going on? Mallory glanced slowly around at the students surrounding her, all watching her with confused looks on their faces, and inside Mallory bristled. She didn't enjoy the sudden spotlight that was shining on her because of this intrusion on their boring lecture of animal classifications. What was going on?

Once they were in the hallway, Mallory asked her to explain, but Ms. Reigns just said that the principal wanted to talk to her about something private and not to worry, she wasn't in trouble. She'd only been in the principal's office on one other occasion, she and her friends had gotten in trouble about a month ago because they had started sneaking behind the performing arts stage to eat their lunch.

Not a huge infraction, Ms. Fredrick, the young principal who had a spatter of freckles across her pretty face, said with a sour voice, but still, against the rules.

Ms. Fredrick's office was small, it only had three chairs and one of those was the huge leather rolling chair behind her desk. Today, the office seemed crowded with adults, one of them a state trooper, an older man with fuzzy gray hair, whose radio buzzed and chirped with voices before he pressed a button and moved out into the hallway, throwing a glance towards Ms. Reigns and Mallory as they entered the room. Just beyond the door, Ms. Fredrick and the new school counselor Mr. Broden stood, talking in low voices with their heads lowered.

"Mallory, hello, come in." Ms. Fredrick spoke up at the sight of her, smoothed her copper colored hair behind her ear and slipped her leopard patterned glasses back on, gesturing towards one of the chairs in front of her desk. "Please, sit down. Mr. Broden and I want to have a word with you."

Mr. Broden was new to the school that fall, just out of college. Every girl in school thought he was super cute and super cool, with his wavy blonde hair and small diamond stud in his ear. Many kids visited with Mr. Broden about lots of things. Mallory wasn't even sure which door was his office.

As she sat down, and Ms. Reigns backed out of the room, closing the door softly, Mallory wondered where the state trooper had gone, the radio was silent. Her dad had been stopped once for speeding, and a state trooper had stopped her mom once for a broken tail light, but that was the extent of Mallory's experience with the law. She hadn't even started driver's training, so what could she have done wrong? She noticed her eye was starting to twitch a little and her lips felt tingly. What was going on?

"There is no easy way to tell you this." Ms. Fredrick spoke from behind her desk, and sitting this close to her, Mallory could see the lens on her leopard colored glasses had spots on them, like she'd been crying and hadn't gotten all the spots off. She was leaning towards Mallory with her hands folded on top of her desk, "I'm so sorry, sweetie, but the highway patrol found your parents this morning. They had a bad car crash. Mallory, we're so sorry, but your parents are gone."

A fog descended that day. It crept insidiously through the rugged and winding mountain passes and skittered up and down the tallest of the white fir evergreens, its heaviest veils shuttering even the hunting of the bald eagles, who perched patiently in their nests on the sheer cliffs, waiting for its damp, disheartening cloak to lift. There, they waited, until they could get back to what they were doing before. Living.

But, it didn't lift, that fog. Not really. Not for her. Even when the sun shone again, burning off the last wispy vestiges of the foggy veil, the damp was still there. The intensity of the sun, the effervescence of it, it had been diminished.

That week strung together one foggy day after another for Mallory, who at fourteen, was soon taken in by the caring parents of her friends until her family could be summoned to Colorado. That morning in the principal's office, however, before it hit home with her what had truly happened, they asked her a lot of questions because they said her student profile didn't have an emergency contact listed.

Did she have any family close by? No, her grandparents on her mom's side were dead, and she didn't have any aunts or uncles. Yes, she had a grandfather on her dad's side, he lived in New York. You know. He's JL McMichael, the author. But, she told them, I don't really know him that well.

Then, Mr. Broden held a cell phone out towards her, saying the state patrol had found it in her parents' car and they would like her to open it if she could, they could maybe find her grandpa's phone number in it. She remembered staring at it as it sat in the palm of his clean hand. It was her dad's cell phone. Normally silver and sleek, that morning it looked old and battered, with a nasty crack in the screen and an ominous dark stain that someone had tried to wipe clean, but they didn't quite succeed.

She didn't really remember opening the phone or finding Grandpa J's number, but she must have, because the next thing she knew, Ms. Fredrick was on her office phone calling Grandpa J. The principal cleared her voice nervously as the phone rang and she glanced at Mallory with a shy smile, obviously the fact that she was going to be talking to the famous author was not lost on her. Plus, there was the reason for her call, someone had to tell him his son and daughter-in-law were dead, and his granddaughter was still here, left all alone.

Mallory felt a flutter deep in her stomach, and as she sat there, the flutter became a flurry that scurried up through her lungs, making it hard to breathe and she noticed her leg had started bouncing, her knee jumping up and down, up and down. She pushed at her knee with one of her hands, trying to make it stop, but she couldn't seem to quiet the storm. Somehow disconnected from the people in this room, she felt Mr. Broden set his hand on her shoulder, and he said something to her, but she couldn't respond. She could only focus on the phone that Ms. Fredrick held to her ear.

Mallory heard Grandpa J's deep voice when he picked up the call, and for some reason, hearing that voice through the phone – the voice that connected her to a family, to her parents – *that* sent her tumbling down a canyon, the tears coming from such a deep and wide place that there was no room left for anyone else in her world. She couldn't talk, she couldn't hear, she couldn't think. All she could do was just sit there on the gray plastic chair in Ms. Fredrick's office and let the waves wash her to and fro, to and fro.

Strange, disjointed thoughts accompanied this rocking feeling, like a memory she had of one of Grandpa J's novels, "I Can't Find the End of the Ocean," a novel he wrote many years earlier, one that she and her dad read together. It was about a sailor whose wife had left him, and he set off to sea looking to heal his broken heart, but instead he lost his mind. It was a sad book. The man died out there, on his boat.

Grandpa J stayed with her at the house the few nights before the funeral, and when Canton's and Jasmine's families arrived, they stayed in town at a hotel. Those days were long and quiet, they didn't talk much, because she didn't really know him. During her early childhood, her dad and her grandfather rarely communicated. Her dad said they were like oil and water, and he preferred to keep his distance. It was a touchy subject.

Only in the past couple of years had her grandpa even visited them in Colorado and they had been out to New York to see him twice. But, even during these recent visits, he rarely talked to Mallory and certainly didn't try to build any type of relationship with her. She knew he grew up on the east coast, he was an author, she had read most of his books, and he had started a small movie production company in LA, but honestly, that's about all she knew about her Grandpa J. Now, with her dad gone, she struggled to find anything that they could even talk about together.

That week, he was required to take care of the details of her parents' funeral and their affairs, so Grandpa J was in town a lot, while she stayed home. When things in the house, like their clothes and their pictures, reminded her too much of her parents, she would escape outside and trek through the snow to some of her favorite mountain places during the middle of the day. She'd think about her friends and classmates at school, carrying on with their lives, together with their parents at night. And, she'd wonder, would she ever feel like those kids again?

When he would return later in the day, Grandpa J usually smelled like alcohol and his bloodshot eyes would be all wild-looking. He would try to say the things she supposed most adults felt obligated to say, things that were meant to fill the hole, but didn't. She would mumble something in response, nod obediently and leave the room, usually finding herself outside again, sitting on a cold boulder by the stream, or leaning up against an aspen tree in the clearing down the hill from their house. Always, the fog followed her.

Finally, the night before the funeral, he told her that she was old enough, he wanted her to know about the things that her parents had set up for her, in the event something "like this" happened.

He was now her guardian, he told her. When she turned twenty-one, this house and the land around it would legally become hers. And, they had a life insurance policy. When she turned twenty-one, that money would become hers. In the meantime, he would pay for the funeral and cremation expenses and any of their outstanding debts and then he would take her back with him. To live in New York. He didn't say exactly when that would happen. When she asked, he told her, just let him figure it out.

His words, as soon as he spoke them, they became like everything else that week, they just drifted away into the fog. All these adult-sounding commitments - twenty-one was a lifetime away - all these plans, they were like mists that hung just over the pool at the bottom of the waterfall in the mountain pass a few miles from her house. What was real to her, was the book report due Monday and the knowledge that she hadn't even started reading the book yet. And, she had to let her basketball coach know if she would be going to the tournament this Saturday. Things that other fourteen-year-old girls thought about, that was real to her.

The morning of the funeral, while she was eating cereal for breakfast and he sat next to her with a newspaper open on the table, Grandpa J poured his juice glass full of vodka and topped it off with a shot of tomato juice. Mallory gulped down her spoonful of Frosted

Flakes and looked up at him, as cold panic shallowed her breath and squirmed around in her stomach. Wasn't he supposed to stay sober the day of his son and daughter-in-law's funeral? Who would take care of things if he was drunk?

Grandpa J returned her look with a crooked, sad smile and said, "Life sucks, Mal. Remember that."

◆ ◆ ◆

"Before my parents died, I used to lie here in this meadow watching birds flying up there so high that I'd lose sight of them in the clouds. I'd imagine those birds just floating along in the clouds, all the way over the mountains, to a different part of the world. I would daydream about my life, possibly moving away from Colorado. You know, just imagining who I'd become."

Harris sat next to Mallory on the trunk of the downed evergreen, their boots buried in the fluffy snow, with the bright early afternoon sunlight bouncing off the luminous white ocean of snow in the meadow in front of them. As she spoke, he let his imagination wander over what this meadow must look like in the summer; Mallory had told him earlier that it would be brimming with brilliant green grasses, with large swaths of pink, blue and yellow wildflowers, grazed by sheep owned by a farmer who ranched in some foothills a few miles over. What an exquisite place to grow up.

And, what an exquisite woman that little girl - who laid in this meadow, dreaming of her future - had become.

He looked at her as she adjusted her sunglasses and pulled her knit scarf closer to her neck, almost as if to protect herself, even after having bared so much already. Mallory had a lifetime worth of hurt and resentment built up inside her, and if he suspected the letter was just the surface of it, he was right.

He wasn't sure what prompted his actions this morning at breakfast, it was if he was on some kind of auto-pilot, kamikaze mission, one where he *knew* he shouldn't say this, shouldn't do that, but instead of listening to his rationale mind, his mouth would just go ahead and do the opposite. Yeah, like that never got him into trouble.

But, unbelievably, after the initial firestorm, Mallory just started talking. And, talking. And, laughing. And, crying. It was an intense, sometimes deeply traumatic, series of stories about her childhood, memories of her parents and their deaths, and recognitions about what had become of her life as a result of it. As she finished sharing one story, one simple follow up question from him would prompt her to tell him something else until here they sat, in this meadow, the place where she had spread her parents' ashes all those years ago when she was fourteen.

The thought of *that* Mallory, that scared little girl, *doing that all by herself* because her grandpa was drunk at the funeral and spent the rest of the day passed out in the cabin - well, it broke him inside, that's the only way he would describe it.

"I've said goodbye to them, Harris. I've said goodbye to them thousands of times, but I've never really let them go. I've held onto this – pain - inside me, this blame that I seem to need to put on someone, ever since they died. At first, I blamed my dad because he was driving, then I blamed my mom, because it was her idea to go to Durango that day. Then, I blamed myself because they were going to Durango to pick out carpeting for *my* bedroom. Then, of course, I blamed my grandfather because we probably wouldn't even be living here if he and my dad weren't always mortal enemies."

She paused, lifting her sunglasses slightly and wiped a stray tear away with her mittened hand, "I don't know, I've blamed so many people ... I've even blamed God. And, I think sometimes, how can I blame him? He's not even on my radar, it's not like I talk to him about my life, but still, I even find him a convenient scapegoat."

She looked across the meadow, shaking her head in frustration. Harris nodded and laughed slightly before saying, "Well, from what I know, he's got big shoulders. Even if it's misplaced, I think he can handle your blame, Mallory."

"Yeah, you're probably right. But, I'm starting to feel tired. I just want to be out from under all of it."

Harris nodded again, put his arm loosely around her shoulders, and hugged her towards his side. Because sometimes, words wouldn't come easy to him and that probably meant he wasn't supposed to talk. She would just have to feel her way through it. Nothing he could say would make it hurt less.

CHAPTER 21

The bright Colorado sun and trudging back to the house through the deep snow tired them out so by the time they'd returned to the cabin later that day, they were thoroughly spent. She went to her bedroom to do some reading while Harris worked, using his cell phone as a hotspot for WIFI.

As she laid in her bed, the bright sunlight beaming in and with the door slightly open, Mallory listened to Harris talking to his brother about his recent meeting in Grand Junction (which had gone very well, according to Harris) and she heard them discussing the new business merger and employee benefit packages. All of it was very comforting, not so highly emotional, and after the last few hours, it was just what she needed.

As she drifted off to sleep, in a most luxurious afternoon nap, she was struck again by how comfortable she was with this guy – had she really just *shared all that* with him? – and wondered if they would keep in touch when she went back home. Just over a week from now, she would be returning to Baltimore, maybe a job would open, she would return to her life with her friends there. And, Jasper. Maybe.

When a little over an hour later, Harris poked his head in with a knock on her door, saying he was starving, could they get something to eat in town, she knew just the place to bring him.

After the day she'd just had, feeling the effects of the catharsis she'd been through, Mallory likened it to waking from a coma, the patient starving for weeks without physical contact and sustenance. And, while a coma may be a peaceful existence, a hospital drip was no way to live. Sometimes, you just needed some good barbecue, a cold drink and a true friend.

They turned the Jeep into a parking spot next to the restaurant and followed the smells of smoky pork and chicken through the front door and around the bar area to the back where a few tables sat open.

"Oh, sorry, that's my phone." Just barely hearing it above the din of the busy restaurant, she reached under the table for her purse and looked up at the server standing at her elbow, waiting to take their order, "I'll just have the pulled pork sandwich and fries." She swiped open her phone to see that Guillory was calling.

"Hey, Guillory! How are you?" She turned slightly away as Harris ordered, to focus on hearing her phone through the noise.

"Hi, Mallory. Listen, sorry to be in a rush, but I'm trying to catch a cab and the weather is horrid." She heard him trying to catch his breath and she glanced out the window behind Harris, noticing the few cars parked outside, the softly blurred Christmas lights on the grocery store across the street and the whisper of falling snow. It was a different world completely when you left the city. "But, the reason I'm calling, Mallory - I'm so excited to send you something! Consider it an early Christmas gift. It's something you will cherish. Should I send it to your place in Baltimore, or to Minnesota?"

"Okay, aside from driving me crazy now with anticipation, I would ask that you send it to Minnesota. Thank you - for whatever it is -

thank you." She laughed into the phone, thinking about how thoughtful he was. No wonder he made such a great father and grandfather.

"Yes, you're quite welcome. I will send it right away. Call me once you've received it. Oh, I have to go - finally, I have a cab. We will talk later-"

She set her phone down, still smiling. When she glanced across the table at Harris, she noticed he was grinning, obviously listening in on her conversation.

"He's sending me something." Mallory explained, excited at the prospect of what it could be, "He said, it's something I will cherish. I know it can't be the finished novel because he already told me that Uncle Canton had been through Grandpa J's study. If it was there, he surely would have found it." Something I will cherish, she pondered. I wonder what it could be?

"That should be interesting." Harris replied, the wide grin on his face softened into a smile that matched the look in his eyes, "I just have to say, though, if this is any indication of how happy receiving gifts makes you, I may have to go shopping after dinner."

"Well, of course! Doesn't everyone like gifts?" She laughed at the notion, "But, if I'm honest, I really like the surprise more than the gift itself. Something about the anticipation, I guess. Jas always used to tell me that, I think he's right."

She took a drink of her water to pause her conversation because, at the mention of Jasper's name, she realized something just felt *off* with her tonight. Something was simmering inside, like the feeling you had the night before you were leaving on a long-awaited vacation.

"You don't mention him often, you know." Harris stated the obvious noncommittally, as if he was deciding which sandwich to order on the menu, but he was looking at her in that way he had. After the last few days, she knew it was safe with him, she didn't need to use the boyfriend excuse for boundaries, but the truth was, she didn't really know what category Jasper fit in.

"I know. It's because we are in the broken-up-but-still-talking cycle of our relationship. We've been here before. In the past, I've always thought when we break up, *this* time it's *really* over. And, each time I've totally believed that, but I always seem to go back."

Harris and Jasper were two such diametrically opposite people. Worlds apart. But, she was starting to feel so safe with Harris now, especially after today, and she wondered, how could she feel so close with two such radically different men?

"Can I ask why?" He was leaning forward, with his elbows on the table, twisting the ring on his finger as he watched her.

"Why we break up all the time?" She swallowed hard. For some reason, talking to him about Jasper was intimidating and she didn't want to tell him the gory details about the blonde attorney who had lived next door to Jasper last summer or about the redhead ex-girlfriend who was in town for the class reunion or the spiky haired lead singer for a punk rock band that bought a car from him and, after their one night stand, continued to stalk him for weeks by sending pictures of them together to Mallory's phone.

Given what she knew of Harris, how could he understand Jasper's infidelity? He would certainly judge her for condoning it by overlooking it, wouldn't he?

"No. I'm wondering, why do you go back?" He asked quietly, without any judgement in his voice. Which kind of surprised her.

"I suppose it's a defect in me." She paused, considering the answer, "Yes, it's most certainly a defect in me. Any normal person would run as far away as possible."

She couldn't look into his eyes because she knew she'd start crying, so she stared at the wire basket on the table with it packets of silverware wrapped up in a red-and-white, checked napkins standing next to the bottles of barbecue sauce. She took a deep breath, willing herself to just be honest with him.

"I've been hurt by him, Harris. Many times. Not physically hurt but still, hurt. He's cheated, he's broken my trust many times. But, somehow, I always think he's changed. He always comes back saying he's changed. He's saying it again now."

"Aww," He sighed deeply, his body language telling her he wanted to take her hands from across the table, but instead he hugged his arms together and his instinctive body language resonated through his words, "I'm sorry that's happened to you, Mallory. But, it's not a defect in you. You love him, you want to see the best in him, right?"

His question came out like a whisper, his voice was so quiet. She raised her eyes to meet his, not sure she heard his question, just as the waiter arrived with their baskets of barbecue and fries.

"Maybe." She nodded slightly, but suddenly not sure at all what her response should be to that question, she ended the nod as if she was a bobble head, half yes, half no.

"You want this glass just set over here?" Later, after their dinner where they'd listened to live bluegrass music and laughed through some memories of their high school and college experiences, they'd returned to the cabin.

After she returned a call from one of her girl friends back home and Harris got a fire going, she'd opened a bottle of wine and poured them each a glass. Mallory set his red wine on the table next to him, as Harris sat in the chair, his slippered feet up on the ottoman, plucking away at the guitar. He was humming along to the song in his head, and trying to remember it on the guitar, but he was having some difficulty, so he'd stop and start over again. It was that same familiar song he'd been playing last night.

"What song is that anyway? It's driving me crazy, I feel like I know it." She asked.

"Well, I've been butchering it, I know, but it's been stuck in my head since we got out here. Don't laugh at me, I'm going to close my eyes now, 'cause that helps me for some reason. Let me try one more time." He said as he closed his eyes, put his head back against the chair cushions and started playing.

Within a few bars, suddenly Mallory knew the song and as she watched him with his eyes closed, she was glad he couldn't see the expression on her face. It was a song that her dad used to play when she was a little girl; one of many John Denver songs in his repertoire because her mom was a huge fan. And, although she remembered her dad's voice as deep and throaty, almost a country music kind of sound, Harris's voice had a smooth quality, natural, almost like he was talking as he sang:

Sunshine on my shoulders, makes me happy ...

By the time he started into the chorus again, Mallory had given up holding the tears back. It was almost as if her dad was here somehow, singing this to her again like he had so many years ago. Why that song? Why was Harris singing it today, of all days? Who had answers to these kismet questions? In the end, it really didn't matter. She laid her head down on the pillowed arm of the couch near his guitar, and just let the "feels" of the moment wash all over her.

Harris opened his eyes, now secure in his recollection of the music, as he started the chorus again and found Mallory laying her head down on the couch, with her face turned toward him and tears in her eyes. He hesitated, was that a good thing, to make her cry? But, she smiled him on, and told him No, don't stop.

So, he kept playing and singing, all the while, in his mind, thoughts were slow dancing along with the music, I wish I could tell her, I should just tell her, I wish I could tell her.

CHAPTER 22
... *I'd sing a song to make you feel this way* ...

Falling in love is one of those things in life, Harris realized that night. You think you know the signs that it may be coming, you try to prepare and protect yourself ... you try to talk yourself out of it, try to rationalize it, even try to doubt it, but then ... Bam. That's when you realize that you are not the same person you were yesterday. All because of this other person.

Now, where it goes from here ... that's where it can get really dicey. It could be the love story of a lifetime, namely *your* love story and *your* lifetime, or it could be a complete and utter catastrophe. All because of this other person.

"Yes, this is Mallory." She kinked her shoulder up to hold her phone to her ear while removing her boarding pass to hand to the gate agent for the connecting flight out of Denver the following morning.

"Hello, Mallory. This is William Bannon from Windhurst & Bannon in New York. You may remember we met at the reading of your grandfather JL's will?"

"Oh, yes." She followed Harris down the jetway towards the flight attendants standing at the open door of the airplane, thinking there must be some legal issues with the Minnesota house. She did own it outright, didn't she?

"I wanted to inform you that your Uncle Canton has contacted me through his attorney requesting disclosure on a piece of your grandfather's work that is in your possession through your ownership of the house in Minnesota. Are you aware of this work? It's a book."

"Uh, well, yes, I think so–"

"Let me assure you, Mallory, there is no contest as to who owns that work. You do. I know JL was working on something in Minnesota before he came back to New York. He told me as much. Your grandfather was absolutely clear that whatever personal effects were in that house, including that book, they were yours. I just wanted you to know."

"Okay. I guess I should say thank you, but I don't know what will come next. Will I need to hire an attorney?" She found her seat across the aisle from Harris who, after stowing both of their carry-on bags in the upper bin, was looking up at her curiously from his seat.

"No, I wouldn't do anything just yet. I will send them a letter stating our position on ownership and we will see where it goes. I've seen things like this happen before, your uncle could have a change of heart and he could let this resolve itself amicably."

"Thank you for saying that." She sighed heavily as she plopped down onto the unforgiving, stiff surface of the blue airplane seat, "But, I wouldn't count on it."

As she hung up her phone, in her mind, she replayed the most recent conversation she had with her uncle where he seemed to be making an effort to be cordial to her and Mallory was more certain than ever that she needed to come clean to them about the novel. There was simply no way that she was going to complete it. They would have the resources to finish it the way Grandpa J would have, had he lived long enough.

She glanced over at Harris, who had also just received a phone call and was trying to hurry the caller along before the flight attendant reached them and cut him off. Her Grandpa J had been right about Harris; he was an amazing man - a true friend - someone who, for no other reason than wanting to make Mallory's life better, had helped her to see that there was a lot more freedom in living a life of forgiveness than one of bitterness. With his help, she was working on forgiving her grandfather, one memory at a time. So, forgiving the rest of the family? That should be a cake walk.

Harris swiped his phone off and turned to her, so she asked, "Do you think they have finished that Jeep yet? I think I will drive it back home next week. I'm going to give Canton and Jasmine "The Last Chapter.""

No. Don't say that, Harris thought. Would it be written all over his face, he wondered? Could she tell how much he wanted her to stay? As quickly as the thoughts were forming in his mind, the battle for self-preservation was taking over. She's going back home, what did you expect? She's got a life back there, she has a guy back there. This - whatever you thought *this* was - this was temporary. And, most likely one sided.

He finally found his voice again, "I'm sure they have the Jeep ready by now. I can check when we land. You will be going back east so soon?"

"Soon? Feels like I've been here forever. A lot has happened in the past month." She smiled tiredly at him, "And, you must feel like I've turned your life upside down along with me. You've been a big help, Harris, thank you."

Her eyes were so clear and blue, they reminded him of a spring sky. And, as he got lost somewhere in those eyes, he couldn't help but feel he was dangerously close to losing grip on himself. Figures it would happen with a girl who was in a pseudo relationship with another guy.

"You're very welcome, Mallory." He held those eyes for as long as he dared, wanting to communicate with the part of her that he suspected felt something for him too.

But, instead of the look he wanted to see, she looked confused, then scared. *That* look spoke volumes, clarifying with cold precision that he had been wrong, whatever he felt for her obviously wasn't reciprocated. He sat back further in his chair, stretching his legs as he tried to relax and overcome his disappointment. This was not the way he wanted this to go.

"So, you've decided to deliver the book to them?"

"Umm, yes." She was still looking at him cautiously, with questions written all over her face. "My uncle's attorney contacted Grandpa J's estate attorney. They suspect that I have this novel. And, I'm planning to give it to them to finish anyway, so I have decided it's time to just meet with them."

"Well, that's great then. I'm glad you've resolved it."

He couldn't help searching her face again for something - anything - that would give him some hope, but the cautious, questioning look in her eyes had been replaced by one that shuttered him out, putting distance between them where just a moment ago there was none.

"So now you'll go back home ... that's great."

She nodded quietly and reached for the in-flight magazine that poked out of the seat pocket in front of her, shutting him out completely.

CHAPTER 23

... At the end of my exhaustive search, I find my treasure hidden in plain sight

Later that evening, Mallory closed the door behind him and moving her overnight bag aside, through the window next to the front door, she watched him walk away again towards his house. Silently she thanked Harris for the thousandth time for the past few days. While she admitted she was a bit clueless, she wasn't completely unaware of her deficiencies, she recognized that her instinct was to run headlong away from emotion, it was just the way she had grown up, like a survival instinct.

Thinking back over her teens, she recalled the times Guillory and Suzanne had suggested seeing a counselor, even her grandfather had suggested it early on, but she rebelled, seeing those suggestions as just his way of passing her off yet again – let this damaged child be someone else's problem to fix. And the feeble attempts that school counselors had made at the different boarding schools she'd attended, she'd met those with icy resentment too. *Just tell them what they want to hear, and you can get out of this office unscathed.*

But even while he would laugh at the notion he was in any way qualified to help heal a shattered person, whatever key Harris had turned in her these past few days, had certainly unlocked feelings that overwhelmed her, sometimes almost shocking her in their intensity. And, for some reason, she completely abandoned all of her well-established defenses and shared the whole lot with him, tears, hiccups and all.

She shook her head, a little embarrassed now that she was out of that warm, safe cocoon in the mountains, now that she was back in the "real" world.

But, that wild ride already! Telling him all those things, showing him all those pictures of her life with her parents that she kept in Colorado to commemorate their lives there, sharing all those memories with him - memories no other person even knew about - because she was an only-child.

Standing here now, honestly, she felt guilty - almost like a betrayal - that she had never shared this much with Jasper these past two years. True, he grew up in a home where everything centered around covering up his mother's addiction, and he had never encouraged Mallory to talk about her messed up life, probably because he might have to deal with his own baggage if he pushed too hard.

It had been the cowardly way - the easy way - but early in their relationship, they had discussed that if you asked too much from life, if you expected too much from people, you were always disappointed. It was always best to just soldier on and make your life what you wanted. To hell with the rest of it.

Well, if the way she felt now was any indication, this way of living was a landslide better. Even though she felt physically drained; emotionally, she felt more alive than ever before. She noticed things differently, she felt things differently. And, in the back of her mind, as her eyes glanced past the open Bible sitting on Grandpa J's bookshelf, she knew she would make decisions about her life differently.

Moonlight was filtering in through the trees, creating a beautiful pattern of lights and darks across the wide planked floor of the living room and she walked over towards the window to find the moon high in the night's sky. Even though there was a protective, steep hill behind the house that was carpeted in thick trees, it was no mountain, so the moon covered the entire yard bathing it in a tapestry of cool blues, silvers and deep black shadows.

She squinted then, focused on sighting her friend, the owl, who was back at it again tonight, his throaty cadence a familiar sound track by now. But the sound of her cell phone ringing in the purse still hanging from her shoulder, startled her away from finding him.

"Hi, Jas." She had to smile, she'd texted him earlier, don't bother calling until later tonight when she'd be back in Minnesota. And, here he was, calling her later tonight. The guy sure could be persistent when he wanted to be. As all good sales people should be.

"Hey, hon. So, you're back to Minnesota. How was Colorado this year?"

"Everything's still there, I guess. Maggie and Don were gone this year on vacation though."

"So, you were there all by yourself?" And, the unstated question hung in the air, if so, why didn't you invite me to come along with you?

"Well, no." Inside she felt a flutter of panic, why hadn't she ever thought about how the past few days would look to Jasper? Honestly, she was at a loss how to explain Harris to him, and she noticed she felt tense and out of breath suddenly as she hurried on, "I went with a friend, he had some work to do in Grand Junction, so it just made sense for him to come along to Ouray."

"Bradford went with you to Colorado?" At the mention of a male friend, naturally Jasper assumed she meant Bradford. He had never really become close to Bradford, and for that matter, Bradford had never made a point of making friends with Jasper either. Even after her repeated objections, neither of them appreciated the other's strengths, and they both took every opportunity to let her know that she was much too good for "him." She had ignored them both, of course.

"No, he's the neighbor here in Minnesota. I thought I'd told you about him, his name is Harris. He took care of the house for Grandpa J."

"And, I suppose this guy is young, and he just conveniently had work in Grand Junction, so he could spend a few days alone with you in the mountains. Is that what you're telling me? Come on, Mallory, you're not that gullible, are you?"

"Oh, stop. Since when are you allowed to tell me who I'm friends with and what I do with my life?"

There was an awkward pause, and Mallory pictured him smoothing his hair and taking a deep breath, assessing his options on how the conversation would continue, or if it would continue.

"Of course, you're right." He conceded, rather too easily, Mallory thought, "I am just going a little crazy here, waiting for you to return. My mind is conjuring up all kinds of scenarios about us, and most of them end up without an "us," if you know what I mean."

"Well, rest assured Jasper, there isn't a hot romance going on with the guy next door here in Minnesota. He's not the type to take advantage of a grieving granddaughter, so you don't have to worry about him." She resolutely refused to dwell on Jasper's own next-door-neighbor transgressions, but if the words struck a chord with him, so be it.

Though her words were basically true, the bravado in her voice masked the many unsettled feelings still inside her regarding Jasper, and regarding Harris. As she peered out the window at a sudden movement in the dark branches of the tree next to the patio, she saw the shape of a creature, and with a shift on the branch, he allowed the moonlight to glance off his white head. The owl was looking in at her, giving her the impression that he was hearing her words, and he blinked his yellow eyes at her then, with a wise look of doubtful disbelief. Even he knew that she wasn't being completely honest with Jasper, or with herself.

"Yes, it arrived yesterday. The UPS driver brought it over here when he found no one home at her place. Peyton was here, and I had all I could do to stop him from ripping into it. He thought it might be a Christmas present." Paul laughed as he handed the box to Harris the next morning.

The return address was Tom Guillory, New York City and Harris remembered their conversation in Colorado with a smile. She was so excited to receive it and it made him ponder yet another example about how special this woman was. Growing up with all that money could buy, but still is most grateful for gifts that have some connection to the people in her fractured life.

"Okay, thanks, Paul. I will text her to come over to pick it up. Or, you can drop it off with her, I think she's there this morning."

"Well, I just thought you'd bring it over?" His light eyebrows lifted slightly, with a quizzical look, "Did something happen in Colorado? Did she cold-shoulder you, or somethin'?"

"No, nothing like that." Harris thought it over, might as well get it over with and come clean with him now or he will never let it rest.

"Yeah, I guess you could call it that." Harris continued sadly, "She's seeing someone. Actually, she's been seeing him off and on for a couple of years. She's going back east next week to carry on with her life. You know. With him."

Paul's smile faded suddenly, and he winced in sympathy.

"Bro, I'm sorry 'bout that." He reached out and grabbed Harris by the upper arm, pulling him into a loose hug, "That sucks for you, man."

Harris nodded and laughed a little at the gesture of affection, although he would give his life for his brother, and they knew each other's deepest secrets, there was still a midwestern, Scandinavian, unspoken touch-free zone, except in the most serious of circumstances. Like this one.

"Yeah, thanks, Paul. Guess a guy can't win the girl every time." The words to finish his train of thought were floating around in his mind, but he refused to let them reach his mouth - or ever, for me, when it comes to women.

Mallory looked up from where she was sitting at her Grandpa J's desk working on the newest copywriting project when she heard the heavy knock at the front door. Opening it, she was surprised to find Paul holding a next day air UPS package.

"Hi, Mallory. This came for you yesterday, but since you weren't here, UPS brought it over to the shop." Excitedly, she reached for the box, but not wanting to appear ungrateful, she commented brightly,

"Thanks, Paul! How are you doing? It sounded like Harris had a great meeting with your client in Grand Junction."

"Yeah, he did. Connie loves Harris. If she had the space, I think she'd buy everything in our line from him." He stopped, looking down at his leather boots for a moment, "He's really good at what he does, you know, he's a really talented guy, my brother."

"Yes, it certainly seems so. He says the same about you, by the way. You two have really found your niche here in the woods, who would have guessed?"

"Yeah. But, you make it sound like you think it's the end of the world "in these woods." It's not so bad here, some people really like it." Mallory was confused by the sudden change in his tone and the defensive challenge in his normally easy-going brown eyes. She wondered belatedly, was she coming off as a snob?

"Of course, I didn't mean to be a snob about it. I'm super impressed with you guys. And the work you do is amazing! I just meant that the fact that you choose to do it out here in rural Minnesota ... it makes your story even more special."

"We hope that's how people see it." He looked like he wanted to say more, but decided against it at the last moment, "Well, I guess I'd better get back to the shop, we're supposed to be getting on a conference call shortly. Take care, Mallory."

As she watched him walk away, she wondered with a little disappointment, since he must be over there for this call they were going to have, why had Harris asked Paul to bring the box to her instead of bringing it over himself? Of course, it could be that he didn't even know it had arrived.

She wasn't sure what Guillory could possibly send her that he thought she would treasure, but she guessed it was a personal item he must have found in her grandfather's brownstone as they prepared to list it with an agent.

Slicing open the tape and pulling back the flaps of the box, though, revealed a laptop and power cord, nothing extremely personal about that. An attached note listed the access password and explained that it was her Grandpa J's laptop and since Canton had already gone through it and downloaded work related files, Guillory thought the laptop should be hers. Oh, and by the way, he continued, check out the folder marked My Camille Photos, they are lovely and a quite a treasure.

There was still some battery left, so Mallory entered the password, and opened the folder, finding a series of photos dating back to their early marriage, and a series of photos of her dad as a child and then as an early teenager. As Mallory clicked through the photos, she watched the little family as they celebrated birthdays, Christmas mornings, ski vacations and private school band concerts. All the photos were evidence that they lived the comfortable, easy life that was to be expected for a renowned author and film producer at the peak of his career.

Then, she clicked open a photo of her grandmother Camille, her face was turned partially away from the camera and she was wearing a brightly colored scarf where normally her lush blonde hair would have fallen. Her skin looked tight, her eyes looked luminously large in her pale face, but her smile was confident as she looked off in the distance at her pre-teen age son Parker who was kneeling on a beach, petting a dog. This must have been the beginning of the end.

Clicking more photos open, she saw changes in the appearance of all three of them as the disease stole away Grandma Camille's light from their lives. The rest of the photos included a few of her father during his teenage years, usually in his boarding school uniforms or with his guitar. There were even a few pictures of her mom and dad and her as a baby and then as a toddler, that she had never seen before.

Mallory tried her best to envision her grandfather poring over these images as he dealt with the loss of his wife and then his son and daughter-in-law. The guy who could have anything in the world, still, she was sure he would have given it all up to have those people back again. And, now, he was gone too.

Her mind was foggy with emotion, a feeling where she lost track of time and sensation, as she distractedly opened the last file in the list, out of order with all the rest, as if it had been dropped in this spot by accident. It wasn't a photo file after all, it really shouldn't be in this folder anyway.

The page opened with large block letters –

STAND TALL, SON

THE FINAL CHAPTER

(final unedited version.jlm)

Dedicated to my son Canton and my daughter Jasmine,
because I couldn't do this without you

And for Parker, I miss you terribly, my son

And, starting on page three, Mallory found Chapter One.

CHAPTER 24

... euphoria, elation, delight, glee, bliss ... I find it all, and more, in this moment

Oh, my gosh. It's here. It's all here! Her fingers were shaking as she scrolled through the pages, checking off chapters one through six. Glancing towards heaven, without even realizing that by doing so, she admitted Harris must be right about where Grandpa J was now, she yelled as loud as she could.

"I can't believe I found it, Grandpa J!" She gulped air into her lungs with a big sigh, trying to calm herself down. This. This computer in her hands, this held the entire Final Chapter. To do with it whatever she wanted. *This was the moment.*

She took the moment and filtered various scenarios through her mind, one far side of the spectrum of options was to go it alone by hiring an attorney to protect her interests, shop the novel around for the highest dollar and keep all proceeds to herself. On the complete opposite side of the spectrum, just send it to Canton's office it in a plain envelope and tell them that she could care less about them, or her grandfather.

The old Mallory might have gone with either of these extremes, both of which would spite her family and her grandfather. But, would either of those reactions feel righteous to the Mallory that lived inside her right now?

No. It was clear that something had changed. Her view of family had changed. Her view of Grandpa J had changed. All because she had changed.

As she mulled it over, and sitting there with the entire novel in hand, she couldn't help but wonder what he meant in his letter about helping him finish something. It was all clearly here. The only scenario that made any sense was that he must have written the letter during a stretch of writer's block, not even remembering having written it when the block gave way and he finished the novel. As Harris had reminded her a few times, Grandpa J didn't know any of this was going to play out this way.

Harris. She had to tell Harris! He would be so excited to hear of this discovery and she was excited to share it with him, the entire novel. And, as she settled deeper into her favorite chair to read these first six chapters, she smiled as she thought about what her friend's reaction would be when she told him he would be the second person to read JL McMichael's crowning final achievement.

Surprised by her text that she wanted to see him about something and that she was headed his direction, Harris quickly wiped the kitchen counter after finishing his microwave dinner and checked to see what he had to offer her to drink. Nothing but some soda and bottled water. Of course. Guess it's to be expected, he hadn't entertained many guests recently.

He glanced out the window, just barely seeing her bright headband and dark hair as she walked to the front door. Now, just be cool, he cautioned himself about contemplating the purpose of her visit. It's probably something to do with the house, she might need help with something, don't let your imagination run wild. Remember she has a boyfriend and is leaving next week ... these and many other thoughts were stacking on top of each other as he reached for the front door. But, when he pulled the door open, he couldn't help it, something inside him still lit up like a campfire.

"Hey, neighbor. What's up?" He stepped aside with a smile, hoping she'd take the hint and come inside. As she walked past him, he caught the smell of a light, fresh flower scent which seemed to make his senses tingle. Somewhere it registered with him that he would remember that scent for quite a while after she was gone.

"Oh, nothing much–" She deadpanned, then within a moment, broke out the widest smile he'd ever seen, and her eyes started sparkling, the dark edges seeming even darker than usual, playing with the lights in his foyer. "Just the best surprise ever! And, THIS reaffirms that my passion for gifts is not misplaced!" She held out her hand towards him and he saw a single USB in her open palm.

"What?! That's what Guillory sent you in that big box?" She blinked slightly, her ecstatic look faltering slightly, but she continued.

"No. He sent me Grandpa J's laptop, telling me that he found a folder of pictures on it. And they were amazing pictures, by the way, many of which I'd never seen. I was excited enough to find those and then, just for the heck of it, I opened this other random file and guess what I found?"

"Judging by your demeanor, I'd hazard a guess that you found the missing chapters?"

"And you'd be right! But, Harris, it's *all* there and it's beyond awesome, it's incredible!" She urgently offered the USB to him again, so he took it, "I want you to read it. I want you to enjoy it. No one else knows about it except you, me and Grandpa J. For now, it's our secret!"

Something about the whole moment hit him with a feeling of overwhelming camaraderie, like they were two kids who shared an adventure together and, at the end of it, they found the hidden treasure. It was intensely personal, this connection he had with her. And, even though he'd never shared his true feelings for her verbally, by this unexpected offer, she had validated every question in his mind. She felt something for him too. Maybe it wasn't romantic, and that hurt him deeply, but it was *something else*. In some ways, he even admitted, maybe it was s*omething better*.

As he processed through these emotions, he felt tears begin to prick at his eyes. He couldn't help it, he was just so happy to see her happy. Was he really going to cry over something like this? He quickly wiped at his lashes with the back of his hand, and with the other arm, he reached around her, and pulled her into a hug.

He didn't think about it, and he didn't wait to see her reaction, but quickly he felt her relax in his arms and reach around his waist to hug him back. As they stood there for a moment, Harris found himself glad that she was still in her bulky winter jacket, feeling her this close otherwise would have been very dangerous. At least for him.

"You are the coolest girl I know, Mallory. I'm so glad Mike was my neighbor." He pulled back a little to look down into her eyes, "Thank you."

He was sure his true feelings were loud and clear, but he tried to lighten it up by kissing her on the top of her head - like a child, like a sister or a friend - and then he released her as Penny trotted over and rubbed against Mallory's legs welcoming her in her own friendly way.

"You're very welcome." She said as she knelt to run her fingers through the fur around Penny's ears. "I'm not even going to stay and chill with you two here because I want you to read it right away. You don't have any plans tonight, do you?" She asked with a worried tone, as if expecting him to cancel any if he had.

"No, nothing as important as reading this, that's for sure."

"Good." She stood up and turned, preparing to leave. Wow, she wasn't kidding, she really meant it when she said she wasn't going to stay.

"Hey - so finding the entire novel - that doesn't change anything for you? You still plan on going back home and sharing it with your aunt and uncle?"

"No change to that plan. Yes, I will share it with them. Before, I was thinking of doing that because I gave up on trying to finish it, I knew I wasn't up to the task. Now, I'm doing it because it's the right thing to do. Just one look at his dedications and I knew that was the only way."

He reached around her shoulder and opened the front door for her, the blast of cold winter air making his eyes water again.

"Okay, it's your choice," Harris continued, "Just double checking that it's what you really want, and that you won't have any regrets." He watched as she stepped out onto his porch and turned to him with what looked like a hesitant smile.

"No regrets. I choose not to live with regrets." And, then with a small wave and a crooked peace-out sign, she left.

CHAPTER 25
... It's official, I'm back to reality ...

Thankful now that she had decided to park the Jeep in a storage garage near the Minneapolis airport that Saturday afternoon and fly back to Baltimore instead of driving, Mallory waved a short goodbye to the friendly, pink-haired Uber driver, and pressed the security code into the door lock at her apartment building. The thought of driving two days across half the country, in the middle of winter, and all alone, it was just too much for her. Maybe not for everyone, she might be a wimp, but so be it.

This way, by parking the car in storage, she didn't have to ask Harris for a ride to the airport and she would have a way to drive back out to Beck's Creek whenever she had to close on the house. Hopefully, it would sell quickly.

Now, she sighed at the sight of the stairwell that led up to her apartment above the street-level paint store and the large bag she would have to lug up those stairs. Now, she was home.

Everything was getting back to normal again. She had paid her neighbor who ran a housekeeping business to clean her place before she got home, so she knew it would be spotless and on Monday before her interview, she would go to the post office and remove the forward service they had on her mail. She was officially back.

And, the interview! She was elated to receive the call earlier in the week from a Baltimore advertising agency telling her they had an opening, had reviewed her resume and wanted to interview her on Monday.

It all happened so fast that she had to hurry up her plans for coming back east, leaving so many things undone in Minnesota, including a meeting with the real estate agent to take pictures of the place. But Harris had agreed to help the agent out whenever she needed it.

So, after a send-off dinner last night, with Paul, Carissa and Peyton all saying their goodbyes, she felt a sad drift of closure over her stay in Minnesota.

Of course, the hardest part was saying goodbye to Harris. After the others had left, they had hung out late into the night, sitting in front of his fireplace, talking about Grandpa J's wide array of books and movies and his newest novel - which Harris proclaimed a new favorite.

Thinking over the evening while on her flight home today, Mallory cherished how special it was because it gave Harris the chance to better understand his friend Mike as an award-winning author with an impressive collection of literary and film work, industry awards and celebrity connections.

But, even more important, their conversation last night allowed Mallory to experience her Grandpa J as just a normal guy, the next-door neighbor, who enjoyed writing song lyrics and had found a life-altering relationship with Jesus in the months before he died. He was, after all, both of those people.

Harris played his guitar and sang the songs that they had written together, and he reflected on some of the specific moments and thoughts Grandpa J shared with him that proved the transformation he witnessed was real, including the night that Grandpa J prayed with him and Harris gave him his Bible.

Even now, back in her apartment, Mallory was frustrated that, in her haste to leave this morning, she hadn't remembered to bring the Bible with her. She made a mental note that the Bible, along with his other books, were among the possessions she wanted to pack up and ship out here when the house sold.

Finally, after having talked and laughed until they were almost falling asleep, Harris announced he'd walk her home because, "You never know what you'll come across in this neighborhood, ha ha."

As they stood outside her door, with her cheeks tingling in the frigid bite of the December night, he told her that he would miss her, don't be a stranger and don't forget about your friends here in the woods. She had laughed and told him, that was unlikely. And, then they hugged and said goodbye. And that should have been the end of the story.

But it wasn't. As he pulled back from her hug, he'd looked deep into her eyes and told her in a voice so low and warm that it seemed to emanate from somewhere deep inside him, "I wish we could wake up in a few hours and everything would be different."

She stood still, trying to imagine the rest of the thoughts that prompted him to actually say that out loud. And as she held her breath, allowing his words to sink in, she felt desperate that he bravely voiced something she had been feeling for a while. But instead of owning up to that, and all the implications of it, she'd run away, visibly pulling deeper into herself than ever before. Can you believe that kind of cowardice?

When she finally found words, she patted him on his chest, and told him, "Everything is just too complicated." With her life out in Baltimore, and Jasper, and the book, it was all too much. Once she'd finished stumbling through her excuses, she'd finally allowed some truth to come out, telling him she would be "forever grateful to him for his friendship."

But, even though she meant every word of that, even to her own ears, it sounded like she was callously putting him in the friend zone – all the while, knowing full well that what they had shared went way deeper than that. But, that's what she'd said to him. And, once the words were out of her mouth, there was no turning back.

Jasper was back in her life. First, it was dinner at the club the night she got back, the next day it was coffee and a walk around Patterson Park in the morning and an afternoon spent lounging around her apartment, reading the Sunday papers and talking about her job interview the next day and his work and family.

If Jasper noticed her disengagement when he kissed her, he didn't let on to her. If he noticed her dodging his oblique questions about their future, he didn't let on to her. If he noticed that she was thinking about a life back in the woods in Minnesota, he didn't let on to her.

He probably rationalized that the old Mallory had walls around her inner self, he was used to that, and he had fallen in love with that Mallory, so, on some level, this maybe even felt normal to him.

But, inside, *this* Mallory – the new Mallory who confronted her emotions, who *wanted* to feel things again – was dying. It was only a matter of time, and the new Mallory would be eaten alive by the old. And, then the new Mallory would be just a memory too.

CHAPTER 26
... All I want for Christmas ...

"Yes, the web listing looks great, I especially like the pictures of the backyard taken through the window. Okay, I will tell him that you have some showings scheduled for Wednesday so if it snows he will clear the sidewalk and driveway. Yeah, he's great. Well, yes ... he is single. Yeah, go for it, I guess. Thanks, you have a great Christmas too."

Mallory silently agreed with the young woman's assessment of how "nice a guy" Harris was, but didn't really like to think about her real estate agent's plan to ask him out to lunch. It made her wonder, though, how much time was she spending out there anyway?

Suddenly annoyed with the world, Mallory swiped closed the telephone call just as the elevator reached the executive suites of JLM Publishing, housed on the top floor of the historic building on West 22nd Street, near Madison Square Park.

Even though she was thoroughly bothered by the final moments of the call, she was grateful that the call had distracted her for a few moments during her elevator ride up here. She knew she held the all the cards, in the form of a USB that was snuggled safely in the oversized pocket of her vintage, jade green wool coat, but she couldn't overcome her feelings of insecurity about this meeting with her aunt and uncle to discuss the call their attorney made to William Bannon's office.

And, as odd as it might seem to deal with a topic so loaded as the "missing" manuscript today – the day they were having the company Christmas party – it was unavoidable, it was the only day her aunt was in New York until after the first of the year. She glanced at her phone to check the time. Well, the party should be in full swing by now, hopefully, the hosts had both enjoyed a glass or two of wine before she arrived, maybe it would make this ordeal less adversarial.

Because she had checked in with security downstairs, Mallory was expecting Canton's receptionist to greet her at the elevators, but she was still a little surprised to find the young man wearing a hideous green and red plaid sweater vest over his starched white dress shirt and expensive purple tie. The young guy with the artfully gelled hair introduced himself as Brock, from what she could understand, but between the loud music and the large group of employee/party-goers, she wasn't quite sure she heard him correctly. It didn't seem to matter to him if she heard him, he turned on his heel and cheerfully waved her to follow him through the groups of people milling around the lobby, stopping midway at a party bar to offer her a glass of alcohol-laced holiday punch.

As they continued through the group of people, Mallory glanced around, attempting to spot either Jasmine or Canton, but didn't see them anywhere. She wondered, did they ever get out and mingle with the troops, or were they more of the ivory-tower-type managers? If she had to guess, she'd say they mingled only as much as business etiquette demanded.

Just remember, she mentally pumped herself up, they are no better than you, and you have something they want, she reminded herself as she followed the receptionist to the small conference room, reserved for the very most important, private meetings, next to the lobby area.

She glanced down the hallway towards the open door of Grandpa J's old office and noticed it looked the same. No one had cleaned it out yet, or taken it over, by the looks of it. But, then his office wasn't the grand one on this floor, Uncle Canton's was the largest, it was on the corner, with the floor to ceiling windows and with the best view. *That* office door was firmly closed.

"Well, it's good to see you again and congratulations! Guillory was telling me that you've found a position in Baltimore." After making her wait for a few minutes, they had joined Mallory, with their holiday drinks in hand, first exchanging small talk about her cousins. Then, purposefully, Uncle Canton eased into his professional tone of voice again. This was, after all, not a social call, it was about some business.

"Thank you. I know the agency well, and it's growing, so it should be a good job, for now anyway."

"Well, if it's not what you expected, you know you always have a spot here, if you're interested." Canton, wearing his heavy rimmed, brown glasses and dressed in his usual designer suit, sat back in his chair again, crossed his legs and watched her evenly. He was well aware of Grandpa J's feelings on the matter. Mallory was surprised he would bring it up, now that Grandpa J wasn't around, so he couldn't possibly feel any obligation to offer her a job. Maybe he was sincere?

"Well, thank you, I appreciate it and will keep it in mind." Mallory's mouth was suddenly dry, and she noticed her fingers were shaking as she took another sip of the holiday punch. Wow, that had a kick, and she pursed her lips and blinked as the strong liquor passed over her tongue and stuck in her throat.

"Mallory," Aunt Jasmine spoke up, "Forgive me for being blunt, but we all know that it's been years since you've made an effort to connect with the family." She glanced at her brother with a knowing look, "Your uncle and I have discussed this, and we take responsibility for not making it easier for you." With her usual poise, she swirled her drink around a little, making the ice cubes clink against the crystal.

"For years," she continued, "we've allowed father's feelings about Parker's choices to color how we interact with you, and it's not a good look. We would like to ask your forgiveness for that and see if we can change this going forward. You are part of our brother, after all. We both miss him."

At that moment, as her words floated in the air between them, Mallory wished they were sitting anywhere else but the office conference room for this conversation, like maybe at a dining room table. You know, like most normal families.

"Well. I appreciate that, too. Honestly, I want to do the same." For some reason, her aunt was approaching this business meeting almost as a human being would. This was very confusing, and not what Mallory expected, and it left her feeling like Jasmine was playing the lead role in one of her JLM Productions movies. Could this be real?

"Father was acting very strangely in the weeks preceding his death, Mallory. Were you aware that he claimed he "met Jesus," or something like that, in the month or so before he died?" She looked past Mallory's shoulder, focusing on the abstract acrylic painting hanging on the wall above the expensive walnut credenza, deep in her own thoughts, "As strange as it might seem, I can tell you, he *was* different. It was a *noticeable difference*; it changed the way he spoke, and he wanted to make his past wrongs right somehow. With Canton, with me. Just in so many ways ... he was different."

As she spoke, Mallory felt her doubts about Jasmine's sincerity gradually subside, as if they were dust particles swept under the door and out into the foyer. Aunt Jasmine really *did* believe Grandpa J had changed. She had actually seen him change.

After nodding in agreement with his sister, Canton lowered his drink glass slowly, setting it neatly on a drink napkin on the conference room table and spoke.

"I agree. He was never an easy man to please, as we all know very well. But at the end, it was as if his driving mission in life was to repair relationships with people. I know it moved me. I was never prouder of him than I was then, at the end." He looked from Mallory back to his sister, a small, compassionate smile curving his mouth, "It's made us both evaluate what's important in life."

Mallory remembered her conversation with her cousin Geoffrey and noted that he used almost the exact same words to describe his own life reckonings after Grandpa J's death.

"Yes," Mallory spoke into the pause of conversation, "I'm aware that he was trying to make amends. It seems that he made his rounds to everyone, except me."

She faltered slightly, admitting that out loud was a major statement for her, especially as vulnerable as they were prone to make her feel. But what good would it do to hold back now? So, she plowed forward, wanting them to be reassured, when it came to her too, their father wasn't the monster she'd made him out to be for most of her adult life. She wasn't looking for their sympathy.

"For a while, that really bothered me." She continued quietly, "You know - I was thinking I must not make the cut or something. But, I found a letter from him in Minnesota, one he never sent because he said he wanted to tell me all of it in person. Even though I never heard it from him while he was alive, that letter told me what I needed to know."

"Oh." Jasmine let out a soft, regretful sigh and leaned towards Mallory, her perfectly made-up eyes misting with tears, "I'm sorry he wasn't able to tell you in person. When I think about his last hours and how I'm sure he wanted to see you to tell you - well, I'm just glad that you found it."

"Yes," Canton sat up a little straighter, always the one who needed to be in control, determined to get back to business, "And now it's up to us to carry on, we need to continue to build on what he left us. So, with that said, I'm guessing you wanted to meet with us because of the letter we sent Bannon about a missing manuscript for the third in the "Stand Tall, Son" series? I suppose you found that manuscript in Minnesota when you found this letter from him?"

"I talked to Mr. Bannon, yes." Mallory deflected his question, having one of her own, "What I want to know - why do you suspect there *is* a missing manuscript?"

"Because he told us he was finished with it." Canton leaned forward, putting his hands out flat on the table, Mallory's eyes catching on the expensive gold watch that peeked out from under his sleeve, and he continued evenly, "Listen, I know Bannon's position is that it's your property if it was housed in Minnesota. He told me father specifically said you were the beneficiary of a work that was left in Minnesota. But, Mallory, you can imagine how important it is to our companies to publish that. The process was already in motion ... before he died."

"If you have the manuscript, we don't want this to get ugly, Mallory." Jasmine's voice was soft and persuasive, and when she moved in her chair, Mallory caught the scent of expensive perfume, "Our attorneys assure us that the novel is under contract, so we control the rights to publication and film rights. But, even though that's the legal position, we also *feel* that you are entitled to share the proceeds, if for no other reason, then because you're our brother's daughter, and our father's granddaughter."

Sharing the proceeds wasn't something she had considered them offering, and she had no way of knowing what "sharing the proceeds" would even look like. But, in the end, her mind was made up a while ago, it wasn't tied to anything financial.

And, as the three of them sat there watching each other all cagey-like, the words of his dedication floated through her mind as if she was reading them in black and white in front of her and she envisioned their faces, when they read the words of the dedication for the first time. She pictured them as the little children they once were, receiving a gift from their father:

Dedicated to my son Canton and my daughter Jasmine,
because I couldn't do this without you

And for Parker, I miss you terribly, my son

She reached into the pocket of her coat which was draped over the chair next to her. Fingering the USB, she felt the full weight of this moment where she released control of Grandpa J's final novel, and it felt good. No, that didn't quite describe the moment. No, in fact, it felt glorious.

"Well, you're right." Mallory spoke confidently into the quiet room, not even hearing the dull noise of the Christmas party on the other side of the door, and she smiled in satisfaction as their eyes focused on the USB she set on the conference room table, "The missing manuscript you've been wondering about *does* exist. It was forgotten, put in a place that no one was likely to look. But, now, it's not missing anymore."

CHAPTER 27
... Like I said earlier, Holidays are often some of the most difficult days

The soft white light of the moon and the playful multicolored lights that were draped on the decorated jack pine evergreens were blending brilliantly together on the smooth snow drifts in the front yard of his parents' home that Christmas Eve, reminding him of Christmas Eves years ago when he and Paul would try to stay awake all night waiting to catch Santa in the act.

The childhood rite of passage – trying to indisputably prove that Santa was or wasn't real – had been settled rather unceremoniously the year Harris was seven and Paul was six years old. Mrs. Claus had lovingly stowed all of Santa's gifts in the back end of the family minivan, under a blanket, safe from inquisitive eyes. The boys would have never known the gifts were there except their father had sent them to retrieve two gallons of milk after their mother had returned from a trip to the grocery store – "You two go look for them, they must be in the van somewhere."

Guess Santa and Mrs. Claus weren't operating from the same playbook that year.

He glanced down towards his feet where Penny had twitched suddenly in her sleep, most likely dreaming she was chasing rabbits in the backyard. It was amazing she could fall asleep at all given the noise from the other room where Peyton, Paul and his dad were playing a raucous game of Chutes and Ladders, and Nat King Cole was pining away on the stereo while his mother and Carissa tried to talk over him as they sat at the dining room table, drinking their after-dinner coffee.

The family had just finished cleaning up after their Christmas Eve dinner, and now the women were already planning tomorrow's festivities, starting with gift opening early in the morning because Peyton would be up at the crack of dawn, followed by an egg-and-bacon-bake brunch, then turkey and all the fixings mid-afternoon. Another holiday where he would eat too much ... and would love every minute of it. Except.

Harris shifted his gaze from the dining room to look outside again, trying hard not to think about her. Trying his best not to wonder if she was with Him.

But it was a losing battle, and his mind wandered down that path of no return. Again. For the thousandth time since she'd left.

He supposed they were spending Christmas at his parents' multi-million-dollar mansion, she'd told Harris that he came from a wealthy family. Or, maybe they were alone together at his multi-million-dollar mansion, it's likely his home was spectacular too. He could just see them sitting together by the fire, listening to some perfectly romantic music with a professionally decorated Christmas tree in the background. Probably all snuggled up together, gazing into each other's eyes right this very moment, happily planning their lives together.

Ok, that's enough, he had to get over this. He had to get over her. She had made it clear that he was never anything more than just a "good friend" to her.

Those words hurt though, because even as he was trying to be legit with her - trying to be that guy, the one who respected her boundaries and didn't make this into something else - he was sure he was beginning to feel something changing, something deeper happening, with her. But, he must have been living in his own separate universe, one where she was beginning to feel something for him, the way he felt for her. The problem was, in her universe she felt that way about someone else. Not him.

He needed some air. He needed ... something. And, he wasn't going to find it here. This place on Christmas, with all its happy memories and happy people, making more happy memories - he was poisoning it. Penny woke at his abrupt movement and jumped to attention when she saw him take his coat from the arm of the overstuffed chair near the door. She ambled dutifully behind him as he silently opened the front door and walked to his truck in the driveway, avoiding contact with any of the family. Then they drove home together. To be alone.

At that moment, Mallory looked out the window, wondering what was Harris doing this Christmas Eve? Who was he with? Was he laughing or singing? Was he thinking about her?

She pushed the curtain back, it was raining outside. It wasn't snowing, and it was Christmas Eve. Something just wasn't right about that.

He noticed the kitchen light sparkling brightly through the paned window onto the shadowed hedges outside, allowing a clear view into the house, now that it was pitch black night. The agent had texted him yesterday morning saying there was a couple from out of state who were here visiting family for Christmas, they were personal friends of hers, and they would like to look at the house. She must have left that light on after that showing and he hadn't noticed it last night. Might as well check things over and turn that light off.

The headlights of his truck reflected off the FOR SALE sign at the curb and made their way up Mike's driveway as he pulled up, his tires leaving tracks in the light dusting of snow that had fallen earlier in the afternoon. When he opened the driver's side door on his truck, Penny was quick to follow.

"Oh well, sure, you can come along too. Just so you know though, Mallory won't be here." He said sadly to the dog as she trotted alongside him on the path and waited expectantly on the front steps as he fit the key into the lock. Once the door creaked open, Penny headed straight-away for the rug by the fireplace, sitting at attention, her eyes locked on the tin box sitting on the mantle, with her tail thumping on the floor behind her. Now that he knew about the treats, it was obvious what she was begging for.

"Yes, yes. I know what you want. Just wait a second." Harris felt his phone vibrate in his back pocket and, retrieving it, he read a text from Paul:

PAUL: What's up? Did you take Penny out for a walk and get lost?

HARRIS: No, just decided I would rather sleep at home and will come back in early A.M. And hey - Don't get too comfortable in your old room tonight. Santa can't sleep in on Christmas morning you know. He has work to do.

PAUL: Ha, ha. Mrs. Claus already told me that. Merry Christmas, bro

HARRIS: Same to you, brother

Harris wandered into the kitchen, checked the lock on the window over the sink, which he had noticed Mallory liked to leave open a crack if the fireplace was too stoked up, and he checked that the door leading outside to the garage was locked as well. Satisfied that everything looked fine, he flipped the light off and came back into the living room to find Penny still waiting in her spot by the fireplace.

"Okay, good dog." He reached into the tin and gave her a dog treat, "That's a good girl." He crouched down, ruffled her ears and as he stood back up again, his eye caught on the Bible sitting open on the shelf of the bookcase.

He had given Mike the Bible that night in his screen porch and Harris smiled, remembering his deep appreciation at having received the gift. Over the next few weeks, Mike read the Bible voraciously, frequenting texting Harris with questions or comments on verses he'd read. Walking alongside a new believer in those first few weeks after he met Christ was unlike anything else Harris had experienced in his faith. When Mike would thank him, he'd reply with complete honesty - No, thank *you*. You are deepening my faith through yours, we're in it together.

Harris reached for the Bible, curious about the last verses he had been reading before he left Minnesota. As he lifted the Bible, however, he was distracted as something dropped from within the pages onto the floor and slid along the wood planks and under the side table. Not seeing what it was, he knelt, and directed his cell phone flashlight on the floor until he saw the small ridge of the item. Reaching under the table, he moved his hand around until his fingers found the plastic device.

Another USB? He held it in his palm thinking, what's with Mike and all these USBs? What the heck. Maybe it was another copy of the novel. Or, maybe it was another novel altogether. He was beginning to believe anything was possible in this meandering mystery of Mike's last months on this earth.

Dropping the USB into his jacket pocket, with Penny following along beside him, he walked to the door, and breathing in deeply, he was sure he could still smell the lingering scent Mallory wore and the hint of fresh flowers made him smile, despite his mood. Leaving the small table lamps in the hallway shining with just enough light to make it look like someone was still home here, he locked the front door behind them.

A half hour later, after showering and making himself a cup of hot chocolate, Harris fluffed up the pillows behind him in his bed, stretched his legs out in front of him, and clicked on the USB icon to open it on his laptop. The rational side of his brain was saying it was most likely nothing more than Mallory had already found. But, the rest of his whole being was praying that it was something she would find interesting, something so exceptional that he would have an excuse to call her. And he was already looking forward to hearing her voice again.

CHAPTER 28

This Old Man...My Story
JL McMichael (aka Mike Jones)

Dedicated to My Mallory

I am an old man, I've lived a long life. If you were to meet me in person, your first impression would be, "This man is weathered and worn, doesn't he know he can pay someone to erase what time has done to his face?"

It's likely that you would politely avert your eyes from my knobby, curled fingers and my thinning, snow-white hair. And, you would graciously try to ignore my weak voice - with it's disturbing, slight tremor - that most annoying tremor that fills the insufferable delays as I search for words that used to be so abundant in my mind and, within a moment's grasp, readily available to my lips.

But there are few facts in life less inflexible than this one:

"Change - and age - is inevitable."

For years, I have accepted life's changes with barely a passing glance. I have travelled those roads, with all their twists and turns, fearlessly. No doubt, I have lived a large life and I have many experiences, personal relationships and material possessions to show for it.

I have been blessed, as they say. And, because I have been blessed with such a remarkably rich life experience, this truth is startling clear to me now. The older I become, the more my world is shrinking.

My horizons are closer, the road is narrower and the shadows on either side of it are deeper. And, now I realize that I travel this road with increased trepidation and some regret. I ask myself, is there time to tell the story, is there time enough to say what I want to say? I have so much more that I want to say.

When I consider the chapters in my life, I see that they are full of distinct moments, some of them bright and scintillating, some of them dark and disturbing, and many of them deeply moving. As my life's horizon draws closer, each of these moments seem to grow larger, they mean something different - something significant - given the contemplation of time.

It is this way with every life, I suppose, I'm certainly not unique. It just feels so real to me now that I have arrived here.

Now that I am This Old Man.

I've told many stories in my life, but the story of This Old Man is one I've never condensed into written form. Let me attempt to do that for you here ...

The annoying light was burning bright and it was focused directly into his eyes. Maybe if he moved over a little bit here, he could ignore it and go back to sleep. It couldn't be time to get up already, could it?

Harris shifted further away from the light of his bedside lamp and sat up, startled by the sound of his laptop sharply shutting closed with the weight of his arm. What the heck? He looked at his legs stretched out and the blankets and pillows in a mess around him. The memory of reading the memoir came back to him then. He had read the whole thing, or at least to the end of what was written on this USB. Finally, he fell asleep, but it must have been really late. As in early morning late.

Sitting up straighter in his bed, he thought in a panic - What time is it? He knew they would be opening gifts at seven o'clock or so. Glancing at the clock on his bedside table, he breathed a sigh of relief as he realized he still had an hour before he was expected at his parents' house.

Rubbing his sore, tired eyes with the backs of his hands, he glanced again at the laptop with the USB attached to the side. Wow, Mike. Just, wow. He couldn't think of a better way to describe the guy's life, and the honesty with which he'd written about his life, in this memoir.

Mallory had given Harris the basic outline of Mike's early life - that he had been raised in suburban Washington DC, as an only child by his adoptive parents - so that part of the memoir wasn't new information. But Mike's memoir elaborated with details that his father was a decorated WWII military officer, who took a post-war civilian defense contractor engineering position and his mother was a civil service professional at the State Department, whose work required frequent, extended overseas travel.

And, although the memoir was not strictly chronological, the overarching themes of Mike's life, including ones of isolation and loneliness, were evident immediately.

His parents' laser focus on their careers left their young son to fend for himself and this affected him deeply. From an early age, it became clear to Mike that his home life was different from many of his peers of that era, most of whom had siblings and a mother who kept the home and a father whose work provided the finances for the family.

By comparison, although his parents loved him, they did not feel he required constant supervision and many times Mike was left unsupervised after school and on weekends. It was a lonely life for a child and he filled his time writing full length novels in long hand and hiding them in a shoebox under his bed. He wrote stories of boys living life out west in Montana or on the bayou in Louisiana, and in his memoir, Mike remembered these stories as simple, pure imagination, innocent in their longing for a life much larger than what he could see out his bedroom window.

This loneliness fueled his desire to write himself a "second life" in his head and sometimes he struggled to assimilate the real from the imaginary. This was a frustration for his parents who, while they appreciated his gifts with the English language, considered it an altogether different prospect when Mike, as a teenager, shared with them his dreams of making writing his career.

From the beginning, Mike shared with aching honesty, he battled not only his own insecurities with his writing skills, but also a distinct sense of disappointment from his parents. Always in search of what he called unconditional love, by the time he became an adult, he had warped his definition of unconditional love to mean, "you show me love by unconditional loyalty, respect and submission to my ways, my will."

In his world, if you weren't with him 110%, 100% of the time, you must not truly love him, and that was enough for him to cut you out of his life. Unfortunately, he held the people closest to him, his family, to the highest expectations to meet this standard. And, unfortunately, some of them failed.

And, while he recounted a life with many happy moments, mostly from the time while his wife Camille was alive, generally, Mike was not a happy man. He was always searching for something.

Towards the end of the memoir, he spoke about his meeting with his Savior. It was delivered in stark, honest terms, and he didn't elaborate on the specific circumstances, a fact which Harris could appreciate because it was so personal.

Mike was unequivocal in his statement that he had been changed; he didn't judge others with his confessions, nor did he water them down to make them PC. He just stated the reality. He was a new man and he wanted to live his new life the best way he knew how. Each day was an adventure.

Even after reading these promising passages about his faith, it hurt to read this memoir, Harris noted sadly. Not only because of the unfiltered honesty with which he shared the painful aspects of his life. No, it hurt to read the memoir because it was left unfinished.

Mike's biggest regrets had to do with his alcoholism and his fractured relationships, including the ones with his deceased son Parker and now with his free-spirited granddaughter Mallory. It was at this point in the memoir, the very end, that Mike must have recognized that he needed to confront these demons directly with

Mallory and find some kind of resolution before he could finish writing the story of his life.

This was the work that Mallory was supposed to finish with him. It was all too clear now. This was what Mike was talking about in his letter to her. And, even though Harris was disappointed – heartbroken, honestly – that she had begun her life again out east and he was no longer part of her world, he was still thankful that he found this and could send it to her. It was the right thing to do – he would pray for her that she could complete her journey through this and hopefully heal from the pain of her past.

Mindful that is was Christmas morning and a little boy was probably up already, waiting to open his gifts from Santa, Harris quickly copied the file over to a link. While he waited for it to load, he realized he was glad that he was in a hurry this morning because otherwise he would be tempted to dwell on the thought of Mallory, and his despondent disposition would come through loud and clear in his text to her.

As it was, he pulled up her name in his Contacts, copied the link and typed a simple message:

Merry Christmas, Mallory, here's a gift I found for you. I know how much you love gifts.

Love, Harris

As he hit Send, he thought with satisfaction, *There you go, Mike. It's finally in her hands.* Now, Mallory had some writing to do, and this time, she would find the words. It was *her* story to finish. And, as much as he hated to admit it, her story just didn't include him in it.

That's just the way this one worked out. He was sure *someday* he would find *someone*.

A half hour later, after a quick shower and shave, he loaded up the brightly wrapped gifts he'd purchased for his family and held the door open for Penny to jump in alongside him in the pickup truck.

Out of habit, Harris glanced over at her house as he passed alongside it, noting through the almost-still-dark morning haze that the sidewalk needed shoveling after last night's snowfall. And, even though he saw the hall light twinkling through the window, the little stone house still looked vacant. Without her, without life.

Harris shook his head slightly, tore his eyes away from the sight of it, and ruffled his fingers through the copper-colored fur behind Penny's ear, to which the dog replied with a soft moan and a thumping tail on the passenger side seat. Harris smiled sadly, and said aloud to no one in particular,

"Good luck to you, Mallory. I'm forever grateful to have known you."

The End

EPILOGUE

Many weeks later: we move on, life just has a way of doing that to us

"Hey, turn up the volume, would you?" Harris called across the room to his brother, and then bent back to the work in front of him, carefully smoothing the cut of leather over the cushion on the back of the club chair and then securely fastening it along the bottom frame. Unconsciously singing along to the song on Spotify, he settled the ample upholstered seat cushion onto the chair and stepped back with a critical eye focused on the latest combination of leather and rugged, canvas-type fabric in the rich, earthy colors. Something about these materials together, it just felt right. These club chairs would be the perfect complement to the line of fall furniture they were working on.

Again though, thoughts of her, prompted by the John Denver song filtering through the speakers, winnowed their way through his work deliberations. These thoughts would often rumble around his subconscious, as if they were the lyrics of a song, on a soundtrack that played incessantly in the background, and then suddenly someone jacked up the volume, and the thoughts would urge their way front and center.

Sometimes, it would be random memories of something she had said or something they had laughed at together. Sometimes, he would ask himself, I wonder if she would like this or that item in their product line. All random musings, going nowhere, since he hadn't heard from her for almost two months.

His Christmas surprise - when he sent her the memoir - was a fantastic let-down. While she was excited, telling him she was stunned speechless by his discovery, she did not engage much with him after their initial texts. She told him that she was starting a new job after the first of January and she didn't really know what she would do - if anything - about the memoir.

Conspicuously absent was any mention of Jasper and their lives together. When he finally asked because the *not-knowing* was driving him crazy, she texted back, "Oh, you know. The same." Yeah, whatever that's supposed to mean.

And now there was this other situation to deal with.

When the official-looking envelope arrived certified mail from the New York attorney's office, he thought it might be a scam, or maybe some class action lawsuit for a defective car part or something. He didn't know anyone in New York, and he certainly didn't have an attorney there.

The letter apologized profusely for the delay assigning this disbursement, the attorney stating that the original letter had been returned to sender because of an incorrect address. The "disbursement" was a $250,000 check issued on the account of J.L. McMichael trust. Harris couldn't believe it was for real and didn't understand why Mike would feel that he deserved such an extravagance. Once, the initial shock wore off though, he knew exactly what he would use the money for.

Now, today, he was going to call her. Tell her that he wanted to buy the little stone house. As far as he knew, it was still for sale; he hadn't seen any moving vans in the driveway. Not that she would feel obligated to give him a heads up if she sold it, that was abundantly clear.

Resolutely, he walked to his office, took a deep breath to clear his mind and dialed her number. Just stay focused, he schooled himself, don't think about anything except buying this house. She will probably have you work out all the details with the pretty, blonde real estate agent that had been trying to sell it. And, maybe you *should* go out to lunch with that agent Hannah, she's asked a couple of times. She seems nice enough–

"Hello? Harris?" Her voice was breathless, and instantly something melted inside him and all thoughts of a blonde real estate agent were obliterated by a vivid picture of dark-haired beauty with light blue, almost lavender, eyes. Okay, it was obvious he wasn't ready to talk to her - to hear the mellow, rounded tones in her voice - he should have known he wasn't ready for this. That's what texting was for.

"Yes. Hi, Mallory. Sorry to bother you at work, but I have something I want to talk to you about, if you have a minute."

"You're kidding me, right? At work?" She laughed a little, hesitating, "Harris, I'm over here, look out your window."

Maybe his feet didn't even touch the ground, he was sure he must have teleported across the yard, because moments later he abruptly found himself on her front steps. Or maybe he was so focused on protecting his heart - psyching himself out, not to get too excited about seeing her - that he just didn't register the fact that he'd walked over here without even throwing on a jacket.

As he lifted the door knocker, he observed that the FOR SALE sign was lying face down in the snow bank by the street, but he refused to dwell on what that meant. All that was important right now was that she was here again.

"Hey, neighbor!" Mallory felt the smile erupt from somewhere deep inside at the sight of him, a feeling of warmth soaked through her body as she instinctively reached out to hug him close, and a thousand tingles danced along her arms and up her neck as she wrapped her arms around his waist.

She stepped back, pulling him by his forearms into the foyer, "Oh my gosh, it's so funny you called! I was just coming over to find you. Come in and sit down. I have so much to tell you!"

Harris followed her into the living room and silently sat down opposite her in one of the chairs he'd built. Noticing that he didn't have a jacket on, her eyes travelled over his dark blue jeans and the sable-colored comfy knit shirt he was wearing, which drew out the velvety soft brown of his eyes. Just the sight of him prompted her to question her self-imposed torture of the past few weeks again - thinking of him, dreaming about him - all while trying to move on from him.

"First, I want to say I've missed you so much, Harris." Mallory had a list of things to tell him, but this was one of the most important.

"Ah, yeah. Me too." He smiled weakly, but his eyes were shadowed, and although he didn't speak the words out loud, his body language was screaming, "Just so you know, I'm not going to let you hurt me."

Of course, she knew her recent detachment from him would require some time to explain and that he might not understand. She would have to tell him everything, step by step. Eventually he would understand. She really hoped he would understand.

So, she started by telling him that she had decided not to take the advertising job in Baltimore and instead was now working with her aunt and uncle on publishing and promoting the third novel. She was excited by the career change and felt more in place in her career now than she had ever felt before. Harris nodded while she spoke, showing a cordial interest, but not much more. Mallory was beginning to feel the uncomfortable breathlessness of panic inside, but she kept talking, even though he wasn't being overly receptive.

She continued by telling him about the momentous meeting at the JLM Publishing office the day of the Christmas party, and that her aunt and uncle had been actively working on mending their family relationship since then.

This generated a more genuine response from him, with hints of the Harris she used to know. But, still, she was sure he was wondering why she didn't call him. He had been so supportive when she told him how hard this whole dysfunctional family had been on her, he was surely wondering, what reason could she have for not calling him?

Finally, she recounted her shock at receiving the memoir from him and the numb, disjointed sensation she had been experiencing since she read it. Finding it when he did – so close on the heels of the third novel, her new job and the family dynamics – it was just too much for her. She told him how she tried to put it out of her mind, to find some peace, she just couldn't decide how to write the end to it and she couldn't decide what she wanted to do with her life. She felt stuck, emotionally stuck.

This confession generated a look of sorrow in his eyes under his furrowed dark brows and she waited, sensing that he must have something to say about all of this.

The tension was palpable, and agonizing, as she allowed silence to fill the room, the space between the two of them increasing like the high tide of the ocean, when you felt you had to move further and further away from the water, get away to high ground, or else you might drown. Suddenly intimidated by the raw emotion on his face, Mallory turned to look out the window, watching as snowflakes drifted between the branches of the tree outside, falling delicately to the ground.

Moments later, when he sighed deeply, she turned back to look at him and found she was holding her breath, just waiting there to be accosted by his hurt-filled anger, all justified, but still no less daunting.

"Why didn't you tell me any of this sooner, Mallory? All these weeks? Why did you shut me out?"

Of course, this was what he wanted to know, she knew it would be the question he asked. Anyone who had walked alongside her like he had, through all this, would deserve to know. But his voice wasn't harsh, filled with anger. It was soft, filled with hurt.

"I couldn't tell you. At first, I convinced myself it was because I had my life out there and you had yours here." She drifted off, not sure how to organize the thoughts into words.

"And you have Jasper in your life out there, is that it?"

"No. It's over with Jasper. It's been over since Christmas. Since you texted me on Christmas." She met his eyes, fighting to find the courage to put herself completely out there, to finally give up control of her stand-alone, fend-for-yourself life. Was Harris her future? What did it mean to intentionally put someone *in the center* of your future?

Her heart in her throat - oh my gosh, this is terrifying - Mallory found herself sliding out of her chair and ended up kneeling on the floor next to his chair, and without looking at him, she reached for his hands, holding them against her face as tears pricked her eyes, "I'm sorry, Harris. I was a coward. I was afraid. Truth is, I've known it was over with Jasper since I first met you."

After a moment's hesitation - most likely he was locked in shock at her actions and her words - in one smooth motion, he shifted off the chair, joined her on the floor, and wrapped her into a hug that felt as natural as sunlight, the warmth of which she felt straight through to her soul. When he pulled away to look at her, she couldn't see his eyes clearly through her tears, but he smoothed her hair away from her face and then he kissed the path her tears had made on her cheek before he laughed softly.

"Funny you should say that. That's about the same time I knew that I was over Jackie too."

"Really?" Surprised by his playful reply, she wondered, how could he forgive her for blundering this whole thing with him these past few months? What gave him the capacity to love that way? Her mind was full of questions - trapped in her cynical, suspicious reality - when his perspective was so different.

"Yeah, really." He looked into her eyes, smiling gently, not saying anything more, as if he was drawing out the moment because it *just felt so good.* "Now, I have to ask, does this mean you will be here in Minnesota for a while?"

"I guess so-" She smiled at his questioning look, "Yes, I guess that's what it means."

"And ... no regrets about any of this?" He quizzed, squinting his eyes with the question.

"No regrets." She whispered, shaking her head no. Slowly, she reached her hand around the back of his neck, threading her fingers up into the waves of his hair and kissed him, happily drifting along somewhere in her mind where - just out of reach, but she was sure they were there - she saw bright puffs of wildflowers in the tall green grass and felt a light breeze on her cheek, somewhere up in those clouds.

"Mmm, yeah." His eyes were closed when he pulled away, and he opened them lazily, teasing her, as he smiled into her eyes, "Well, I can tell I'm starting to *really like* my new neighbor. She sure is a lot prettier than the old guy who used to live here."

"Well, that's good, because she's not selling. She's here to stay for a while."

Mallory watched as the owl fluttered back onto his branch in the tree outside the living room window. What was he thinking about, that owl? How long had he made that tree his home? Had Grandpa J ever talked to that owl like she talked to him? Did he share his deepest thoughts with that owl like she had today? Thoughts about life's twists and turns, and what love means and how God works through it all. How even the simplest of events, coming out of the blue, like meeting a neighbor, could all be part of something more, something big.

Harris. Just to think of him made her happy. This was what happy felt like. And to think she had to come to this forgotten house to find *happy*. And, maybe someday – no, not maybe someday, *definitely* – she would live over there in the big house. Someday she would be married to the owner of the big house. They would live there as a family. Because she loved him, and he loved her. Mmmm.

With a contented sigh and a whisper of a smile, she turned from the window, and moved to the Harris Original chair where her laptop sat open, ready for her to begin work. She had informed Canton and Jasmine about the memoir, and now her uncle was waiting for it – he had the wheels of the publishing "machine" primed and ready. And, she was in the center of this one, just as Grandpa J intended.

Spreading the crumpled letter over the arm of the chair, she read through it one more time. And, as she scanned it, she found herself speaking them out loud before she even read the words, she had committed them mostly to memory.

After she finished reading it, she contemplated her computer screen where the cursor blinked in the memoir, at the end of the last line Grandpa J had written before he died. As she sat there, in the quiet of his living room, she indulged the sad, but so true, thought to drift around in her mind – these really were the last words he had ever spoken to her, they were the last words she would ever hear from him – how did she feel about that?

And, as naturally as if he had written them expressly for the memoir, as if somehow, he knew they were meant for this purpose, she started typing the words of his letter right where his memoir left off. When she finished that task a few minutes later, she double spaced and watched again as the cursor blinked, waiting for her response to these final words that had been spoken from his heart.

She took a deep breath and as she let the air out slowly, she found her thoughts were forming together like a colorful mosaic, with the shadowy somber and the brilliantly luminous moments of her life blending together into an exquisite work of shattered glass art. As she contemplated her life from this angle and tried to encapsulate how she felt about all this, she hesitated to say the word, even to herself, because it was so overused that it sounded cliche'.

But, man, the journey getting her to this point – her odyssey – it had been rough, and none of that was cliche'.

Forgiveness. That's the word. She had finally found forgiveness – for her family, for her Grandpa J and for herself. Because the love that had been forgotten somehow over the years had now been remembered, and she vowed to never, ever forget it again.

Then, she started typing. And as the words started spilling from her mind and trickled down through her fingertips, she found the stark, white wilderness of the electronic page was not daunting at all. There was so much to say.

Dear Grandpa J,

I miss you terribly...

◆ ◆ ◆

AUTHOR BIO

J. Marie is the author of the inspirational debut novel FIND YOUR WAY HOME (March 2018 Amazon) and a second novel THE FORGOTTEN HOUSE (October 2018 Amazon).

After raising three children while also working in consumer products marketing and general management for over twenty years, she left the corporate world to better focus on managing various family businesses.

It was then, even though her days were filled with the telephone calls, spreadsheets and financial statements, suddenly voices of characters and compelling stories of their lives became too much to ignore. So, she wrote it all down and hasn't stopped writing ever since. Snippets of a third novel now play through her mind, so it won't be long, and it too will be written down.

In addition to writing, in her spare time, she enjoys volunteering with various organizations, and spending time with her husband and their family on their farm near Canby, MN.

Book Club Discussion Questions

1. Although this book travels between various places, the author wished to connect the reader to these places. Can you identify ways that was accomplished? Can you give examples of how Mallory was connected to these various places in her life and how they affected her?

2. What were the key influences in Mallory's young life that affected her most as an adult? Can you list a few moments in the book when Mallory reckoned with her past and seemed to find peace with it?

3. Name some of the characters in the book that you felt had the biggest impact - both positive and negative - on Mallory. How did Mallory interact with these characters? Did her relationship with these characters change over the years?

4. What overarching themes did you identify in this book? Can you give examples of how the characters lived these themes?

5. Have you personally struggled with the loss of family members like Mallory (and Grandpa J) did? Were any of these feelings/reactions similar to yours? How did you learn to "live" with the loss of someone close to you?

6. Faith is integral to which characters in the novel? How is it demonstrated? Find examples of how it impacts their daily lives.

7. If, while reading the majority of the book, you had to choose a one-word descriptor for the relationship between Mallory and her grandfather, what would that be? After you finished reading the book, do you feel the one-word descriptor would change?

8. Even though Grandpa J was not physically present in the novel, he was very much a central character. Give some examples of how he touched the lives of the characters even after he was gone. Do you still feel the impact of loved ones who have passed away? How so?

9. What surprised you about the novel?

Made in the USA
Columbia, SC
09 January 2020

86434237R10181